The Last Stage

The Last Stage

Mary

I hope you enjoy my Books! Feel free to read them @ Beeftalk! Best!

Jim Cherry
10/8/15

Jim Cherry

writing under the Influence of Rock & Roll
www.jymsbooks.com

To order additional copies of this book, contact:
Xlibris Corporation
1-888-795-4274
www.Xlibris.com
Orders@Xlibris.com
28779

Contents

"It's time to speak of unspoken things."

Jim Morrison

INITIATION

Is Everybody In?

I'm dead. Not the cold corporeal type of death, but a warm, living death, a ghost trying to regain what he has lost. A death where everything is a faded, pale facsimile of the life I had. I went into my study and sat at the desk, it's an old theatrical make-up table with a gilded mirror surrounded by those old fashioned bulbous lights, naked, astringent, that push light into every crevice and nook, no where to hide. Every night I sit surrounded in this room, a shrine to my "career." The desk is stuffed with my newspaper reviews, photographs, journals, scrapbooks and notes. The mirror was cleaned up and glimmered, a relic of an age gone by, salvage from my past.

I lit a candle and popped a tape into the player on the desk, I watched the candle flicker and dance, casting shadows against the wall, hoping it would set the mood. A voice from the speakers said, "ladies and gentlemen, from Madison, Wisconsin, *The Unknown Soldiers!*" I cleared my mind and let the music transport me back, opening the flood of memories. It was a ceremony I've been practicing, a little ritual to help induce self-hypnosis. I closed my eyes, and I could see the audience cheering, an impressionistic flash of colorful clothes, and faces looking up at me. I had been the singer in a Doors tribute band, The Unknown Soldiers, it seemed like if I could concentrate hard enough and remember all the sights, sounds, smells, and feelings, I'd find myself on that stage again. The music was raw but powerful, then my voice came booming out of the speakers, it was huskier than Jim Morrison's, but I was able to tear out screams as well as his. We sounded like what *The Doors* had on a night Morrison wasn't too drunk. I remember those days like the touch of a lost lover, the sensation lingers. More salvage.

I liked playing Morrison it made me feel powerful. Getting a reaction from the audience, and being able to move them to ecstasy, despair, or joy. I imagined it to be something of how Morrison had felt. People had given me things, presents, trinkets, beads like Morrison's, poems that they thought I'd be interested in, women gave themselves to me because of it. I later realized they were only trying to get close to me, so they could touch something of Morrison, a ghost of someone not even myself. It had also gotten me to Los Angeles and my chance at fame, I can still almost feel the "whoosh" of air as fame rushed by me. I opened my eyes to the usual disappointment, I was still in the here and now. No audience, no cheering, no applause.

Jim Morrison, was the charismatic and controversial lead singer of *The Doors*, the 60's rock group that had such hits as *Light My Fire*, *Touch Me*, and *Riders On The Storm*, but also songs like *The End* which at first glance was a paean to lost love but in the end had a modern telling of the Oedipus myth, like many young men Morrison worried about death, every twenty year old feels like he'll never live to thirty, while simultaneously feeling immortal. Since I was a teenager people, friends had told me I looked like Jim Morrison. I hadn't really paid that much attention to Morrison, or his music, but I took the compliments to heart, it had boosted my ego to think I looked like someone famous, and that's how my life took its form.

I looked into the mirror. I had the idea that I could look into myself to find the questions of my life, and I hoped the answers lay within the formulation of those questions. But all I could see was my craggy face being torn by the toll of time that Morrison never had to endure, kind of like Dorian Gray without the luxury of a portrait.

My friends and I had missed the 60's, on a geologic scale it was only a stones throw away, on a cultural scale it was ancient history, it was like looking back to the age of heros, and beholding past glories through the ambered memories of our older brothers and sisters. So we tried to recreate that time, our own Summer of Love, going out to the park and smoking dope, at the feet of our very own Dion, listening to him play James Taylor songs on an acoustic guitar.

I wanted to be a rock star, everybody wants to be a rock star! Including you! You become something more, something special, it's like alchemy from lead to gold, the mortal to the immortal. Being a rock star is power, power over authority, power over women, power over the truths of reality, by definition, a hero!

And why not *The Doors*? *The Doors* had both mainstream success and a cult following since their inception. Rock 'n' Roll is a lifestyle, high volume, dress, attitude, rebellion against authority, and nobody embraced that better than Jim Morrison, he's the model of a rock star to rock stars. And *The Doors* were a truly revolutionary group. The music was primal, and Morrison's lyrics and his confrontation of his audience was a message of revolution, not storm the palace walls, but a subtle revolution, an exhortation to change from within, the revolution within yourself, and that's what scared people, because real change is always from within.

But I wasn't a rock star, maybe a simulacrum of one, a modern Prometheus, ever changing, facile. I'd had a taste of what being a rock star was like. Probably a shadow of what it really was like, but I'd been closer than most. I saw the top of the mountain through the mists. Performing had been the best high I'd ever experienced. Better than any drug I'd ever tried. I'd had a taste of what most people can only fantasize of, only dream of, and will never experience, nor can they imagine what it feels like even as they sing along, play air guitar, or beat out a rhythm.

I looked at the blank page staring back at me from the desk. I've been trying to write my autobiography on and off for years since the band broke up. I have to write it while I can still hear the chorus of voices of those I met, those I befriended, those I cheated, those I loved. The band had been my idea I was the lead singer. I'd gone through a lot of things with the band most people wouldn't understand. As the lead singer, I was the focal point of the band. I'd experienced a lot of things even they couldn't understand, but they had never understood me, or what I was trying to do. But if I can get this one thing right, if I can put this together and make you understand, then maybe others will understand. The one thing Morrison taught me was to have some irreverence for art, maybe I should sit here and write 'fuck' a hundred times

My 'fame', my 'celebrity' were now things of memory. Things were different now that I was a chef, albeit in a "fancy" restaurant. I had to "take orders" from people, and conform to other's expectations, such as wearing a uniform. I learned the trade by going to one of those six month schools you see advertised on TV at three in the morning, financing and student loans available, it was either this or gunsmithing. I spent a couple of years working as a prep cook doing most of the actual preparation while the chef heated up the food, put it on a plate, added a colorful garnish, and took all of the credit.

I haven't been to work on time in weeks. I try, but something always seems to get in the way. Tonight was typical I was running late and as soon as I walked in the manager, Sergei, was on me, pots clanking on their hooks as he rushed passed. He caught me in the prep area as I was trying to make it look like I'd been there a while. He came up to me, close, I could almost taste the decades of garlicky food on his breath.

"Hey rock star!" He yelled, his thickly accented voice reverberating harshly off the stainless steel. I had told all my coworkers of my past "celebrity", regaling them with my tales, on and off stage. "You're late again, Michael."

"I know, I'm sorry, it was . . . ." A smile crossed my lips as I tried to find the right lie. I was beyond any pretense of caring if I could think of one or not. I was beyond caring whether or not I kept the job. My wife would be the only one to care, but only momentarily because she would understand, and support whatever decision I made. From the moment I met her she believed in me.

"I don't want an excuse, I've heard them all from you," Sergei said, looking me up and down with disgust, "and look at your shirt, it's starting to look dingy." Every night sweat stained the shirt a little more, and a little more dirt clung to it. It became just a little dingier, just like the work, "do me a favor, Gray," he said moving even closer to me and pulling at the shirt, "wash it."

Then there were the customers and invariably the complainers, 'the soup was too hot', 'too cold', 'how is the fish prepared?', 'the steak is too well done' 'too rare', 'not done enough', and inevitably the less satisfied they were, the 'ruder' I became. But Sergei couldn't fire me because I was too good a chef, and had a small local following asking for me whenever they came in. Finishing this book is the only way I can get back what's been taken away.

Rock 'n' Roll Dreams

To understand me you have to understand my story. I had an idyllic childhood of backyard adventures and playground heroisms. I grew up in the 60's watching the trembling lift-offs and cool blue splashdowns of the Astronauts, first in Mercury, Gemini, and finally Apollo. I remember the front porch conversation of the neighbors after Bobby Kennedy was killed, peace signs, baby sitters that were hippies, beads, and bellbottoms. I remember the excitement of the times without being a part of it. When I was a boy I wanted to be an astronaut so my mother enrolled me in all these classes at the planetarium but all the mathematics were a drag when all I really wanted to do was look at the stars. My father was military even after he wasn't. When I was a kid we had lived in a typical white picket fenced in house, several of them. Eventually settling in a suburb of Chicago, so I could identify with Morrison. His father too was military and the family had been Navy nomads moving around the country at every change of assignment. Like the young Jim Morrison, I retreated into books, one subject leading to the next. Curiosity was my only guide it was formless, without direction.

In high school I got a taste of the Rock 'n' Roll lifestyle I was a roadie for a band, although it was more a ruse to get into parties. Through a friend of a friend I met the band at a party and they asked if I could help bring their equipment in, I said "sure!" and being the resourceful guy I am, and wanting to keep my party schedule full I asked where the next party was they were playing. I showed up at the next party and brought in the equipment, and that lead to a summers worth of parties, but I never took out any equipment when the party was over I was either too busy throwing up or making out with a girl, nothing was ever said about it.

The summer between high school and college I followed a band around because of Cassie Leighton, the beautiful apple cheeked ministers daughter who was 'in love with the snake' who wasn't me, it was the leather jacketed lead singer of the band. They played sweltering outside gigs, the phosphorus flash of smudge-pots as he struggled to read lyrics off a notebook he had stashed on-stage.

After high school I went to the University of Wisconsin in Madison. It was one of the more liberal of the liberal arts schools. The town had a counterculture post hippie feel to it. In college I started hearing songs I remembered from my childhood. I asked around and discovered the songs I liked were *The Doors*. I read everything I could find out about *The Doors*. I became enamoured of Morrison. I saw my reflection in him, a disaffected youth who had some problems with his parents, who didn't want the world imposing its rules on him. I discovered the legendary Rock 'n' Roll stories I'd heard as a kid were Jim Morrison stories, like, a band was getting on a plane and a groupie tried to board the plane and someone asked her what she did and she answered "ornament", or a rock star in a restaurant orders one of everything on the menu just "to see what everything tasted like." I started reading all the same books Morrison had, Nietzsche, Blake, Kerouac, Huxley, Ginsburg, seeing a path in the wilderness I was in. It became my real education. I dressed in black jeans, and reenacted everything I'd read about, I did balancing acts, took stage dives, I hung off balconies, and drank to excess trying to find the palace of wisdom. I became a minor hero, someone to invite to your party to make it interesting, then an object of ridicule.

After graduation, I wanted to do post graduate work, but my parents pulled the plug on the money. They refused to pay for any more schooling insisting my choice be practical, get a job with the education I had, and to pay for any further schooling that way. I liked the lifestyle in Madison so much I didn't leave. I guess I subconsciously chose nothing, but got experienced in everything. The atmosphere was stimulating, nonjudgmental, and there was an acceptance of a range of thought leaning towards the experimental. It was around this time that I met Colt and his wife Jessie, I used to hang out at their second floor apartment smoking hash. They were newlyweds, their furniture was all new looking like it had all been bought from the pickings of wedding envelopes. Colt was a good looking guy with long blond hair, he always wore a buckskin jacket and behind one of the couches in the living room stood his guitar case, he looked like a cross between Custer and Eric Clapton. Jessie was a pretty blond who always wore white billowy blouses that were popular in the 70's. And when she looked at Colt her eyes gleamed with admiration, she had obviously hitched her star to Colt's, she unflaggingly believed he was the next Eric Clapton. They were contemporaries, the first married couple I knew working towards their Rock 'n' Roll dreams, but I didn't know how to get there, yet.

Post –Graduate Work

I lived simply to keep my freedom intact. I bought a trailer outside of town picking up jobs as I needed them, janitor, convenience store clerk, telemarketer, gas station attendant, everything except Indian Chief. I only took the jobs to finance the buying of bootlegs and books. I didn't want the things that my contemporaries sought out a kick ass stereo, a hot car, a big house, those things that salved their conscious' of abandoning their dreams. I wanted more. If a job started to last too long, or started making too many demands on me, I quit. I wanted to be free.

I found the buying of bootleg concerts provided the same thrill as scoring dope. You had to know someone, who knew someone who was "dealing." Connections were loose, people tenuous. On the way to a "score" I'd look over my shoulder to make sure I wasn't being followed, and that no one suspected what I was up to, which may have lead people to suspect I was up to something much more illegal. And you had to be wary of new people. Were they trying to rip you off? Were they trying to sell you a commonplace concert that everyone has and they just added on some songs from another concert or cut a tape short? Were they "narcs" from the RIAA's police, or cool like you, just trying to score some stuff? And once you got your "stuff" you ran off to the secrecy of your own pad to ingest the substance. In this case, listening to your contraband concert. A totally furtive lifestyle.

In a college town there's a new influx of excitement and adventure every fall, in the form of a new class, especially the girls. My brother and sister always teased me, asking if my girlfriends were at least eighteen, it was just that as I got older, my girlfriends didn't. Most of the girls thought I was a local and didn't fit their definition of success. They were unimpressed with my dreams, and they would soon be off to trendy careers and successful husbands anyway. They were interested in one thing, and it wasn't the one thing I was interested in. The girls I did interest ran from the neo-hippie chicks who loved to wear tie-dye and have sex, which they considered a form of rebellion, but as their graduation loomed and their rebellion came to an end, so did our relationships. Then there were the girls I always seemed to fall for, the girls with purple hair and problems. They were the wildest. But I was saving myself, not from sex, they were the type of girls that you could take to the bars and concerts, but I was looking for someone more in line with my ambitions. I started to see the passage of classes as the passing of seasons, one piling upon the other. First there were a few, then a handful, then more and more, until I became worried the passage of seasons was becoming too many.

I had just broken up with my last girlfriend, Deidre. We'd had an on again, off again relationship for about a year. Whenever we had a fight, or she was acting like she wanted something more from the relationship, I sent her home. She wasn't beautiful, but she wasn't ugly either, and there was something latently sexual about her. She was twenty-one to my thirty, and I liked her because she wore low cut blouses, and short skirts. I guess I wasn't very good on waiting for all the rewards later, there were other benefits to be had, namely blow jobs, I knew luxuries would come later. The ironic thing was she turned out to be a local, and not from the college. She was a Rock 'n' Roll chick through and through. She had a collection of black concert T-shirts from the 70's, which in some kind of relativistic universe should have made them antiques. The glass of her vanity mirror was almost obliterated by the ticket stubs of every concert she'd ever been to. She was not quite a groupie, and something more than a fan. It was like she lacked the imagination or perhaps the ambition to be a groupie, I knew almost from the start it wasn't going to work out. I met her at a party. I didn't notice her until she came up to me.

"You look like Jim Morrison!" She shouted above the music. I was already drunk and being complemented by a pretty girl added to my euphoria. We started talking, she agreed with everything I said.

"I want to move to Los Angeles."

"Me too!" She enthused.

"What're you going to do there?" She asked.

"I don't know, see what comes up."

"Me too!" I couldn't believe how much we had in common, she was infectious and I was enthralled. She was also lying about everything, but I didn't notice until later when we had nothing in common. She was a neo-hippie chick who had never met a hippie, or a counter-cultural thought, break the skin and she was like the surrounding town, conservative. I knew from almost the beginning that it wouldn't work out but she came along at a time in my life when I was feeling particularly vulnerable, and didn't want to be alone, I should have known better, but I consoled myself with a steady supply of sex until she discovered the truth. There are times of our lives when the answers to our problems is to bury our flesh in that of others. And what happens when you make compromises? You end up compromising yourself.

As time went by I felt trapped with her at the trailer, like any good college town Madison has its own strip of bars. So, to avoid the realization of the inevitable, I'd taken to spending afternoons in the various bars, alongside the locals avoiding wives, girlfriends, and responsibilities. Whenever the phone rang someone invariably yelled across the room to the bartender,

"Hey, Sue, if it's my wife I'm not here." I was avoiding going back to my trailer, dreading one of those crushing relationship ambushes when the other person is there at an unexpected time, and you know you're in for one of those heavy talks about the relationship that you usually experience right before you break up. The death of our relationship was my ambition, and hers was to be married. It was beginning to look like any other relationship, I was beginning to look like any other resident. I was looking for a new world.

The View From the Audience

While Deidre and I were waiting for the truth to reveal itself, we still had Rock 'n' Roll in common, we went to Milwaukee's Summerfest. We walked around the grounds, arm in arm, to all the different pavilions. First checking out all the typical carnival rides, roller coaster, merry-go-round. We visited the little bijouteries selling silver rings and gold crosses. We wandered in and out of the maze of booths of various craftsmen selling their homemade leather goods, caricaturists, artists, all the way down to women selling macramé plant holders. Then came the food pavilion where you could get the all American favorite pizza, fresh hot pretzels, shish-ka-bobs, corn on a stick, and Baklava. After eating we decided it was time for a beer, so we walked over to the Oktoberfest tent. We sat down at a picnic table in the pavilion to drink our beer.

"We still have a while before any of the bands go on." I said.

"Do you want to go on some of the carnival rides?" She asked enthusiastically.

"No!" I said facetiously, looking as shocked as I could, "did you ever see those guys that put them together and run them? I'm surprised there isn't a tragedy every year, trust decreases as the number of tattoos increases." She giggled.

"Let's go over to the Marcus Amphitheater and see what time the different concerts start." She said looking at a brochure she taken out of her purse, which always made me flinch as I had an abhorrence of brochures and itineraries, a leftover from rigidly scheduled family road trips as a kid. "By the way it looks on the map it's right around the corner from here."

"Let's have another beer, then go over." I said.

The Marcus Amphitheater rose out of the concrete like a shrine, the Taj Mahal amid the temporary or semi-permanent buildings of the rest of the fairgrounds. It was closed, a swinging gate chained and locked impeded our path to venture any further. There was a placard in front of the building listing all the shows, including the free ones. *Huey Lewis and The News* was the headlining act. It was thirty-five dollars a ticket to see them.

"I thought all the shows were free."

"Do you want to see them?" Deidre asked.

"The question is do you want to pay to see them?"

"Let's see *Blood, Sweat, & Tears* featuring David Clayton-Thomas." I said, reading the placard. There seemed to be three levels of show business visible, the headlining act playing the amphitheater, the 60's nostalgia acts were playing on the concourse, and a couple of stages were set up out in 'the meadow' playing unknown up-and-coming bands.

Bands from the 60's had been touring the nostalgia circuit for a couple of years usually only with a key player or two from the original band. The names of the bands of my youth, *Uriah Heap, The Strawberry Alarm Clock, Bread*, were all ancient history to me, relics of my past. I can't even tell you what most of them sounded like now or the titles of their songs, but to Deidre they were a rich living history. The world she grew up in was a response to the 60's, so seeing these groups was like a chance to see John Kennedy alive, or a Civil War reenactment.

As we walked up the concourse the stages were nothing more than trailers backed up onto the concourse, parked sideways, and the sides opened and propped up to make 'the stage.' A little green fence kept the spectators separate from the band. Everyone pushed to the front to see the band, and get off the concourse. If you weren't paying attention as you walked down the concourse you could find yourself part of an audience and not even realize it. We found the pavilion where *Blood, Sweat, & Tears* were playing, the band was already on stage, waiting, talking among themselves, their guitars hanging at their waists. They all seemed to be nineteen or twenty, they were lean, dressed in dark pants, wide belts, dangling earrings, headbands and pouffy hair. They looked like refugee's from bands like *Duran Duran*, or *Flock of Seagulls* or any other 80's band. There was a surge of excitement as David Clayton-Thomas walked onto the stage. People pressed in from behind to get closer. He was dressed in a white shirt and Khaki's, the tight fitting clothes and flowered patterns of youth gone. A thrill ran through me as the band started the first song. I found myself part of the faceless crowd, yelling to distinguish myself from them, as they were trying to distinguish themselves from me. I listened to the band. They were sloppy, missing cues, not bothering to play the songs faithfully. Even though I was never a *Blood, Sweat, & Tears* fan, it bothered me that the band didn't know the songs well enough to play them well, or didn't care how well they played. Didn't they know they had a job a lot of people would kill for? They had the spotlight and adulation, but they didn't have to sacrifice for it, it wasn't theirs, it was a job, and they might as well have been washing dishes or slinging hamburgers, they were refugees from their dreams, hired guitars too young to remember when the band who's name they were playing behind was alive and vibrant, and had meaning.

"I can do better than that." I yelled to Deidre.

"What?!"

"It should be me up there."

"Men always want to see themselves as the hero of the story."

"What?" I asked.

"I read somewhere that people have the propensity to see the human face in random things, men want to see themselves as the hero." I had to admit that was the most insightful thing she had ever said.

"I still say I can do that better myself."

"Then why don't you?"

"Do what?"

"Ever since I've been with you, you've said you can do this or that better, or that someday you're going to be great. Why don't you do something?"

"I am." I said.

"What is that?" She asked, her voice suddenly changed, she was angry, she let go of my hand, "do you want me to tell you the truth?" This wasn't the first time we'd been through this, but it was the last.

"No, I don't want to know the truth, the only truth is what I create."

"Well, what is that?" She snapped, and went back to listening to the band.

"Never mind." I said.

"See, you won't even tell me what plans you have. You vaguely mention how someday you'll be famous, but not how. You're not in school, you don't do anything that I can see. It's like that *Steely Dan* song," and she quoted the lyrics, "you've been telling me you're a genius, since you were seventeen, in all the time I've known you, I still don't know what you mean." All you do is sit around getting stoned, and listen to *The Doors*." She stood there looking at me.

"I'm searching for something new, some new world of thought and feeling."

"What the hell does that mean?" She asked.

"I don't know, but when I find it I'll know."

"You know, we could do anything together, if you'd just trust in me enough to let me in on what you want to do. You never know, I might surprise you, and might want to come along for the ride."

"I don't know all I have is this vague feeling that something great is inside me. I don't know how, what, or why. I just feel it, but I can't ask you or anyone else to wait for anything that ambiguous. I want to be interviewed, I want leather pants, I want groupies, I want to scream, I want to dance."

She put her arms around my neck, looked into my eyes, I could feel her breasts sliding across my chest, "you're my rock star."

"Knock it off." I said, pushing her away.

"Why can't you just be?" She asked me, "why isn't any experience enough for you? How come I'm not enough for you?" I knew the answer she wanted to hear, the answer I probably should have given her, the answer she probably deserved. But I didn't know what to say. "Fine." She said coldly, "if that's what you want, do it, you deserve it. Do it with some little girl who doesn't care enough about you to tell you the truth, go to L.A. and find the happy ending." People had started to notice our argument, a small circle had formed around us, little did I know how soon it would be when again I'd be at the center of a circle with spectators all around. It was a small conception. The next day she moved out of my trailer, only coming back later that week to pick up her things. A couple of months later I heard she had moved in with some guy and they lived happily ever after, I guess.

A door closed on that part of my life.

The Place

'The Place' was one of those local, cleverly named college town bars that don't have much to look at inside. It survived by reputation, generation to generation, brother to brother, senior to freshman, and in the off college season relied on atmosphere and local characters for survival. It was your old fashioned type of establishment with a mahogany bar, a few booths and tables, and a mirror behind the bar to make the room seem larger. There was an adjoining room with a stage for local and touring bands to play. When it wasn't in use, the room was dark and closed off, the darkness spilling over into the bar. One afternoon, while I was still getting over Deidre, because doors don't close as easily as we'd like, and chapters of our lives don't end as neatly as chapters in a book. I don't remember if I was in a good mood, bad mood, I was just trying to feel something. There were only a couple other people in there, I was playing *Doors* song after *Doors* song on the jukebox. There was a guy sitting two stools down from me, he looked to be in his late thirties or early forties. The music made the place seem hopping, we were bopping around on our stools, hands and fingers tapping out the time to the music. We were both singing along. Although we were both digging the music, we hadn't said anything to each other, but if you hang out in bars long enough you'll drink enough to talk to everybody.

"You know," I said, to the room "I probably know the songs better than Morrison, I've been singing them longer."

"You like *The Doors?*"

"Yeah, Morrison was great," I said. He nodded his head agreeing with my ridiculously simple assessment. "You know," I said, "I should start a band that covers *Doors* songs, and everybody would think they're originals, especially some of the more obscure ones. I mean I saw *Blood, Sweat, & Tears* a few weeks ago at Summerfest, and David Clayton-Thomas was the only original guy from the band. The band he had didn't look at all interested in the music, except to pickup a paycheck. I know some other bands from the sixties are touring again, but with Morrison dead we'll never see *The Doors.*"

"I saw them live a couple of times back in the sixties." He said.

"Really!" I asked excitedly, "what was it like?"

"You saw Morrison up there on stage, and he was just singing those songs," He said, holding up his cigarette, punctuating each statement by stabbing it in the air. "But somehow you knew just by looking at him he was singing about existence. You know what I mean?"

"Yeah, I think so," I said, thinking about it for a minute, "most people don't even seem to remember them much anymore."

"It's the kinda feeling I wish I could get into my writing." He said.

"You're a writer?" I made a mental note, you never knew what form your big break would take.

"Yeah. Just a little local journalism, nothing to write home about, as it were." Then he looked at me "You really like *The Doors*?"

"Yeah! I think I can link *The Doors* to any modern band."

"I bet you could!" He said, "Ray Manzarek is playing down in Chicago tomorrow night, wanna go with me?"

"Really?" I asked. "Cool, yeah, I'll go!"

"I'll meet you here tomorrow about three, all right?" He asked.

"All right! I'll be here at three!"

"Well, I gotta be going, nice talking to you." He said as he got up.

"Hey," I said, "what's your name?"

"Jim," He replied. "Weird huh?"

"Yeah, I guess." I said, puzzled why he thought it was weird.

Meeting Ray

Jim Morrison and Ray Manzarek were one of the best teams in Rock 'n' Roll history, but nobody seems to have given much credit to Morrison/Manzarek and they never achieved the legendary status of Lennon/McCartney or Jagger/Richards, but maybe it was because the credits on the records read *The Doors* instead of Manzarek/Morrison. Ray was the linear mathematically precise keyboard player from Chicago who loved the blues. He met Jim Morrison at UCLA when both were there in the film school; the rational and irrational working together. Soon after, Ray met John Densmore and Robby Krieger at a meditation center, and *The Doors* were born. Morrison lived on the edge and pushed the others to those extremes. He was the artistic center of the band, the spark, the indefinable something that led *The Doors* beyond their boundaries of the rational into the irrational fires of creativity, a landscape never before seen; their new world, a sensuous wild west. Robby, who wrote most of the 'hit' songs followed Morrison's lead, adapting Morrison's imagery and themes. While all three were talented musicians, after Morrison died they never again hit the creative or popular high Morrison had driven them to.

Ray was playing with Michael McClure at Lounge Ax on the North side of Chicago. The trendy Clark Street area where the St. Valentine's Day Massacre had happened, but now was just old buildings filled with Starbucks, bookstores, and upscale theme restaurants "owned" by sports legends. The club had always enjoyed a cult status, even to a suburban boy like me, as one of Chicago's premiere clubs to see bands. So, when we got there it was disappointing. The reality clashed with my idea of what it was going to be like after years of hearing how cool it was. We walked right past it at first, we stood on the sidewalk looking for the address. When we turned back the way we had come, three girls came out of a blackened storefront. They were dressed in spandex and lace tops. I yelled to them "Hey! Is this Lounge Ax?" They looked back and sized us up before answering.

"Yeah," she said. I looked over the facade, there was nothing announcing its presence, no sign that said Lounge Ax, no fancy logo, or neon sign just the blackened out front window. I guess you were just supposed to "know" this was it.

"Is it open yet?"

"Yeah, go on in."

Inside, Jim and I stopped to pay the ten dollar cover charge. As we ventured deeper into the narrow space the rest of my romantic illusions were thoroughly dashed. The nightclub was wedged into the storefront. The bar ran almost the length of the club, at the back was a riser for the 'stage' that rose maybe eighteen inches above the floor. The space between the bar and the stage was four feet of linoleum for a dance floor, and opposite of that, of all things, were wooden bleacher seats, four or five seats high. It looked like there were five or six of the stage risers stacked on top of each other and bolted together. In the middle of the linoleum floor was a music stand and a keyboard, surely Ray's. The keyboard was being given a respectful space by the growing crowd in the shrinking room. The crowd seemed an even mix of women and men, but every third guy had on leather pants and a white shirt, concho belt optional for individuality, waiting to be discovered by Ray. We got a couple of beers and chatted away time until the show started.

Without announcement Ray and Michael McClure came out from behind a black curtain. Michael McClure, the beat poet, was friends with seminal beat writer Jack Kerouac who was an early influence on the young Jim Morrison. Later, after *The Doors* and Morrison's fame, McClure met Morrison, and they became friends. On this night McClure was dressed all in black with a *Dr. Who*ish multi-colored scarf. While he was arranging his manuscripts on the music stand, Ray adjusted himself behind the keyboard. He turned the power knob on and waited for McClure. Ray's graying hair was in a short spiked crew cut, he was dressed in latter day Carnaby Street fashion. Ray looked to McClure who nodded and Ray started to play. The crowd pressed in, a solid mass from stage to door, the waitresses pushed their way through the crowd. I lost track of Jim, but could feel his presence close by.

Ray played the accompaniment to McClure's words. Filling in the holes where words ended. Ray added his own statements, describing the indescribable. And McClure's words complimented the music, filling in the holes of Ray's music, giving form to the formless, interweaving to create aural textures. I closed my eyes bopping my head, grooving to the whole thing and letting the eurythmia carry me away. McClure's words invoked Morrison, Ray played the ribbon of notes that make up the iconic opening of *Light My Fire*, "do-do-do-dew-do," the crowd pressed forward as one, I opened my eyes, and for a moment I saw colors! The music had taken me on a trip! They had stripped away the boundaries of ordinary perception. For a moment I had stepped through the doors!

Ray looked up from his keyboards "any questions?" He asked the audience. While McClure leafed through the pages on the music stand "What was Jim like?" Someone yelled from the back.

"I could tell you what he was like, man," Ray said, in his gravelly voice, "but what you really want to hear is, he was a cool guy, and fun to hang out with. He was, but he also could be a jackass, but that was only when he was drunk."

"Is Jim dead?" Another disembodied voice asked.

"Now, that wouldn't be much fun, would it?" There was a kindly, but condescending tone in his voice like a somewhat stern schoolmaster in his twentieth year of explaining an overly simple problem to students, "if I told you Jim was alive, and living at 1349 California Avenue." Then it hit me could it be as simple as going to that address to find Jim Morrison alive and well? But what if it was reverse psychology? I let myself be intoxicated by the thought for a moment. What if Ray were telling the truth? What if it *could* be so simple as to find Jim Morrison alive, as to just knock on the door at that address! What would I find? A middle-aged Jim with a white beard and a world weary smile relieved it was all over? Or a cantankerous Morrison, pissed off at being discovered? Either way, I would be the greatest hero of the *Doors* world! Maybe of the Rock 'n' Roll world! Maybe of the world! I reined in my imagination from its fantasy, I knew Ray had been born and grew up in Chicago, I figured that address was probably his families old house or his Grandparents house or something much more prosaic like that.

"Seriously," Ray said, "Jim was a great guy but he denied himself his birthright, to see the future. So take his example and lead as an extraordinary a life as you can, push beyond your boundaries, see as much of the future as you can, and report back." During all this McClure had been standing at the music stand listening to Ray, without a signal Ray went into their next piece.

When it was over Ray said, "I'll only sign albums or things like that, no bar napkins." A collective groan went throughout the crowd, "really, what's that anyway?" He asked facetiously, "a napkin?" He and McClure were immediately surrounded by their admirers, the crowd around Ray was a little larger. As the admirers dwindled, a line formed. I stood at the end of the line and watched as Ray signed albums and chatted with girls. I stood there like an acolyte awaiting consecration, 'but of what?' I asked myself. While standing in line, I don't know how many times I heard people ask 'what was he like?' or some variation of that question. I wondered how many times Ray had heard that question in the almost twenty years since Morrison's death, and how many times would he hear it in the next twenty, thirty, forty or fifty years. Finally it was my turn.

"I don't have anything." I stammered out.

"Well, good luck," he said, smiling down on me as he stood up and went backstage.

Jim and I sat at the bar having another beer, waiting for I don't know what. Hoping to glimpse, one more time, the life I wanted. The styled hair, the fashionably elegant clothing, enough money in my pocket to buy whatever I desired, people hanging on my every word and rushing towards me. Or hoping Ray would see something in me, or that he'd even leave by the front door. I was beginning to feel like a stalker. I was tired of being a spectator I wanted to be on that stage. I wanted to be the one people were screaming for, trying to be with. I saw a long white limo pull up. From the back, Ray and Michael McClure came walking towards the door.

"Mr. Manzarek," I blurted out, just before they were safely out the door, and then I didn't know what to say. I knew I had only milliseconds to formulate, and say something to him, so I said the first thing that came into my head, "I'm going to start a cover band. Maybe you can come see us and give us a recommendation?"

"Sorry man, but I've been down that road. If that's your path, its success or failure is your own challenge." And they left. I felt even more foolish than before, like a tourist caught on the wrong side of the velvet rope.

A couple of minutes later Jim and I were walking back to the car. It was about midnight, the night was cool and crisp, the sky dark blue, the streetlight halos like a starry starry night.

"Let's do it!" I exclaimed.

"Do what?" Jim asked.

"Let's go to that address Ray mentioned. 1349 California Avenue and see if Jim is there."

"You're crazy, it's not close."

"Closer than Madison." I said.

"So, we're going to knock on these people's door in the middle of the night and ask if Jim Morrison is there?"

"Sure, why not? We'd be the greatest hero's of Rock 'n' Roll!"

"Or just two drunk guys arrested for bothering people in the middle of the night instead of going home." My enthusiasm deflated, I knew I wouldn't knock on that door by myself. I'd never know what was on the other side of that door. You either are something or not, I was neither. What did I have in life? My trailer? My Collections? Maybe Deidre was right, and I didn't even have her any more. Where was that new world? I trudged on to the car. Then, I had the one moment of pure genius in my life, maybe there was another way to find Jim Morrison. It ceased to be a dream and became something more tangible, it turned to power as it manifested in my mind and I saw how I could do it! I'd been flirting with it for months and even said it to Ray. It was like I had been wandering in a wilderness and the path was now before me, the dream was over, I had woken up!

"I'm going to do it!" I exclaimed, jumping around, flapping my arms. Maybe it was from my new found sense of purpose, the excitement of meeting Ray, maybe it was the cold, or maybe because I was just a little drunk.

"Do what?" Jim asked.

"The cover band, *The Doors* cover band idea I told you about!"

"You were drunk." He said, as we walked down the street.

"Yeah, and I am now. But the more I think about it, the more I see it can work. I can't get it out of my head."

"Well, can you sing?" He asked.

"No."

"Are you in a band?"

"No!"

"Do you know anyone in a band?"

"No! Jesus, don't be so hung up on the details. If you let the little things like that stand in your way, you're never going to get anywhere. I'll start this band, then maybe Ray will come and see us! And maybe even endorse us!" Then I had a vision, "or even think I'm good enough to perform as Jim, and we'll get together with Robby and John. I can tour with *The Doors*!"

"You're crazy."

It was a long drive back to Madison. As we sped deeper into the night, I tried to sleep, but couldn't. I rolled around fitfully in the seat, no matter which way I turned I couldn't get comfortable. I couldn't wait to get back to Madison to put my plan into effect. I knew I was running out of time to do something in life, but did I really have the balls to open that door?

The Master Plan

I woke up the next morning, excited. The cover band idea still seemed like a good one. The test of any barroom idea is, if it's still a good idea in the light of morning, in the light of your hangover, it's a good idea. I'd had the idea for a couple of years but didn't know how to go about it, or as Morrison said, "I could never allow myself to rationally fantasize about doing it myself. I guess all the time I was accumulating inclination."

To put my plan into action, the first thing I had to do was find a band. That seemed simple enough, and there were plenty of bands that played the bars in any college town and Madison was no exception, but which one? The next problem seemed a little harder, I didn't know anything about music. For instance, how would I know if a particular band could play the music? Or if they could play it, did they play it well enough? It bummed me out for a few hours. I couldn't see any way around it, short of taking music classes to get that expertise. That would take at least a semester in even a survey course. I didn't have that time, I needed this as soon as possible! Then it hit me, I didn't need to! Morrison was a film student at UCLA, living on the beach and he didn't know anything about music beyond a few childhood piano lessons. I didn't even have those! On that scale I could be a bigger success than Morrison! I would solve the problem the same way Morrison had, he found Ray Manzarek and I'd find that person for me. I'd seen a lot of bands live and figured I was a pretty good judge of music. All I had to do was find a band that played well, knew what they were doing and they would work out the music problems. All I had to worry about was what Morrison worried about, the lyrics and the performance. I already had the blueprint for that. So, all I really needed to do was find the right band.

I spent the next few days working out the criteria. The highest priority I would have to find a band with a keyboard player, nothing else could recreate the distinctive sound of *The Doors*. I would need musicians who didn't have any long term goals towards a career of their own. Either a band that knows they're not good enough to make it, or they're on the opposite end of the spectrum, a band that had already given up its ambitions, one that had tried, didn't make it and has come to terms with that, but are willing to do anything to keep their hand in the game, and stave off having to get straight jobs for another year or two. And finally, they had to be somewhat local, so that we could have rehearsals with a minimum of logistical problems, like lugging their equipment across state, or me driving hours on end for a rehearsal.

I started by reading the classifieds in the Milwaukee area entertainment magazines listing bands and the venues they were playing. The first problem I ran into was most of the bands that advertised seemed to take themselves too seriously, listing requirements such as must have stage presence and own equipment, or no drinkers or drugs, what was the point of being in a band then? None of the bands mentioned having a keyboard player. Plenty mentioned having a lead guitar and bass player but were looking for a hard rock drummer. It also occurred to me that I needed a band that was indebted to me, or at least they thought they were indebted to me, so they couldn't get rid of me when I'd outlived whatever usefulness I had to them.

The more I looked through the listings I found they wouldn't be of much help. None of the ads listed *The Doors* as an influence. There were mentions of just about every band that had ever existed from *Zeppelin, AC/DC, Metallica, Michael Bolton* to contemporary bands like *Ratt*, but no *Doors*. Which, strangely enough, encouraged me. I knew that there was a cult following of *The Doors* out there. Even though *The Doors* had had mainstream success they were unique in the rock world in that their sound was so distinctive that no one ever tried to duplicate it. In *When The Music's Over* the psychedelic roar of Robby Krieger's guitar is so original as to be trademark. Heavy metal bands used *Deep Purple* and *Led Zeppelin* as a starting point, but *The Doors* were a world unto themselves. Up until *The Doors* rock songs were about your girlfriend, your car, and surfing. After *The Doors*, girls were still in the songs, but it was about sex, and cars weren't for picking up your girlfriend and cruising around, cars were vehicles to something else, somewhere darker, and suddenly rock was free to delve into subjects that up until that time had been confined to the realm of literature, death and existence.

Since the ads weren't going to be of any help, I turned to the listings of what bands were playing where. I would have to go to the gigs themselves, and scout the bands. I started by going to the local clubs to see bands, but none met the criteria I had established. Either, they weren't good enough period, they were obviously ambitious, selling their own tapes and t-shirts trying to get a following and major label attention. Or they didn't have a keyboard player you wouldn't think finding a band with a keyboard player is all that hard, until you actually go out looking for one.

I gradually increased my search pattern until I found myself going to clubs as far as Milwaukee. There were some commonalities of all the bands I saw and talked to. One being that all the singers said they were sick and I should come to their next show and it would be better, the other was I missed all their big shows. The second problem I ran into I hadn't anticipated, although I probably should have, was that I took to the nightlife like a fish to water. I'd always liked the excitement, the energy of the clubs, the allure of meeting women. Adventures every night provided a new opportunity. The net effect was I ended up drunk, a long way from home, and no band. I started questioning my motivations. Was I looking for a band, or a reason to go out drinking? I had decided to take a week or two off from the search to recuperate physically and psychically. I was burned out from the amount of energy I was dedicating to the search.

THE BAND

Ghost Dance

One Saturday afternoon I was in 'The Place'. I wasn't looking for a band, I wasn't looking for a woman, I wasn't looking for trouble, I was looking to relax, I had decided to take a sabbatical from the search, and some times when you're chasing a dream too hard if you step back it'll come to you.

The bar was dark, cool and empty. It was early in the afternoon a couple of weeks before the fall semester was scheduled to start. After the school year started, the college crowd that frequented here was mostly a weekend crowd that came to get drunk and laid, and inadvertently see whatever band was playing. In the next room, I could hear Reggie, the owner of 'The Place' auditioning a band to play for that crowd. As one of the better customers I knew Reggie and talked to him when he sometimes sat in the bar having a beer. Reggie struck me as being a hustler, always on the make, there was something sweaty about him, he fancied himself a high powered rock promoter, his clothing was hip, but always about five years behind any trend.

"This one's an original composition of ours, one, one two three . . ." I heard coming through an amplifier from the other room. The band went into their song and by sheer force of habit I listened to their playing. I found myself nodding my head in time to the music.

"They're not to bad." I said to the bartender, who just shrugged his shoulders, probably having heard countless auditions, myriad bands, and endless original songs countenanced by their creators to be the next number one hit record. He retreated to the opposite end of the bar to read a newspaper. All of a sudden, I couldn't believe it miracle of miracles, a keyboard came in. I went over to the doorway to watch the audition. The lone light in the room was from the single spotlight on the band on stage. The lead singer stood stridently in front of the microphone, yelling the lyrics just under the sound of the music. He was dressed in ripped, patched jeans and T-shirt, guitar slung low. The keyboard player was off to stage left, the lead guitar player to his right, and of course behind them on a riser, the drummer. The lead guitar player wandered the stage, eyes closed, 'feeling' the music like any good guitar player was supposed to. The drummer was hidden behind his drums, and they were good! Their playing was above average, their music hit some interesting ideas, but they didn't explore the note or concept when they were already off to the next thing musically, trying to fit in as many interesting things as they could before the end of the song. A quantity over quality approach to music, but their really big drawback was they were totally uninteresting to watch. They could have been any one of a number of garage bands around, but they were good enough for a cover band.

"OK!" Reggie yelled to the band and they stopped playing, "do you guys know any cover tunes?" The lead singer stood at the microphone, one hand shielding his eyes straining to see and hear out into the darkness. He looked at the other band members. They exchanged looks amongst themselves. "You know, like *The Beatles, Stones, Zeppelin.*" Reggie said impatiently. The lead singer turned towards the other members of his group then shrugged his shoulders they looked like they had been playing together long enough to read the other's mind. They started to play *Light My Fire*, and a shot went through me! I struggled to contain my excitement, just as I had given up hope, destiny dropped them right in my lap, it's like the forces of nature conspire to bring everything you need to you, there are certain times in life when you're in tune with the universe, when no matter what turn you take, no matter what wrong turn you think you made, turns out to be right, it was almost enough to make you believe in a higher purpose or predestination. As the band got to the instrumental, Reggie once again yelled.

"OK! Thank you!"

Returning to my stool at the bar, I settled into another beer to calm myself. As the band sullenly packed their equipment I watched them struggling with it as they lugged it out. When they were taking out the last of it, I was still riding the wave of excitement of discovering them, and was just drunk enough to talk to them.

"You guys are pretty good." I said to the lead singer as he came by.

"He didn't think so." He said, motioning with his head back towards Reggie still in the other room.

"Ahh, don't worry about him, he's always trying to find an angle. Some day when you guys hit it big he'll see the error of his ways, and probably claim he discovered you. Can I buy you guys a beer?" The band members looked at one another, another silent conversation taking place.

"Sure." They sat at the bar, in what seemed to me in the pecking order of the band. The lead singer closest to me, the lead guitar player, keyboardist, and finally, farthest down from me the drummer. He was wearing what seemed to be the Rock 'n' Roll uniform of the day, ripped jeans and T-shirt but with the addition of blue hair.

"I'm Johnny Rydel," the lead singer said, introducing himself, "this is Brian, Mitchell, and Ian. Who're you?" He asked.

"Oh, sorry, Michael Gray." I said extending my hand. "So, how long have you guys been playing together?"

"Well, Mike, it's . . ."

"My name is Michael, not Mike."

"Sorry, is that some religious thing or something?" Johnny asked, they all shared a chuckle between themselves.

"No." I said, "so, what's your band's name?"

"Ghost Dance."

"That's cool, I like it. Where do you guys know each other from?"

"Brian, Mitchell and me have been playing together since high school."

"What about you Ian?" I asked.

"I was a music major at the school, these guys were playing some house party that I had crashed. During a break I was goofing around thumping on the drums, they were a little out of tune so I adjusted them."

"His tuning was better than our drummers drumming, so we brought him on."

"Let me tell you," I said, "I think you guys are pretty good. A couple of rough edges, but you'll work them out."

"Yeah, that's what we're trying to do, we want to get out in front of an audience and get some experience and some exposure for our songs. Maybe make a couple of bucks. Here," he said, reaching into his coat pocket and pulling out a tape and handed it to me, "it's a tape we made of our songs. Listen when you have a chance."

"Thanks." I said. I looked at the tape he handed me. Small bands like to identify with the bands they idolize so when they make a tape they usually title it something that's a play off of a title of their favorite band. This one was titled 'Pieces of Fate,' I smiled as I put it in my pocket, no matter how good they were they weren't going to make it any time soon, they wore their influences on their sleeves. I leaned conspiratorially over to them, "you guys want to go to my place and get high?" They looked amongst themselves, hesitation and distrust in their eyes "no, no, no, I'm not some kind of weirdo, we'll just smoke a joint."

"Okay."

The Trailer

My trailer was outside of town on a small piece of land I rented from a farmer. The trailer had been used for hunting, but the farmer needed some extra money so I bought it. Since the farmer had run a phone line and electric out to the trailer, I left it where it was and rented the land. We walked along the path through the weeds to the trailer. I really hadn't been planning on bringing anyone over, between Deidre leaving, and running around looking at bands, the trailer, which had already been cramped with books, records and tapes, had a layer of empty beer cans and days old pizza leftovers covering and overlapping each other from every flat surface available. I quickly tossed some things off the couch as they walked in, pushed others to the side, and there was enough room for everyone to sit down. The next step was to feel these guys out, and see if they were interested in my cover band idea.

"You guys want a beer?" I asked, taking five out of the refrigerator and putting them on a table. As they settled in, each nervously surveying the surroundings, I sat down, and pulled a joint out of the chaos of the table, lit it, sucking on it hard, before blowing out the smoke and handing it to Johnny. I sat back letting the smoke emanate through my body. I didn't say anything until they each took a hit off the joint. "I noticed when Reggie asked you guys to play a cover tune, you played *Light My Fire*. Do you guys like *The Doors?*"

"Sure." They all nodded, "we use it at practice to warm up."

"Here, listen to this." I said, jumping out of my chair. I pulled a record off a shelf and put it on the turntable. "I collect *Doors* bootlegs. You know, concerts people taped, soundboard recordings." I dropped the needle on the record. There was a pop and a hiss, and the sounds of long ago concert goers flitted around the room. Then the dark, pulsing beat of Ray Manzarek's organ came on, the first tentative twangings of Robby Krieger's guitar, the boom-ka-boom-boom of John Densmore's punctuating drums, and finally the scream of Jim Morrison filled the trailer. I looked at their uncomprehending eyes, I hoped the music would provide the soundtrack to sway them. I tried to sense their mood, but couldn't. I was nervous and tried to hide it by acting cool, but it only added to my nervousness. I was all nerves and energy I couldn't stop, I plowed into the proposal I had gone over and given time after time in my head. "I have a proposition for you guys." I said, my voice wavering and cracking from the strain.

"I knew it! We're so out of here." Brian said.

"No, no!" I said, settling them back into their seats, "it's an idea I have about a band."

"It better be man."

"What kind of an idea?" Johnny asked.

"It is, listen. A while ago I saw a show called *Beatlemania*, and I thought somebody should do that for *The Doors.*"

"That was a play, right? With guys pretending to be *The Beatles*, and doing the songs?"

"Yeah, it was, but my idea is simpler, just a band playing the songs and a guy 'being' Morrison, doing his antics." They didn't seem to be following me so I launched into my sales pitch, "Morrison was completely spontaneous, he acted out the songs, he recited poems, he fell, he dived off the stage into the audience."

"You mean like an Elvis impersonator?"

"Yeah."

"Man, that's a bad example, those guys are a joke."

"What's the show gonna' be? A casket on-stage, you open it and out falls a skeleton dressed in leather pants?" Mitchell said, laughing.

"But it doesn't have to be, we do it in clubs, the same environment *The Doors* preferred. We play it straight, no camp, no winking, and no making it seem like a joke."

"And who would the guy 'being' Morrison be?" Johnny asked.

"Me."

"And who would the band be?"

"You guys." They looked at each other with varying degrees of shock, skepticism, or amusement. The pot must have been kicking in because the moment seemed to freeze momentarily in a tableau reminiscent of The Last Supper.

"Excuse me," Ian said, "but Johnny is the lead singer of this band." they all nodded in agreement.

"Sure, sure," I said, "you guys have your band, but we can do this until your band is getting gigs, making a demo, gets a contract, whatever you want. This way you're performing in front of an audience, getting paid, and you can do a couple of your songs each set."

"What do you get out of it?"

"The reason Morrison said he started writing songs was because he said he 'was taking notes at a concert in his head.' Well, I'm hearing a *Doors* concert in my head, with me singing. I want to know what it feels like to be up on stage, I want to know what it would be like to be Morrison."

"You should see a doctor about that."

"So, why would people pay to hear a band play a bunch of old songs they can buy on an album?"

"Or hear on the radio."

"Aren't you listening? Listen to the bootleg I have on. We can give people something they can't buy, that they can't get anywhere else."

"Which is?"

"Something real. The hair bands are all hype drinking tea out of Jack Daniels bottles, the rock stars themselves are getting old. Mick

Jagger looks like a freeze-dried version of his younger self, Dylan, a jowly legend." I stopped, a little exasperated. "People want something real again. I was born at the tail end of the baby boom. By the time I got old enough, it was like I could hear the sound of receding thunder. And I was asking 'what was that?' While everybody else was saying wasn't that cool."

"So?"

"I remember hearing their songs when I was a kid, but I was too young to do anything about it."

"What're you talking about?"

"The sixties, there are a lot of people out there just like me who were too young to be part of the sixties. The younger brothers and sisters who raided their older siblings record albums, and could only listen to their stories. Or those more your age who weren't there at all and want to experience some part of the whole thing. It's like our mythic age of heroes and gods."

"What thing?"

"The experience of seeing a *Doors* concert live. They never played a song the same way twice, they did medleys, solos, and long jams. They were like *The Dead* only Morrison was wilder. I'm just saying I know more about *The Doors* than just about anyone else, I've read everything about them, I have all the bootlegs," I said, I hung my head in exhaustion, I didn't know how many more ways I could explain it, "I've thought about this for a long time. I've thought it all the way through, the band will be called The Unknown Soldiers, after one of their songs," I looked nervously between them trying to gauge how it was going, all their faces registered skepticism, but I couldn't stop, I was too far in, "and people have been telling me all my life I look like Morrison." I saw smiles of an in joke cross their lips again. So, I decided to throw in a little flattery "I know you guys are going to be successful, you know how I know that?"

They all looked at each other, "no, how?"

"Because of that right there, that silent almost psychic communication you guys seem to have with one another. It's the same camaraderie *The Doors* had."

"You think so?" Johnny asked with as much false modesty as he could muster. I could tell he was proud of the band.

"Oh, yeah." That got them to relax, and they at least seemed to be considering the proposition.

"Can you sing?" Johnny asked.

"Why is that the first question everyone asks?" I said, "no."

"Awww, man . . . ."

"But neither could Morrison at first. Here, look at this." I grabbed my well read, dogged eared copy of *No One Here Gets Out Alive* from somewhere out of the rubble of the table, and tossed it to Johnny. "Read it. Morrison couldn't sing either." Johnny held it up looking at it before handing it to one of the other guys.

"I've read it," he said. "So, the idea is we play the songs and you sing and act like Morrison, right?"

"Yeah, and dress like him. I'll wear a pair of leather pants, and grow my hair out."

"How old are you?" Johnny asked.

"Thirty-one."

"That's four years older than Morrison was when he died." Johnny said, "and Morrison was ten years younger when they started *The Doors*."

"It's not that much that anyone will notice, a little make-up and stage lighting, and no one will even notice."

"Dude, it's getting to be a forced perspective." Ian said.

Everyone was quiet. "And you have me." I added.

"What does that give us?" Brian asked.

"I have what Morrison had, a philosophy."

"So?"

"It makes me dangerous." I watched the silent deliberations and decided to add a closing argument, "c'mon, Reggie was right, people want to hear something familiar, it's comforting, it's something they can identify with, then when you have them, you can spring the originals on them and they're more receptive to them. What'd ya say?" They all looked at each other registering their votes with their different reactions, then deferring to Johnny.

"Nah, man," Johnny said, "we're a band, we got our own songs we wanna do."

"I've had this idea a long time, and looked at a lot of bands. You're the first band I've asked. This can work to your advantage. People will hear your band, you can play your songs, we'll tour all over the country like a real band. Think of the exposure. We can become rich, and famous, it'll be great! We'll split everything fifty-fifty like *The Doors*, we'll share all the expenses, we'll share any profits, and any offers we receive."

"That's cool, but fifty percent of nothing is nothing." Mitchell said, "and that's what I already earn."

"But a cover band is guaranteed. There aren't many bands out there doing this, so it's a niche waiting to be filled. Club owners will love it because they're hiring bands that play proven hits without having to pay the bands with the hits."

"Haven't you heard man, punk is the new music." Brian said.

"Morrison practically invented punk!" I said, "the leather pants, the slouch, the attitude, confronting the audience, the poses in the publicity stills, it's all Morrison!"

"You think so?" He asked thinking it over, "how do you know people want to hear a band that plays *Doors'* songs?"

"Because, I just do." I said, "there are books coming out. There's even talk of a movie coming out, probably with John Travolta or Tom Cruise."

"No, man," Johnny laughed, "that's way too screwy, we gotta go."

The Deal

I hadn't heard from Johnny and the band for a month or so, but I knew sooner or later that I would. They had fairly reeked of desperation that night in my trailer, and I knew sooner or later that some vicissitude of life would send them my way.

While I hadn't known any of them before I met them, at heart Madison was a small town, so I knew some of their stories, gleaned from the information that floats around any small town. They were small town boys trying to escape the inertia of the college town they grew up in with the velocity of Rock 'n' Roll, but they had neither the inclination nor the desire to use the college they had so readily available. After I got to know them I found they were well versed in the history and lore of Rock 'n' Roll, they talked endlessly about it when they were moving their equipment, and after I got to know them that was all they talked about. They knew what their instruments could do and what sounds they could get out of them, but about the rest of the world, general knowledge was lacking.

Johnny's family was fairly well off. Even though he wore ripped jeans, they were fashionably faded and ripped jeans. His father was a vice president of some corporation, and active in the community. By Johnny's comments and demeanor I assumed his musical aspirations clashed with his family's wishes. He could play guitar, but he looked a little grungy and had little or no charisma. Brian was the good looking one and probably got most of the girls. Mitchell was the punk rocker dressed in the most outrageous combinations of clothes. In such a small town, it was outrageous and probably meant to offend the prevailing standards. It's somewhat of a myth that college towns are liberal bastions. A facile observation of parents as they visit the campus, they see the experimental idealism of the students, and the insulated radicalism of the professors. But the real town, the town where people have lived for generations without a thought of leaving, the town which the college itself grew around, the town where once their children reach eighteen they buy a trailer, get married, and live quite different lives and values than the artificial society of the college. I met plenty of them in the barrooms. And Ian, well, Ian was the drummer. Most people don't give drummers enough credit. They have to carry the tempo of the band and most of the time they get written off. Read any rock biography, drummers are the quirky ones, or an after thought.

Then one afternoon my phone rang.

"Hi, it's Johnny, um.. can I talk to you?" His voice quavered and sounded hesitant, and I knew I had a band.

"What can I do for you?" I asked.

"Well, it's like this . . . uh, are you still interested in doing *The Doors* cover band thing?"

"Yeah."

"It's like this, uh, . . . we lost our rehearsal space and we don't have any money for a new one and umm . . . well, we'll do your *Doors* thing if you can provide money for a rehearsal space. The band will still be ours, but we'll do the *Doors* thing. We'll be able to play a couple of our original songs every gig, right?"

RS Article

Former Cover Band Has Break Through Album

Ghost Dance's self-titled debut album is a curious mix of influences that strangely enough work. With songs like 'Testament' and 'Last Stage' to their hit 'Girl Wild' which is currently racing up the charts, Ghost Dance demonstrates a hard rock base with punk influences. Leanings, that give them a different and wildly original sound from their contemporaries. While they're young and new to being recording artists they're old hands at touring, having paid their dues, crossing the country playing small clubs and bars.

"Ghost Dance very clearly has its origins in classic rock."

"Yeah, we all grew up listening to the radio when rock from the seventies was played a lot, *Springsteen*, *Aerosmith*, *The Stones*, but we also have a punk element that we're trying to expand on all the time."

"Where did you guys get the name Ghost Dance?"

"We grew up in the Madison, Wisconsin area," lead singer Johnny Rydel answered. "There are still some tribal remnants up there. I visited a reservation quite a few times with my parents when I was a kid and I always thought these trips were the greatest things in the world. Once I kind of had a mystical experience on the reservation, so I became interested in Indian things. And I thought the name was different and cool sounding."

"A mystical experience?"

"Let's just say I thought I had discovered a new science." He said chuckling.

"Kind of like Jim Morrison."

"Kind of." He smiled, wanly, "but Jim Morrison doesn't have a monopoly on mystical experiences."

"The reason I mention this . . ."

"The time we toured as a classic rock band." Lead guitarist Brian Leto cuts in.

"I read somewhere you guys got started playing in a tribute band."

"Not exactly, we were already a band, we just couldn't get a gig, and one day we met up with this guy. We grew up in Madison and he went to school there or something. We'd seen him around town when we were growing up. We considered him something of a weirdo, a dude who wanted to be young so he hung around the college years after he graduated. He had this idea for a cover band. We couldn't get a gig, so we did it to keep the band together and be able to practice without having to work some lame day jobs."

"Of course we admired *The Doors* and their accomplishments, we just didn't want to be forever tied to them."

"Forever a tribute band."

"We knew we always had something to say and we wanted that voice."

"Well, he did manage to unite us as a band."

"Yeah, he gave us a common enemy."

The House

We stood on the lawn in front of the house I had rented. It was white and hadn't been lived in for some time, the paint was chipped and peeling in places, smudged and dirty in others, but the important thing was, it was far from any neighbors.

"It doesn't look like much." Johnny said.

"It's not supposed to, it's a rehearsal space." I said. "Come on, let me show you the inside." I led them up the stairs and into the house. "How do you like it?" My voice echoed in the empty rooms, "see, we can set up the equipment and practice down here in the living room, the kitchen's right over there." I said pointing, "and the dining room is adjacent to both." They wandered around the room in ever expanding circles, looking at everything and taking possession of it with their eyes, getting the feel of it with their bodies as they moved from room to room, "upstairs are some bedrooms. I'll be living up there, but we can throw some mattresses in the other rooms in case someone needs to crash here," I said.

"Where'd you get the money for this?" Johnny asked.

"I sold my trailer." I said, "to show you how serious I am, and to show you how much I believe in this." Everyone was quiet at this realization, it grew awkward, so I hastily started talking again, "and I've put all my bootlegs and books over here. I spent the morning setting up my stereo, and TV and VCR," I said going over to a bookcase built into the wall, "so we can have an instant reference library. Feel free to look through these at your convenience they might give you some insight into the whole thing we're trying to do. Oh, yeah, there's a basement if we want to have a party or something and come over here, look at this." I said, rushing over to the kitchen just off the living room and opened the refrigerator, "have a beer," I'd filled it with beer.

"Pretty cool." They said.

"Looks like a good place to bring pussy!" Ian's voice echoed down from one of the upstairs rooms. We laughed.

"That's real classy." Johnny said.

"It's always the drummer." Brian said, nodding his head. We spent the rest of the afternoon moving in their equipment and drinking beer. We had our first party in honor of the house. We'd start to work out the music and our hangovers with a real practice the next day.

Metamorphosis

"Let's start with a song you guys know," I said, "*Light My Fire.*" It was early afternoon, the boys all had slept here overnight and we were all wearing the same clothes as we had on the night before. The pounding in our heads, or at least mine, had been reduced to a dull thud.

"Easy enough." Johnny said, they looked at each other and went into an album perfect renedition of the song. No mistakes except what was on the album, a clean, antiseptic feel to it, technically perfect, but there was no soul to it, nothing of themselves in it.

"No, no, no," I said, "you guys are making it sound too much like the album. We have to make it sound spontaneous."

"Man, I thought that's what you said people wanted to hear, the songs?"

"Yeah, but Brian was right we can't give them what they can hear on the radio, but if we give them a show that was like a *Doors* show they'll feel that integrity. They may not know it with their heads, but they'll 'know' it with their souls. Here, listen to this." I grabbed a bootleg from the bookcase and put it on the stereo, from the speakers came the notes that open the song.

"See, it should sound like we're inventing it right at the moment."

"We?" Brian asked, "how do we do that?"

"I don't know, you're the musicians." They looked at each other, and for a split second I really thought they were going to put down their instruments and walk out. It was like one of those scenes in a movie where everyone has a gun drawn on everyone else and it's either everyone gets blown away, or someone uncocks his gun and everyone breathes a sigh of relief.

"What do you mean, you don't know?" Johnny asked.

"I don't know," I said, "you guys are the musicians, you take care of all the audial details." They all looked at each other, again.

"Audial? What's that?" Johnny asked, and the rest suppressed a smile while I looked puzzled, "man, there's no such word as audial."

"I don't know, man, just don't make the tuning perfect or something, and I'll sing a little off key."

"We won't have any problems there." Ian joked.

"What about your part?" Johnny asked, "what's this 'performance' you're going to do?"

"Start *Light My Fire* again, and I'll show you." As the band played I sang the first verse, "you know that it would be untrue, you know that I would be a liar." I delivered the lines in the deliberate almost languid delivery that Morrison had used finally screaming the last line into the instrumental, "try to set the night on fire!" Then I stood hanging on the microphone with my eyes closed, feeling the music, like Morrison did. As they went into the instrumental I twisted away from the microphone doing a few of Morrison's patented staccato Indian hops.

"Hold it, hold it," I heard Johnny saying as the music stopped. "That, uh, seems a little flat, doesn't it?"

"That's what Morrison did for this song," I said, "he usually left the stage as an excuse to have a beer while the band played the solo's. Don't worry it'll work itself out. Here, I'll show you." I went to the dining room and rolled out the videotape player and TV.

"Cool, visual aids." One of them said sarcastically.

"What's that?" Johnny asked.

"It just came out, *The Doors Live at the Hollywood Bowl*." I held up the cover of the tape I had watched the night before after everyone else was asleep. We watched it from beginning to end. When it was over, there was a second of silence of the boys looking at each other.

"That's it! That's going to be our show!" Brian said incredulously. He picked up the videotape cover and read off the back 'the greatest agent provocateur of Rock 'n' Roll', the guy just stood there for most of the time, he barely moved!"

"Look, things he did are documented in the book. It's not really what something is, but what people expect that something to be, if we give them what they expect they'll be happy."

"I've been looking through this." Mitchell said, holding up a copy of *The Compleat Lyrics of The Doors*, "I just don't see it either. I thought there was supposed to be so many levels to *The Doors'* songs, they all seem pretty simple."

"A lot of that was insinuated by Morrison and the music added the mysterious feel to it." They looked skeptical, "look, most lyrics *are* pretty simple. And Morrison liked it that people were reading all these deeper meanings into his lyrics. He thought art was a two way street and the audience brought something to the experience too."

"You know what the songs mean?" Brian asked.

"I like to think so." I said.

"Why was he so hung up on serial killers?"

"That's an easy one. It's your own death, that's the killer on the road that we're all going to pick up one day on the trip of life, death."

Mitchell, who was still leafing through the lyrics book said, "some of the lyrics, you know, it sounds like he was just using things he saw around him."

"Yeah, I'm sure he used things he saw in everyday life in his lyrics, but Morrison read a lot, especially Mythology. He understood the symbolism behind the things he used, you have to give the artist credit for transforming life into art. You can't dismiss it because you know he was at Robby's house and saw his cats and then wrote about lions or panthers."

"What about *Five to One*?" *Five to One* has been the subject of speculation since the instant Morrison put together the combination of the ratio's 5 to 1, and 1 in 5 into the song.

"I read that the numbers meant the number of baby boomers to those over thirty."

"I heard it was the ratio of pot smokers to non pot smokers." I smiled, knowing Morrison must have gotten a good laugh as people all around him volunteered explanations of what the five to one ratio meant, and every one of Morrison's associates has a different version of what they say Morrison confided to them the numbers represented.

"Maybe, five to one means us as a band." Mitchell said, "the five of us against the world."

"No, it's nothing that simple, you've got to remember Morrison was a genius, it's nothing as mundane as statistics."

"Then what is it smart ass?"

"OK, I'll tell you, Morrison liked the poems of William Blake, right?" They nodded agreement, "well, in the Songs of Experience or Songs of Innocence, I don't know which one I get them confused but it talks about the five senses each person has, five senses to one person, five to one."

"Then what's the 1 in 5?"

"The reverse one person has five senses." They all looked at me and as the thought exploded in their minds they all got excited.

"That makes sense!"

"You're a genius, how'd you think of that?"

"It's not my idea, but I think it's the right one, but don't tell anyone it would ruin the mystery, now can we get back to work?"

Over the next few weeks, as we moved on to other songs we hit a snag I hadn't anticipated. It was easy to find the guitar tabs and arrangements for the hit songs, *Light My Fire, Touch Me, Hello, I Love You, Love Her Madly*, but for the lesser known songs the guitar tabs and arrangements for those songs simply didn't exist. There wasn't the information available as there is today, it was like being out in the wilderness. So Johnny and the band had to work out the songs one by one. We'd listen to the live album and my bootlegs starting and stopping them over and over again until they got the sound right, sometimes it went note by note, even the video helped in that we could see exactly how they were playing, where their fingers were on the guitar, or where their hands were over the keyboards or drums. It was a time consuming and tedious process, but it had the unintended side effect of teaching them how to build a song from the inside out.

It also taught me a few things about music. For instance, they gave me what I thought was some bullshit musical theory that they tried to make sound mysterious, but what it boiled down to was you weren't supposed to change tempo in the middle of a song, which *The Doors* did. I also learned John Densmore should have had a better rapport with Morrison, the drummer is an uncontrolled element in a band because it's almost impossible to tell a drummer how to play something, there's no way to notate or have sheet music for the drums, the drummer is the one chaotic element of a band. As the weeks went by I found solace in the music, to float along in the notes, lost on a river, to give yourself to the music, the moment, to really let go, to feel free and scream! It was only a few weeks before that I was making fun of the band for 'feeling' the music as they played, but I learned to love the members of the band and their talent, how Brian cradled the guitar, and during L.A. Woman did a slide that gave me hard-on, how Mitchell mashed the keys of the organ to create the discordant *Doors* sound, or Ian the Indian staccato of the drums. I don't know if we became friends but we did learn to respect what the others brought to the band.

After a day of practicing I would lay awake on my bed into the night, the room darkened, the light from the TV flickering like lightning at twenty-four frames per second. I watched the tapes of Morrison over and over again memorizing his every move, and intonation, and likely as not, falling asleep and dreaming of when it would be my turn. As they mastered each song, I worked out the theatre, sometimes I instinctively knew when to fall, or dance, I could see Morrison in my mind's eye doing it. The key was spontaneity and feeling it, and then acting it out that would recreate Morrison's mind-set.

Practice Gig

We'd been practicing for a couple of months, the band had worked out the arrangements on most of *The Doors'* songs. They sounded perfect, but not too perfect, they just left in any mistakes, not that they were playing sloppy, it's just those random elements gave it the needed spontaneity. It was a delicate balance. I decided we were ready to find a gig. First of all to see how the act would go over, and secondly the boys were getting anxious and starting to make noises about all the rehearsal being a pointless exercise, and that it was taking them away from their own music, and lastly some money in their pockets would go a long way towards relieving all those feelings. One afternoon I skipped rehearsal and went to 'The Place' and talked to Reggie. When I got back to the house the boys were rehearsing a song I didn't recognize. I looked around the room and realized it had become, and looked like a place where four guys lived.

"We gotta get this place cleaned up." I yelled. They stopped playing and looked at me, trying to figure out if I was serious or not. In the time we'd been practicing we had developed a good working camaraderie. Not quite friendship, but bordering on it.

"Hey man," Johnny said, "when do you want to learn more about the music?"

"I don't want to know too much about the music it might lose it's magic for me, I don't ask you to do any of the singing, do I? But I have some good news."

"Like what?"

"I got us a gig!" I yelled.

"We got a gig!" They all said, excitedly, jumping towards me, wanting to hear all the details.

"Where?" Johnny asked.

"At The Place."

"How'd you do that?"

"I'm friends with Reggie." I said.

"You're friends with . . . Reggie? You said . . ." Johnny started, then blew out a breath in frustration. He didn't seem as excited as he had been the moment before. "Well, thanks for saying something to Reggie about us the day we auditioned."

"It's his business which bands he hires."

"But he booked your cover band idea without even listening to us?!"

"Well, he did want to hear the band," I said, "but when I mentioned that he'd heard you guys before, and I told him who you guys were. I guess your performance impressed him enough, it clinched the deal for him."

"But he hired the cover band sight unseen . . ." Ian said.

"If you thought we were good enough for your cover band idea, and you seem to have some influence with him, you could have mentioned something to him that first day."

"No, I couldn't have," I said, "what makes you think my opinion would have changed his mind?"

"If you believed in our music you could've said something, it might have *said* something to him."

"Well, I thought you guys would be excited that I got us a gig."

"We are." Brian said, "maybe just in shock."

"So, what're you guys rehearsing?" I asked, trying to change the subject.

"We're rehearsing our stuff."

"Oh, you guys are rehearsing your songs?"

"Yeah, dude, we've been rehearsing every day after you left."

"Oh, well, . . ."

"Do you mind?" Johnny said, "this is for the band only."

"Well, rehearsal is over, . . . uh . . ." I stammered, "I guess . . . I, OK." I went back to the kitchen, opened a beer and listened to them work up their songs.

Trial Run

I arrived at 'The Place' at about eight on the night of the show. I was dressed in black leather pants, a white Mexican wedding shirt, and silver concho belt that I bought that day. I got a pair of leather pants at the local Harley distributor right off their rack. The shirt and concho belt were a little harder to find because where do you find a Mexican wedding shirt in Madison, Wisconsin? I ended up in the woman's department of a local retailer. There were no Mexican wedding shirts, so I found a shirt that closest fit the picture in my mind. And the concho belt? Well, just about every woman's department in America carries them or a similar design. The sum of the whole was greater than its parts. Since we had started practicing I had let my hair grow out. It wasn't as long as Morrison's, but altogether I looked like Morrison at his apex.

The band had spent the afternoon setting up their equipment and doing the sound check, while I was shopping. I had spent the morning calling the local papers, including Jim who had taken me to see Ray only a few months prior. I went back stage and found the boys in the dressing room. It was small and cramped. On the far wall there was an old couch that was dirty and stained that Johnny and Brian shared. Ian and Mitchell were sitting in feeble looking chairs with their backs to the door, a rickety table was jammed between the couch and the chairs, and all this was only a few steps from the stage out of sight of the customers.

"Well, lookit here, our own Mr. Mojo Risin'!" Brian said, as I walked into the room.

"I never would've believed it, if I hadn't seen it with my own eyes." Mitchell said.

"Well, all right, Michael! We just may pull this off after all."

"What song should we start with?" Johnny asked.

"How about *The End*!" Ian blurted out, "that way we can make a quick exit, if we need to."

"Ha, ha, very funny," I said, "how about *Break On Through?*" We sat there waiting to go on. I had plenty of time to think as we sat killing time until we went on. Johnny and Brian were lucky they could pass the time tuning their guitars, or playing little impromptu tunes on the guitars which sat in guitar stands by their side. I tried to get into character I was trying to think like an actor, trying to get Morrison's character in my head and how he would act in this situation. Morrison himself came from a theatre background, having studied at Florida State, he went on to UCLA to study film. Theatre was always one of his intentions. For the feeling of the song I envisioned the promotional film *The Doors* had done when *Break On Through* was released as a single, all in black except for a couple of colored lights blinking, each of *The Doors* in a spotlight separated by darkness, Morrison pouting, trying to seduce the invisible audience.

"Whatta ya gotta do to get a beer around here?" I asked.

"Buy it." The unanimous reply.

We decided to start with *Break On Through*. It seemed to make sense, it was the first song on the first album and this was our first time in front of an audience. The band went on first. They started to play a drawn out introduction which was typical *Doors* strategy. They liked to let the pressure in an audience build until the last moment. Then Morrison would come out and release them from the musical trance. I walked out onto the stage and was standing above the heads of the crowd. The room was densely packed and the clamor of voices died down as everyone in the room looked up at me, the audience in anticipation of the show, and the band to see if I could actually do it. The only routes of escape were, singing, or jumping off the stage, pushing my way through the crowd, and out of the club. The band hit the vocal cue for *Break On Through*. I sang.

"You know day destroys the night." As I sang the words I didn't feel the tension of the audience break, they didn't move, they just sat there staring at me, or carrying on the conversations they were already involved in. I closed my eyes so I wouldn't have to see them and hit the words of the next lyric hard "**tried to run, tried to hide**" to shock them into some kind of reaction, nothing. During the instrumental I danced around the stage trying to engage them and when I got to "the gate is straight, deep and wide," I made it as suggestive as I could. Nothing. I finished out the song as best I could. When it was over there was silence, no clapping. All I heard was the background noise of drinks being ordered and continuing conversation. The audience didn't seem to be paying any attention to us. I stared at the audience frozen, not knowing what to do. I could see all my hopes ending there, after one song, the shortest career in music history, one song long. The band started playing *Roadhouse Blues*. I didn't know if I should get off the stage, or stay for whatever humiliation still awaited me. I missed the cue for the vocals to come in, but the band seamlessly went back into the song and started over. I don't think the audience noticed. Then something switched over in me, I wasn't going to allow them to humiliate me. I wasn't going to let them control how I felt. I was in control, I screamed one all for nothing scream, venting all my anger and rage towards the audience, torn from my throat. Then I hit the vocal cue.

"Going to the roadhouse, gonna have a real GOOD TIME!" The audience started clapping and cheering. The infection of the music moving them past the reservations they had, or maybe they were more familiar with 'Roadhouse', or maybe it was just a more up tempo good timey blues song, or just maybe I had shocked them into realizing we couldn't be ignored. During the rest of the set I pulled out all of Morrison's moves that I'd worked up during rehearsals. During the solo on *Light My Fire*, I went over to Mitchell and watched as he dibbled at his keyboards almost as intently as Ray Manzarek himself. I went into the audience and let a few people scream or sing. I acted out the firing squad scene of *The Unknown Soldier*. I fell on the stage writhing and contorting, I shocked the audience. In short, I gave them a real *Doors* show.

To end the show we were going to end it the way *The Doors* usually did, with *The End*. From the first lilting tones of the guitar,

I was immersed in the song. I became part of the song. I didn't need
to remember when to come in, I didn't need to remember the words,
I didn't need to react, just act. I just was. I was the song, I was Jim
Morrison! When it got to the Oedipal section after delivering the
lines, "father? Yes, son? I want to kill you. Mother, I want to . . . fuck
you!" I screamed again as the band lashed out into a musical torrent
of primal torment. I whipped myself into a fury, twirling, dancing
with the music, no acting, no rehearsed moves, being on-stage was
like having sex, you exist outside of time and space, you're immortal.
I fell to the floor hard and delivered the last lines from the floor. I
laid on the floor for a second or two, one arm hanging off the stage,
the shirt matted to my skin, my chest heaving, I was empty, devoid
of everything, I stood on the precipice looking out into the darkness,
as I pulled myself to a sitting position, then it happened . . . applause,
real applause, people waving and cheering. It filled me with a warmth
and became a power within me, it was birth, a metamorphosis, new
worlds lay before me that hadn't existed before, I felt as if I were
becoming larger than the room, like the room couldn't contain what
I was becoming, I rose up out of my mind "I AM!" I could go on
for hours. I didn't want the feeling to end, and I understood why
Morrison had wanted to keep the party going. Why he needed to
drink just to slow it down so he could feel normal again, to quell the
excitement, keeping the hounds at bay. This is where Morrison got
that energy.

"Thank you! Thank you!" I said. I decided to throw in an
improvised Morrisonesque rap. Not the exact words he ever said, or
that I ever heard, but they had the feel of Morrison.

"All right! All right!" I said, "this is work for me, I wanta get outta
here and have some fun, fun, fun, and some other words that start
with fu!" A final cheer went up as we left the stage.

Back stage we were celebrating, people were crowding into the
dressing room to congratulate us. Pressing in to shake our hands
and/or tell us how cool we were. It seemed the whole audience had
packed in backstage. It was the seed of addiction, I wanted to get up

there again and again. I wanted to sing and dance! We were having a beer reveling in the success when Reggie finally was able to make his way to us.

"You guys were great!" I could hear him shouting over the crowd, to Johnny. Johnny looked excited, "I'll book you guys! This *Doors* act really packed the people in and you guys were really good. If I closed my eyes I could almost see *The Doors*. I'll book you guys for a couple of weeks, that'll give you some money. If you want, I can set you up with a booker who can get you guys a tour, at least through the Midwest. It'll be a lot of riding around in a van together, sleeping in cheap motels, or in the van on the way to the next gig, but you can get some bucks for it and maybe some groupies. That is if you want to do it?"

"Uh, I, we, uh . . . ." Johnny stammered, and the rest of the band looked sheepish.

Reggie noticed their reaction "This *Doors* act wasn't just some kind of ploy to book your original act, was it?" Johnny looked at his band mates trying to decide what was the right answer to get the gig.

"No, no . . . this *Doors* thing is our act, it's Michael's idea." Johnny said motioning to me.

"OK, then." Reggie said, shaking his head.

"All that doesn't sound too appetizing." Johnny said.

"The groupies do." Ian said.

"C'mon you're in your twenties!" I said trying to motivate them, "this is the time you'll spend sleeping on your friends' floor, not eating, and screwing women you don't know anyway. Why not do it for your career, making some money, and the spirit of adventure? How many people can do that? Do you want to live your life or read about it when some other band becomes famous because they did it?"

"Who's this guy? The booker, I mean," Johnny asked.

"His name is Swifty."

"A little Runyunesque don't you think?"

"Where'd you hear a phrase like Runyunesque?" I asked.

"Probably the same place you did, a book."

Breakfast of Champions

The next morning the house was buzzing with energy, I woke up after a few hours sleep, refreshed and energized. There was the hum and excitement of women in the house and domestic smells of breakfast being made. Sausage and eggs were in the air. I could hear the radio playing from the kitchen. I went down to the kitchen to find the boys sitting at the kitchen table, each with a girl I recognized from last night's audience. They had finished eating, their plates pushed away from them. The boys were leaning back in their chairs. The cats that ate the canaries, they were all engrossed in their own conversations until I walked into the room.

"Welcome to the Rock 'n' Roll lifestyle," I said, "I see the fruits of your labor are paying off, already."

"Good Morning, Michael!" Greeted me in chorus.

"What happened to you last night?" Johnny asked.

"I went down to the lake to think things over."

"Annnd?" Ian prompted.

"I noticed during *Five to One* Brian was a little sloppy on the solo."

"Man, can we talk about it the next time we practice? I mean let us enjoy this."

"That's not the right attitude for success."

"Cmon, let's bask in our glory a little." Johnny said.

"OK," I said, "did anyone get the paper and see if we got a review."

"Nah, we didn't check the paper."

"A good review might get us a better deal with the agent Reggie was talking about."

"Man, you really need to get laid."

"I've fucked most of the girls in this town," I said. I walked out to the front porch to get the morning paper. I wanted to see if any of my efforts to plant a story, or get a review in one of the papers had succeeded. I leafed through the paper until I found Jim's column. It had a badly printed but recognizable picture of him at the columns head. The headline jumped out at me, but I couldn't bring myself to read the review. I knew we did a good show. I did my best, but what if someone else not as close to it saw something different and didn't like it? It was only a mention in a column anyway, I rationalized, but like my grandmother used to say "you have to start somewhere." I heard the phone ringing, one of the boys took the message. It was Reggie telling us of our appointment on Wednesday with Swifty, the booking agent, and the directions to his office. I made a note to myself to call Swifty first thing Monday morning.

Madison Capital Times Column

Left Behind

by James Ozell

The headline is tongue in cheek. As in many small towns the columnist knows many of the people he writes about personally, this is one of those times. And when you're wrong you have to fess up to it. A few months ago I was sitting in one of our town's finer establishments of adult refreshment, when I met Michael Gray. We shared an interest in *The Doors* and when I mentioned I'd seen them in the 60's his eyes lit up. We also had occasion to see Ray Manzarek down in Chicago, after which he told me he was going to start a cover band. I blatantly scoffed at him and didn't believe. Well, he whipped a band into shape and last night he opened with that band, 'The Unknown Soldiers', which just goes to show you the type of person you can meet in bars. True it may be a dicey proposition, but every once in a while you'll meet someone of ambition and drive. He made a believer out of me. He's someone from our area to keep an eye on and they're playing at that establishment of adult refreshment, 'The Place' for two weeks, so go and see them and don't be left behind.

Swifty

Swifty's office was in Milwaukee. We found the address Reggie had given us without too much trouble. It was in an old building that must have been from the 30's or something, but I don't know enough about architecture to know what style or period the building was from. Standing in the building's vestibule we realized we had a problem.

"Do any of you know Swifty's real name?" I asked, running my eyes up and down the directory, nothing immediately popping out at me, and nothing looked right. Then Mitchell said,

"Here it is, Maxfield Leonard Representation, LLC."

"Are you sure?"

"Nothing else is even close."

The office was on the 22nd floor. As we walked in I pulled up short. I was expecting an outer office with a secretary, or at least a big office, but the first thing I saw was a window with what seemed a downward view of the city. Immediately behind Swifty's desk was a big wooden frame window that had a latch on it and you could open, like any one you would find in your house. We were only a few steps in front of the desk the floor had a 'creaky' feeling to it. I thought I could feel the building swaying as we stood there, or maybe it was just a sudden fear of heights or claustrophobia. On one side of the room were four or five filing cabinets, the walls held pictures of bands that no one would recognize with the possible exception of the bands themselves, and their mothers. In the middle of the room was a big desk with neat columns of papers lining its top. Behind the desk sat a startled looking Maxfield Leonard, Swifty. He seemed to be of average height, thinning hair. He looked like what you would think someone named Swifty would look like, a cigar stuck in his mouth, the buttons of his shirt straining to contain what was underneath. Not the svelte, well coifed, well to do agent I had imagined, but this was the reality of the dream. He looked like he might have been a gumshoe from a Damon Runyon novel. From that moment on,

I started thinking of him as a cliché. Clichés, legends, myths, and stereotypes wouldn't exist if there weren't some truth at the bottom of them.

"Swifty?" I asked.

"In the flesh." He said, as he rose to greet us. "You the boys Reggie sent?"

"In the flesh." I said, matching him with an enthusiastic response.

"Come on in, close the door." We all arranged ourselves around the cramped office. Johnny and I grabbed the chairs in front of the desk. The rest of the boys leaned or perched themselves on the surrounding furnishings, adjusting themselves to look cool.

"Can I ask you something?" I asked.

"How'd I get the name Swifty?" He smiled, paternally, "that's always the first question." I shrugged my shoulders sheepishly. "It was sort of a joke. My father was a very dignified old world man, and he disapproved of this as my choice of a career, and he asked 'what's next? being called Swifty?' and it stuck. It became a self-fulfilling prophecy." He looked at us, "now that we have that out of the way ready to get down to business?"

"That's why we're here, man."

"Good, first things first," he paused for dramatic effect, "you should've never taken the gig at 'The Place', to put it in your vernacular, you got ripped off."

"But we . . ." I started to protest, Swifty held up a hand to quiet me.

"I understand you had to do it to get on the map as it were, but whoever did the booking is done." He looked at each of us to see if there was any disagreement with the terms. There were none. "Now I understand Reggie wants to book you guys, for a couple more weeks."

"Yeah," I said, with a sinking feeling in the pit of my stomach.

"Well, don't worry about it. Luckily, I know Reggie fairly well. I'll call him and we'll work out a more advantageous agreement. All right then, that's old business. Now about the tour." And he pulled out of his desk drawer a map of the United States and unfolded it spreading it over the top of his desk. He looked genuinely excited like an explorer plotting an adventure. I looked at the pictures on the walls again. How many bands had he sent off on voyages of exploration in search of gold and silver? A journey ultimately he himself could never take. Had any of those he sent off found their new worlds and treasures? I didn't recognize any of the pictures, I was his Columbus I would find those treasures of the New World. I wondered if Swifty had any treasured stories of conquest. "Here's the tour I booked for you boys. It's a tour of the Midwest that'll get you to every major city and just about every podunk bar and club outside of them. The bad news is you won't get to see much of the scenery because you'll either be playing, sleeping, or traveling. Chicago first, St. Louis, Kansas City, Dallas . . ."

"That all sounds good," Johnny said, "but how do we get from city to city? Or is that our problem?"

"Good question, young man. I bought you a second hand van, but it's in good condition and has enough space for the equipment and for everyone to fit in."

"A used van!" Brian exclaimed.

"And you're paying for it from the receipts of the shows I have lined up."

"So, we're in debt?" Johnny said.

"Welcome to show business boys." Swifty said, matter of factly.

"I also got you a roadie. He'll drive as well as help move equipment and set up."

"We don't need any help." Johnny said, "we're used to moving our own equipment and setting up."

"He's also my proxy," Swifty said, sternly looking at each of us to see if there were any more challenges, "in addition to driving and being your roadie, he'll count heads at the clubs so you don't get screwed by the owners. He'll collect our share of the receipts from the venue, make the deposits and I'll send you each a check every week."

"And who pays him?" Brian asked.

"His salary also comes from the shows."

"Who is he?" I asked.

"My nephew, Tom."

"Nephew!" Johnny said, incredulously.

"Wait, wait, wait let's go back to this check thing." Mitchell said, indignantly, "if I wanted a job, I wouldn't have joined a band. I would've gotten a fucking job at McDonalds."

"Then you're welcome to. Any of you are welcome to pursue any path you want, but realize this is a business and a job the same as any other." Swifty said firmly.

"You don't have to make it seem like one." Mitchell grumbled.

"One more thing boys, Michael will be paid more than everyone else."

"WHY!" The band said in unison.

"Because he's the performance, the attraction that will be drawing people in." There was grumbling all around. "Mr. Night and I have discussed this, and from what I hear of the show it sounds like it's justified."

"You're going to take his word for it?" Brian asked.

"I called Reggie at 'The Place' also. It seems he was impressed with the performance as well."

"Wait a minute, wait a minute," Johnny said, and then looked at me, "I thought you said we'd share everything equally."

"You didn't take that offer. You called three weeks later, so I felt free to make a better deal." Johnny looked at his bandmates. They all looked upset, but they were in too deep. With the couple of months of rehearsing *Doors* songs, and paying gigs lined up, if they walked out the door they'd be right back where they started. Stuck in small town USA without a gig, with no one hearing their music, without any money, and nowhere to rehearse, but their integrity would still be intact. "Fine." Johnny said, controlling his temper, "and what do you get for all of this?"

"The standard ten percent," Swifty said. "I also make sure you don't get cheated on the gigs. I do advance promotion buying ads in the local papers a day or two before you hit town and coverage in the papers when you hit town, everything from the Tribunes and Times' down to the Beacons and the Heralds. All you have to do is sign the contracts I've drawn up and you start the tour a week after you've finished at Reggie's."

"If we don't?"

"Then you play at 'The Place' for however long Reggie wants you. After that, if you don't have any other local gigs, it's back to whatever you were doing before."

Johnny's Father

It wasn't twenty-four hours after we got back from Milwaukee when somebody rang the doorbell at the house, which was unusual. No one had done that since the first week I had rented the house. I would wake up at all hours to find one of the boys watching TV, smoking pot, or having a party with some friends, I'd also heard about a lot of parties that happened while I was gone, but no one rang the bell any more. I answered the door, standing there was a distinguished looking middle-aged man with short gray hair, in a three-piece suit.

"I'm William Rydel." He said, walking in, "Johnny's father." He surveyed the room with a look of disdain on his face.

"I'm glad to meet you." I said, holding out my hand.

"Why do you think I stopped giving my son money for a rehearsal space?" His condescending attitude took me aback momentarily.

"I don't know anything about their previous arrangements." I said.

"It was because I was trying to discourage him from such a risky career choice. I had them on the verge of breaking up. Ian graduated last spring. Without a band he was already looking for another band, or thinking about moving back home to find a job. Even Brian was at a loss as to what to do, and he's the one who usually pulls Johnny back into this fantasy."

"You forgot Mitchell in your little rendition." I said.

"He's useless. He'll do anything to avoid responsibility, just like you."

"Thanks for the recommendation."

"Then," his voice was stern, "you come along and get a tour for them. And the dreams and fly by night ambitions are back. Now, thanks to you I get to take a different tack. I get to be the hero with my son and the band when this all falls apart, I get to pick up the pieces, I'm not the villan anymore. Do you know what I'm talking about?"

"Other than the band, no."

"I talked to my son about this situation last night."

"What situation would that be?" I asked.

"Your making more money than my son and the rest of HIS band."

"It's fair," I said, "I'm not the only one who thinks so. The agent . . ."

"Be assured," he said, in a controlled voice, "that I will be contacting Mr. Leonard in this matter." He stared at me sternly, "but if my son wants to be in the music business he's going to have to learn it the hard way. And you're part of that lesson. Personally, I hope your deceit dissuades him from pursuing this career any further. I don't know where you get your sense of entitlement that you think you can . . ."

"It's not their band now," I said. "It's OUR band, it was my idea for the cover band. Before I found them they were just local wannabes. Without me they couldn't even get a gig."

"That may be true, but at least they would've succeeded or failed on the merits of their talents or lack thereof, without someone negotiating for them who only has his own self-interest at heart."

"That would make me laugh if I didn't know you were serious. Your son is old enough, he knows what he wants to do. He made a deal and he'll be held to it."

"I'm just letting you know I'm looking into smoothing out the inequities for my son and his band. If you try to take anymore unfair advantage of those boys; I will see to it there will be a day of reckoning for you."

"I know how to handle parents like you." I said.

"We'll see," was all he said as he walked out.

Calling Deidre

I turned the volume down on the TV, and fiddled nervously with the phone cord as the phone on the other end rang.

"Hello?" Deidre said, a little groggily.

"Guess where I am," I said.

"I couldn't guess." I could hear the exasperation in her voice when she recognized my voice.

"I started a band, we're going on tour. I just wanted to talk to you before I left."

"That's cool. I read the review in the paper. What did you want to talk to me about?"

"I miss you."

"Don't be doing this Michael." She said.

"I'm doing this for you."

"You should be doing it for yourself, not me, and not us. I'm happy with my life and if you remember," her voice got a little harder, "it wasn't my choice, really."

"I'm going to make it big in this band."

"Just listen to yourself Michael, you sound like a gambler looking for the big score and you'll live happily ever after. But it never happens, the big score is always right around the next corner. I just hope you'll be happy with the life you've chosen."

"Aren't you even going to ask me what it's like on tour?"

"No."

"Oh." I said, disappointed, "It's not really the tour yet anyway, we just finished playing 'The Place' we leave next week for the tour. I never knew what you wanted."

"I used to think you were going somewhere, Michael. At first I thought you were . . ."

"You thought I was your ticket out of town."

"Oh, Michael, all I ever wanted was *you*. Happy, sad, famous, a farmer, whatever. I think that'll be your downfall."

"I didn't want to hurt you. I was just doing what I thought was best for the both of us." There was a cold silence on the other end.

"Well, good-bye." I whispered. I realized this was the end, this was the song, and I knew the finality of good-bye. I hung up.

Hollywood Today!

Hollywood Today! Was on, it's one of those shows that thrives on celebrity gossip. It was part of my campaign to keep myself informed of what was going on in Hollywood. Merri Caldwell, a cotton candy blonde plastic confection, a television projection for viewers fantasies was the host. I lay in my bed listening to her report.

"Where is Jimmy Stark?" She said, "Once the star of the late 60's TV show 'Family Muse', and known as 'America's little brother.' We all grew up with him. Jimmy's mother noticed his talent early and got him cast in TV commercials." They cut to a very grainy black and white TV commercial, with an almost infant child that, in hindsight, is recognizably little Jimmy Stark. "Then came Family Muse, the late 60's sitcom in which he played the precocious son of a mother trying to make it in the music industry." They showed a clip from the show featuring Jimmy which is now considered a television classic, "after 'Family Muse' his career stalled. Hitting the wall a lot of child stars do, not being taken seriously in adult roles. In his late teens Jimmy got married," they showed still photos of Jimmy and a young girl in a wedding dress, running down the steps of a church through a gauntlet of friends throwing rice. The pictures juxtaposed to create a jerky stop motion sequence ending with a picture of Jimmy, his wife and two children, "but they divorced after five years." They cut back to Merri in the studio, "in his twenties it looked like he was making the transition from child star to actor, starring in several movies, including an Academy Award nomination for 'Tender Fury'." They, of course, showed clips from the movie, followed by a still photo of Jimmy and his wife going down the red carpet into the Academy Awards ceremony, "he was also known as Hollywood's enfant terrible, making headlines for a series of police arrests and drug problems." There was a flash of white light that faded to a newspaper photo of Jimmy being lead away in handcuffs by cops on either side of him. A headline read: Former Child Star Arrested. "But he has long since disappeared from movies, TV, personal appearances, the police blotters, and even the tabloids." Then came the big finish to their story, "Jimmy Stark had fame, money, a glamorous career. Why did an actor with such a bright future toss it all away with such ruthless abandon? Well, we here at Hollywood Today! want to know too. Going on the adage, to find out where you are, you should examine where you've been. In future reports we will try to answer those questions."

I fell asleep.

Dream

I was at a party, the room was crowded with people. A stranger I knew asked, "hey, want to go to a concert?" Then I was walking the familiar hallways of the school, the light coolly reflected off the waxed marble floors. I heard the sound of faraway music echoing in the halls. I was alone. I followed the sound through the hallways of the labyrinth school. It became louder and louder as I approached the auditorium, I recognized the music, it was *The Doors* at their peak playing a *scorching* rendition of *Light My Fire,* played only as they could have early in their career. It was loud and Morrison's voice was a growl, then the music stopped. I was walking backstage, there were velvet curtains, backdrops from plays, tied off ropes running up to sandbags and wooden catwalks. Suddenly, there was Jim Morrison. Lean in his leather clad glory wearing a white shirt that accentuated the shiny black leather of his pants. He was sitting at a table having a beer. He pushed out the empty chair across from him with a tap of his boot.

"Have a seat man. Want a beer?" Before I could answer he pulled out an open beer from somewhere. "Replenish those precious bodily fluids." He said. "So, I understand you're going to be me."

"I, I don't think I can do it. I can't sing. I can't dance. All I have is this stupid idea."

"It's as easy as falling down, man. Go ahead, fall down and get back up. Make it look like a part of the act. I fell down a lot."

"You think I can do it?"

"Sure, consider this my blessing and just remember, it's all a dream." Then the bearded poetic Jim Morrison was sitting back in the chair smiling benevolently at me. "Well, I gotta be in Kalamazoo by two AM, hahaha." Then he was gone and so was the beer.

THE TOUR

The Van

Our first look at the van was underwheleming. It was your standard commercial van a little larger than your average family van, stripped down to its welds and the joists of its skeleton. Swifty was right, there was enough room in the back for the equipment and us, just enough. He was right, again, in that it was used, there were dents and dings everywhere on it, but it was road worthy. I learned to love the van, when you got it up to seventy-five miles an hour or so, it started rattling, we'd take turns driving, when it was my turn to drive, I would get it up passed seventy-five until the band and the equipment were bouncing around like flowers in a storm, yelling at me to slow down.

"Should we paint it like the Partridge Family bus?" Mitchell asked

"Nah, that's kind of lame," I said, "how about Kesey's bus, Furthur. That might be the better reference."

"Well, I think we should christen it something?" Mitchell said.

"It's just a van." I said.

"How about the van-ity?" Ian said.

"The what?" I asked. I wondered if it was one of their smirking inside jokes, I looked around trying to see if any of them was suppressing a smile, but they weren't.

"The van-ity. It's a van, right? Like in chitty, chitty bang bang, get it?"

"Not really."

Then there was Tom, the 'roadie' bequeathed to us by Swifty, also underwheleming. He looked like a headbanger who had banged his head one time too many, he had long frizzy hair and his clothes looked dirty, he was a rocker who knew the history and lore of Rock 'n' Roll, but that knowledge mysteriously stopped at 1979 with *Pink Floyd's The Wall*. He talked about *Shine On You Crazy Diamond*, or some triva about *Black Sabbath* for no other reason than that's what he thought was expected. Or maybe he was a little slow, but in the end, I could see he was malleable. I hoped the reason Swifty had put so much trust in him went beyond Tom being his nephew.

"Have you been a roadie before or is this your first time?" I asked.

"Oh, man, no, I've been doing this for a while."

"You tour with anybody we'd know?"

"Sure, *Cheap Trick*."

"*Cheap Trick*!" We all said, shocked. Then I asked, "THE *Cheap Trick*, the band that played Budokan, *The Dream Police*. That band? And not some band that spelled Trick with a y, or something, was it?"

"Or cheap without the A and a thing over the e?"

"No, dudes. They're probably the biggest band I ever toured with."

"How'd you get to roadie for them?"

"Total accident, man. I grew up in Rockford, right? I was out one night, you know, I went to get a burrito and there's this guy in front of me. He had on a jacket with John Lennon on the back of it. I was in a boisterous mood, you know, so I said, 'oh, it's John Lennon,' and the guy turned around, looked at me and said 'are you a lawyer?' I had no idea what he was talking about, but we started talking and it turned out this guy was Rick Nielson. But not Rick Nielson from like CHEAP TRICK. Just Rick and he kept talking about his band and he asked if I wanted to be a roadie. I figured it would a good way to get into parties and bars for free, so I said 'sure.' This was when they were still playing around Rockford and just about to start touring around the Midwest, way before Budokan. I've also toured with Scratch Happy and Thor."

"Never heard of them."

"No one has, dude."

"Do you like being a roadie?" Brian asked.

"All the traveling is fun, there are the chicks who'll do anything to get to the band. The only bummer is a band can leave you any place they want. You can get fired in the middle of nowhere. I've had to hitch home a few times."

"Why'd you have to hitch?"

"One band just ran out of money and it was, sorry dude we can't afford you anymore." Then he turned to Johnny, "what instrument do you play?"

"Guitar."

"I thought so, man. You should grow your hair out."

"What for?"

"You need hair to play guitar, man, or it's really boring."

"All right," I laughed, "let's load the van and get going."

"Anyway, I doubt I'll be left behind on this tour." Tom said.

On The Road

Once we got out on the road, distance and motion seemed to lose all meaning. The odometer turned and signs whizzed by. The horizon was always just out of reach, we were riding the snake of American commerce and dreams, the highway, I'd always watched trucks and cars paas on the highway and I'd felt as if life was being transacted, and now I was on that road. But somehow it didn't seem real, it felt like we were standing still, like we were in a simulator or something, but we were having a good time. After all, we were a rock band touring on the road! The radio was blaring, the boys were goofing around, joking, playfully throwing things around. We were about half way to Chicago when the van started to slow down.

"Hey guys! Tom said, "there's a hitchhiker, should we pick him up?" The boys leaned up from the back to look. The hitchhiker looked like he could've been Tom's twin brother in torn jeans, plaid shirt and backpack. The boys all looked at each other, and yelled,

"No, man! That could be the killer on the road, step on it!" We all laughed as Tom hit the accelerator.

The time and distance gave me a lot of time to think. Since Kerouac, America has become convinced that some existential truth about itself can be found on the road. Morrison himself bought into the theme. In his songs, poems, and HWY, the movie he made was about a serial killer as existential metaphor. The randomness of death on the highway of life, the killer on the road we'll all eventually meet. Travel as catharsis and transcendence. When asked what *Doors* songs were about, Morrison said "sex, travel, and death," they were meant to be a journey. We think there are no worlds to discover, we forget about the monsters that lie just under the surface. What would we find at the end of this road? I didn't know, maybe visions, sex, madness, some great promised adventures in the American wilderness, and maybe we were going to find out some truth about ourselves. Kerouac and Morrison saw it as a search, I thought of this as transformation.

I pushed back in the passenger seat across from Tom, my boot resting on the dashboard. Johnny and Brian got the two seats behind us, while in the back Mitchell and Ian were variously draped over the equipment or sitting braced against it. I guess a new pecking order had been established. My leather pants creaked against the seat whenever I moved. With the money I had leftover from the sale of my trailer, and selling off the last of my collection I bought more leathers and other clothing that had the right look. The boys called it my Morrison uniform. Morrison lived the role. He didn't differentiate between real life and the stage. To him Rock 'n' Roll was a stark theatre, a place where life and death are enacted, it wasn't safe on the edges, it was dangerous and you could die and that's what makes life real. To Morrison, theater and life weren't separate. Shakespeare said, "all the world's a stage," and Morrison wrote, "this ancient and insane theater," so if I was going to be Morrison, I needed to live the role too. Writers have always been identified with the lifestyles they've lead. Hemingway let the man and the myth become inseparable and convoluted until even the man couldn't remember what was myth and what was truth, and that's the problem with an image, it's the flickering light of TV, it's pliant, it distorts, and turns on you. Morrison discovered this. But I knew all those pitfalls, I read all the biographies and learned from the mistakes of others who've gone down this road, I could see the traps and landmines ahead and avoid them, a real artful dodger.

Chicago was the first stop of the tour. The club was actually in a suburb of Chicago. We veered around the outskirts of the city, as the skyline came into view. "Sweet home Chicago," I sang under my breath. I remembered that L. Frank Baum had used Chicago as the description of Oz in the book *The Wizard of Oz*. I could kind of see it, a cluster of buildings hiding in the opacity of haze, which seemed to form a bubble around it. I remembered the line from a song by *America*, "Oz didn't give anything to the tin man that he didn't all ready have." I felt like I was the man behind the curtain, at the same

time controlling everything, but still a fraud. I hoped like hell the
boys didn't find out.

Morrison had sung about Chicago, or at least included a reference
in the song *Peace Frog*. "Funny name for a song, huh?" Morrison used
to ask in concert. "Because even *The Doors*, in 1970, couldn't name a
song Abortion Stories," Ray answered years later in an interview. I
sang a verse from the song, "there's blood in the streets it's up to my
knee, blood in the streets of the town of Chicago," probably one of
Morrison's most personal songs, it includes a lot of autobiographical
details. There's a reference to New Haven, where he managed to
be the first rock star arrested on stage. Also mentioned is Venice,
California where he had lived on a friend's rooftop and by all reports
ingested an extraordinary amount of LSD while writing the poems
that would make up most of the first two albums worth of songs. And
there's the incredible Indians bleeding on dawn's highway section,
which recounts an incident from Morrison's childhood. So, why in
the face of all those autobiographical mentions is there a reference to
Chicago? It's a minor Rock 'n' Roll mystery. A lot of people like to
think it's a reference to the police riot at the Democratic convention
in '68, but Morrison wasn't there. Why mention places and events
that have a deeply personal autobiographical connection, and one that
has no personal connection? Morrison, if anything, was the master
of his own mythology. So, why the Chicago mention? What people
tend to forget is Chicago is where Morrison consciously provoked
his audience to riot for the first time.

Besides Swifty buying ads in the local papers, the plan was
as we hit each city the boys would run around plastering the
local neighborhood with fliers. They would get the artsy, trendy
neighborhoods with the coffee shops and bookstores, and then to
the club areas, while I would give interviews to the local papers.

The living accommodations for the tour were supposed to be the
band would share two rooms, and Tom and I were to share a room.

I was the star, and the boys were at the age where they would be sleeping on friends' couches, anyway. I was a little passed that. Since I had the money, I got a room of my own and paid the difference between a single room and a double out of my own pocket. Tom was the inheritor of the unexpected luxury of his own room.

Illinois Entertainer article

Doors Music Revived

by Terence Moore

With Francis Ford Coppola's use of the Oedipal epic, *The End*, in *Apocalypse Now*, and the almost simultaneous release of the Morrison biography *No One Here Gets Out Alive* at the beginning of the decade there's been a resurgence of interest in all things *Doors*. One consequence of this is there's a new kind of rock band touring the country today. Not exactly new, cover bands have been quietly playing clubs across the country for a couple of years now. In case you're not familiar with the concept, the cover band is a band in which one or more of the band members play members of an already famous band. In this case the covered band is *The Doors*, and the band covering them is "The Unknown Soldiers", taken from *The Doors'* controversial anti-Vietnam anthem of the same name.

The cover band is a concept, the band says has its roots in *Beatlemania* and Elvis impersonators. "The Unknown Soldiers is an attempt to revive the music of *The Doors* for those who are curious as to what *The Doors* were like live, for those people who were too young to see them the first time around, or for those who want to relive the experience." Says lead singer Michael Gray, who seems to live in Jim Morrison's skin as he came to the interview for this article in his Morrison drag.

"How did you and the band get the idea to cover *The Doors*?"

"It was my idea really. I was never in a band before I just had the idea. I was a *Doors* fan and was one of those people who were too young to see them. Part of *The Doors* appeal was their theatricality, so I thought it would be a natural that *The Doors* would translate easily to this format."

"What are you trying to accomplish with this cover band?"

"I'm trying to create a truth through fiction. I want to give people the experience of what it was like to see *The Doors* live because *The Doors* will never be able to tour again."

"I was able to see one of your rehearsals and you really seem to have Morrison's moves down."

"We've all seen videotapes of *The Doors* of course, but I seem to have an affinity for Morrison. I've read about him and I can just see him doing these things. Although I don't consciously recall seeing them, I just do what I'm seeing in my head. I don't know, maybe I just have a vivid imagination."

"How long have you guys been performing together?"

"Not long. This is really our first performance away from a hometown audience, and the public at large. We don't really know what to expect, but we've been getting a really good response."

"You and the band seem to have a great rapport."

"We all love *The Doors*, the band and me. That's what drew us together in the first place. We even split everything equally like *The Doors*. We're a unit, no one any more important than the other." With that kind of ethic this band could tour for a very long time.

The Unknown Soldiers are playing at *Fitzgerald's* this weekend and are currently touring the Midwest, signed for small clubs, and a couple of the outdoor fests. If you saw *The Doors* in concert and want a bit of a nostalgic return, or if you want to see what a *Doors* concert was like, see The Unknown Soldiers this weekend at *Fitzgerald's*.

First Gig

The van pulled into the parking lot of *Fitzgerald's*. At first I thought we were in the wrong place. It looked just like a house. Although, how many houses have parking lots in front of them? We all got out and stretched. Tom and the band started unloading their gear while I headed into the club when I heard a voice behind me.

"Hey! Aren't you going to help us move the equipment inside?"

"No. You guys are the band." I went into the bar and got myself a beer. *Fitzgerald's* was a small room. It seemed to be built on the box principle. A large box with several smaller boxes placed inside. One of those boxes was the stage at the head of the room it was built up three or four feet off the floor and looked like a stage for grammar school plays. It faced seating for what looked like would be an audience of a hundred, tops.

I wasn't completely convinced of Swifty's trust in his nephew, so I watched everything Tom did under the pretense of hanging out. I watched as he brought the equipment in, setup the amps, mic's, and sound board. Since the room was so small, Tom commandeered a table in the middle of the room and set the sound board on that, running all the cables from the amps, mics and guitars into the mixer and set the levels during the sound check. It wasn't that hard of a setup. We didn't have any special effects like dry ice for fog, no smudge pots, not even any colored lights except for whatever existed at the club.

While this was going on I was trying to figure out which song we should open with. We hadn't rehearsed 'sets' of songs because *The Doors* never did. They usually planned the first few songs ahead of time, but after that they frequently stopped between songs to discuss which song they were going to do next. If you listen to the bootlegs there are huge gaps in the shows where they're doing exactly this. That's why the band and I learned all *The Doors'* songs, so we could recreate this feeling and play any song that came up or that the audience called for.

The dressing room at *Fitzgerald's* was literally two steps behind the stage, as would become the usual, if there was any dressing room at all. It was small. There was an out of tune piano pushed up against one wall, a bunch of music stands were pushed into another corner. Against a wall stood an old-fashioned gilded stage mirror with light bulbs that run around the outside edge. Of course all the sockets were empty and there was a layer of grime on it. I wondered how many lives it had? Did it start out life in vaudeville reflecting the likes of Bob Hope or Jack Benny? Maybe it had come from a theatre of Barrymore or O'Neill? Maybe the owners of this place had just bought a replica, a facsimile of the real piece and no longer had a use for it.

I thought I had worked out my nervousness at 'The Place'. Maybe it was because of the hometown advantage, or because I thought it would all go up in flames anyway, so I hadn't been nervous, but now I was and didn't know why. After all, I did have Morrison's blessing from the dream, but the dream made me more nervous. It really was just a dream, a little wish fulfillment courtesy of my subconscious. I didn't have Morrison's blessing or anyone else's for that matter. Maybe my nervousness was me trying to tell myself something? Or maybe it was because now it was more real. Everything was on the line. Everything I had dreamed of, all my hopes.

This was the make or break point, there was no going back for me. I'd sold my trailer for the money to rent the house. When I gave up the house, I sold all my possessions and collections, just as Morrison had when he started *The Doors*. He severed his ties with his family, going so far as telling people they were dead. Morrison knew there was no going back. The boys had homes and families to go back to. Everything I had known was gone. Everything I had worked for was to get me here, everything I wanted was in front of me one way or another I wasn't going back. Nothing would be the same for me after this. It was either fame and fortune, or failure. What if I did fail? At least that was something I could understand. I've felt the cold hand of rejection before, I could understand rejection. But what really scared me was what if I succeeded? That I couldn't imagine, I couldn't even imagine the feeling? Joy? Exuberance lifting me to the heights? I couldn't even imagine what it would be like, outside of anything more than an abstract, or a cliché that didn't really seem to be a definition or even satisfy. Is that why Morrison acted so confidently, he knew that joy? Would I ever feel that? I thought I could feel it welling up inside of me, spreading like a warm smile. I'd felt it the first night at 'The Place', but suppressed it. I couldn't allow myself to feel it then because it was a beginning. The question was, could I allow myself to feel that now?

When it was time to go on there was a knock on the door and Tom stuck his head in the room with the rhetorical question "ready?" We crowded into the hallway. I was behind the band. I would go on last for heightened effect. The club was darkened, except for the spotlights on the stage. I could see figures, unknown, moving in the darkness. I could hear the chatter of a hundred different conversations. Then I heard Tom say from the mic at his improvised sound booth, "ladies and gentleman! The Unknown Soldiers!" And I felt a shot of excitement and adrenaline surge through me. The band took the stage each took his place at his instrument. Then it all seemed to slip into slow motion, the walk out to the microphone, my hand reaching out towards it and in my head I saw a movie of Morrison's hand reaching out to grab the microphone. I knew somehow I had to play somewhere *The Doors* had played. I had to see if that hand could reach out across time and touch me.

We opened with *Peace Frog*. The club went wild when I sang "blood in the streets of Chicago," just as I knew they would. My voice was a shriek compared to the screams Morrison used to jolt his audience from their complacency. But that wasn't enough I wanted them on their feet.

"*Celebration of the Lizard.*" I said to the band. I rattled a tambourine to give the snake slither to the piece, the feeling of a story being told around a campfire, a preface that Morrison usually invoked when

priming his audience. The band hit the first discordant notes of
the 'song' it was a poem, really more theater, a loose narrative of a
post-apocalyptic world where the survivors gather to tell their stories.
Morrison variously acted, screamed, or moaned through the piece.
It was supposed to be the long theater piece at the end of the third
album, like *The End* and *When The Music's Over* were on the first and
second albums, but they couldn't get it together enough for it to be
on the album. *Not to Touch the Earth* was the only remnant to survive
to the album. They usually used *Celebration* as a punishment when an
audience was unruly demanding to hear "the hits," or to shock their
audience into submission if nothing else worked. I recited the first
few lines, and let the sounds vibrate around me and into the audience.
I looked passed the lights into the audience and I could tell by the
shocked look on their faces that they weren't familiar with this facet of
The Doors, or the surprise that awaited them. We were going to give
them the abbreviated version. As Mitchell hit the last note he held it,
sustaining it, letting it linger in the air. I raised my arms, every eye in
the club was on me and I knew I had them. I dropped my arms and the
band went into the opening notes of *Light My Fire*. There was a gasp
of recognition. The tension that was holding the crowd suspended was
released and erupted. People were dancing others rushed the stage. As
we got better in our show we'd do this over and over again, we'd play
something like *5-1* letting the pressure build until the audience was
ready to 'POP' then we'd let them off the hook with something like *Love
Me Two Times*, it almost always provoked the same reaction, near riot.

After we played the last set, the audience was energized and
still wanted to hear songs, and we still wanted to play. We had gone
through the songs we had rehearsed the most, so I fell back on a
device Morrison had used.

"What do you guys want to hear?" I asked the audience. Somebody
shouted back,

"*Land Ho!*"

"You're kidding, right?" I asked. A hint of a laugh in my voice,
"let me ask the band." I turned back to the boys, "you guys wanna

play *Land Ho?*" They shook their heads no. "The band doesn't want to hear it either!" Everybody laughed. "Let's slow it down a little, here's a song I identified with too much in my tragic youth, *End of the Night.*" The boys started the slow waltz of the song. I had always thought *Pink Floyd* had heard the song and adopted the feeling and used it for *The Darkside of the Moon.*

"All right! All right! All right!" I said, as we walked into the dressing room after the set.

"That was so cool!" Johnny said, "I've never seen an audience do that!"

"Unfuckingbelivable!"

"Let's do that again!" Brian yelled.

"Jim! Jim!" I heard someone yelling. I turned to see the manager of the club grabbing me around the shoulders, trying to be my friend.

"Uh, it's Michael actually." I said.

"Jim, Michael, whatever. Look, I understand what you're trying to do here," He said, above the din, "I like *The Doors* too. That's why I booked your group, but you need to tone down the histrionics. We can't have everyone in the club running around. There are fire laws and I'm trying to sell drinks here."

"All right, man." I said. And I knew I was successful.

The 'Rents

Chicago was the slow start of the tour. We didn't have another gig until the next weekend, so we had a couple of days to kill. The next day, Sunday, I slept in until one or two in the afternoon. Since my parents lived nearby, I decided it was time to tell them what I was doing for a living, it was a chance Morrison also took and it was the last confirmed communication he had with his parents. He sent them a letter telling them he was in a band and, "what did they think of that?" They, especially his father, had disapproved citing failed childhood piano lessons. I wasn't going to be as confrontational as he had been, I hoped. My parents were quite a bit older than me. I was a late life baby for them. As a matter of fact, my older brother and sister were often mistaken for my parents. My father answered the door. He was a tall, lean man even in his seventies. An Annapolis graduate. After he left the military he had become a corporate lawyer who took stock in lieu of his full salary. Around the time I was in high school he owned so much of the stock he was given the chance to buy the company, which he did. Then he turned around and sold the company again within the year. The new owner breached their contract and my father took them to court and won. Winning several more millions of dollars. He had a cocktail in his hand when he answered the door.

"Hello Mikey," he said, as I breathed out a sigh of exasperation. Surprisingly, he didn't seem surprised to see me, "come on in, your Mother and I were just having a cocktail." My mother was in the den. She was still a handsome woman, who had helped my father's career by being the charming, witty hostess, wife and mother, for both the military and corporate worlds. Her only real failing in life was wearing perfume that was much too rosy smelling.

"Mikeee!" She said, as she got up from the couch to give me a hug, "its so nice of you to come down for a visit."

"I didn't come down, for a visit. I'm actually in town on business."

"That's good to hear," my father said. "What business would that be?"

"Here, take a look." I said, handing him a scrapbook that I had put together with the few reviews there were. He handed it to my mother. After a couple of minutes of leafing through the pages and skimming the headlines my mother asked,

"I don't understand this, Mikey, what do you have to do with this band?"

"I'm the lead singer."

"Oh, Mikey!" My mother said, disappointment clearly in her voice. "You have so much potential, you could be doing so much with your life."

"I am doing something with my life."

"Mikey," my father said as mildly as he could, "your mother and I gave you so much more than even your brother and sister. You were practically raised as an only child we had such great hopes for you. True, a great many things were expected of you," he paused, "but then again as of late, not that much has been forthcoming from you." My eyes started welling up from the usual litany of disappointment. I tried to think of anything else to staunch the tears.

"That's really not true," I said, "you gave money to Jonathan for medical school and money to Ilene to buy into that software company."

"All loans that were paid back with the appropriate interest. Look Mikey, your older brother and sister were always more self-directed than you. You got a liberal arts degree and then you wanted to go to graduate school. I'm still not sure what you were planning on getting a post graduate degree in."

"And since then what have you been doing Mikey?" My mother asked. "Doing drugs, and living by that college and dating those little girls."

"Michael," my father said, "your mother and I have been talking." My parents looked at each other. My mother, tears streaming down her cheeks, nodded her head to my father almost imperceptibly. "I'll loan you the money for graduate school. You'll have to give up this band thing of course, get a job in the area of the graduate degree, and pay the loan off within five years. The same deal we gave your brother and sister." I started gathering up my scrapbook.

"Mikey," my Mother said, "you don't have to give us an answer now, take a couple of days."

"That's all right," I said, "you've never believed in me or let me do what I wanted to do anyway. You made me take all those science courses when all I was interested in was music."

"Mikey, we've always encouraged you in your endeavors. Like when you got that job as a disc jockey."

"And what happened with that?" My father said, sternly.

"I didn't take the job."

"And why not?"

"It was a small market station, I didn't want to move to the middle of nowhere New Mexico. It was beneath my talents."

"Mikey, you have to start at the bottom. How many times have I told you no one is going to come to you with a job no matter how talented you are. You have to go seek them out."

"Thanks for the moment of failure, I was trying. I am trying," I took a second to compose myself, "never mind. This is what I want to do," I said clutching the mostly empty scrapbook. And I left.

On We Go

After we left Chicago we started the tour proper. This is when we settled down into the long haul, over the road touring. Gone were the slap-happy antics of the day trip to Chicago, mooning people, or flashing Penthouse centerfolds at other drivers. After a couple of days of laying down some hard mileage, there was no more good natured joking, tossing things around, and listening to music at party levels. We started noticing the habits and idiosyncrasies of one another. At least when we were at the house we could leave, get some perspective on things, or just get away, but in the van, on the road, it was a shared isolation tank on wheels. A band is a really compressed thing, the most severe living conditions imaginable outside a family. The fault lines show early and erupt under the pressure of constant exposure with the possibility that any one thing could be interpreted five different ways, or magnified beyond its true proportions. There was always someone's itch to scratch, or someone's ego to soothe. The only escape were the thrice daily stops for food and washroom breaks, at most an hour. I noticed that whenever Tom had some spare time when he was done loading or unloading the van, when we stopped for lunch, or he just had some time to kill, he would take out a sketch pad and start to draw, the boys had noticed it too, but he never let anyone see what he was doing. Brian took up the challenge and was continually trying to sneak up from behind to see what he was drawing. Tom was vigilant, almost like a Shaolin monk in his ability to perceive someone coming up from behind. Otherwise, Johnny and Brian kept to themselves most of the time. From what I could gather they'd been friends since grammar school. It was hard to crack the familiarity and solidarity they had, but they were the musical heart of the band and that was what I needed the most. Living day to day in such close quarters, it's a wonder any band lasts more than a few months. The only sound in the van would be low playing music as a soundtrack, Ian tippy-tapping out some rhythm on whatever surface was available, it seems drummers have to keep their hands moving no matter what. Mitchell would intermittently read from whatever guidebook or free pamphlet of local sites he had picked up on a break.

"What kind of word is en new I?"

"Let me see that." I said, reaching back for the book, "which word?" I asked, Mitchell reached over and pointed to the word. "It's pronounced 'on we'."

The View from the Stage

As the tour progressed and we got more gigs under our belts, I felt the band and I hit our stride musically. The boys were into it, I could tell by the way they played and their expressions. They were having a lot of fun. I became more confident in my delivery of the shows. I was hitting all my cues to come into the songs and I had some fun with the audience. I became more spontaneous, leaving behind the stiff choreographies I had worked up in rehearsals, I discovered freedom, I could do anything, say anything I wanted up there, there were no limits, no laws, it was my canvas, it was my blank page. I learned how to control the elements of the environment like colors of a palette, the stage became MY stage. If somebody heckled me, I stuck the microphone under his nose and invited him, and it was almost always a guy, to, "say your thing man." Whatever came out was usually enough to embarrass him. The couple of hours on stage a night made up for all the travel and screwed up hours of going to sleep when it's light, waking up when it's evening, and fast food instead of real food. I was able to relax and take a look at things from my perspective. I became proficient at reading all the different "types" in the clubs. For instance, the clubs themselves all started to blur in my mind, they all started to look alike. Only the shapes became discernible, round, square, cavernous, cramped, oblong, elongated. The names of the clubs broke down into two categories, those named after someone, Otto's, Charlie's, Rick's, etcetera. God knows if these people really existed or the owners just thought it was a good name for a bar. And the cleverly named bars like The Dew Drop Inn, Who's In There, or Stop Rite Inn.

Next were the customers. There was the high school quarterback who couldn't get into college, his high school girlfriend, still at his side, who hadn't lost faith in him, yet. The barroom savant who no matter how long he'd been drinking could answer questions on Jeopardy faster than the contestants, and the bartenders demonstrating examples of barroom physics. I noticed there was usually a visible gap in the ages of the waitresses, they ran from the young and hopeful for whom the job was only temporary until they got through school. They did their jobs bouncing from table to table. And the older waitresses, those that hadn't gone to school or had just plain missed their chance and knew they were there to stay. They conserved their energy, taking a puff or two off a cigarette at the bar before going to check their next table, each day sliding blissfully into memory.

Then there were the growing signs of our success. We had gathered a following. I started seeing some of the same faces at gigs that were close to one another. Another was the gigs themselves started to blur in my memory. One night's *Backdoor Man* seemed the same as the previous nights *Riders On The Storm*, or *Hello, I Love You*. It was also around this time people started giving me things, phone numbers, rings, necklaces, keys, poetry and artwork. I don't know if they thought I could get them published or "discovered," or they just wanted an audience, someone who might understand, some of it was pretty good. As word about us got out, Swifty was able to fill in more and more of the empty dates in the tour.

If we weren't traveling, or at a gig, there was a lot of down time. It was downright boring. The days we played were filled with drama and excitement of the gig, the bustle of loading and unloading equipment was completely counter balanced by ripping boredom. No wonder

Morrison found ways to amuse himself by hanging out windows, ledge walking, and later drinking. Because Tom was closer in age to me than the band, on off nights or when I was bored I'd visit his room and we'd smoke a joint, or drink some beer. He'd tell me his road stories, having lived pretty much of his life on the road, never settling anywhere, no family of his own. In between bands he lived as well as he could, depending on how much money he had saved from the road. He'd partied with rock stars and drank with winos, but he never showed me what he'd drawn.

One night when I got on stage, in the front row was a table of four truly beautiful girls. All decked out in their finest wares, dripping with sequins and pearl necklaces. They looked uncomfortable and awkward in the clothes, like kids playing grown up, still tripping on their mother's high heels. I knew the boys had girlfriends, which is how I came to think of their little troupe, as 'the girlfriends'. Thinking back, it was a gradual process. It started with one girl at a table close to the stage, then two, until the night I walked on-stage and was confronted with their glittering entourage. These weren't your average Rock 'n' Roll chicks, these were your exotic type. They were amateur groupies trying to move up the food chain. Not the type of girl the boys were used to, nor would have been able to attract had they not been in a band. Which just goes to show you, no matter how unattractive you are, if you're in a band you can always get a beautiful girlfriend. They were the boys' own group of sirens, each with charms and songs of their own.

Kaja, was tall and dark, and had a mysterious look to her. She was of Eastern European descent of some sort and had lean supermodel angles to her body. I've never been able to figure out how so many Eastern European women are beautiful when young, but when you see pictures of them as old women they're all fat, sprouting mustaches and wearing babushkas.

Sofia, wisdom, the irony was she was the one truly troubled soul of the group. She wore lace and her mother's pearls. The band called her the suicide queen. If you tried to break up with her she threatened to kill herself. If that didn't work, she would corner one of the other band members and try to cry on his shoulder, for a little drama.

Michelle, she was always dressed in black. From the concert T-shirts she wore to the stylish combat boots, and in between diaphanous skirts. She was one of those people who tried never to say an uninteresting thing, or do anything remotely mundane in their lives, never. She always had a story to top yours, no matter how bizarre. I tested her by telling her the most fantastic stories I could think of. She was never at a loss for a story to trump mine. She had either done a lot of living, or was a gifted liar.

And finally, Alex, she was the one truly dangerous one, capable of breaking up the band if her influence became too much, she was smart and the problem was her whisperings in Johnny's ear. I would guess her name was probably Alexandra or Alexia, no one ever told me, and I never asked. She was my type. Or would have been in the past, but I was beyond them now. She wore leather pants, assemblages of torn T-shirts, handcuffs and chains, and every time I saw her she had different colored hair. And she was smart. One night between sets I talked her up a little.

"Why are you so into Morrison?" She asked.

"I bought the book *An Hour of Magic* when it came out, and when I opened it, it just had this incredible picture of Morrison, a shiver just shot through me."

"A little latent homoerotic reaction?" She asked.

"I'm not gay."

"Are you sure?" So much for showing my vulnerabilities.

We also started getting invitations from our 'fans' for after show parties, which sometimes added an element of danger and adventure. One night, there was a table almost directly in front of the stage with two couples on a date. One of the girls was truly beautiful. Each show I tried to find someone in the audience to sing to, the seduction was easy, just sing a song and look into their eyes as if you were looking into their soul. Playing Morrison made me feel like I could move the world, picking up whatever girl at a gig was easy, sex became a liquid to me and unlike the boys I didn't have a girlfriend, there were plenty of women who wanted to be with "Jim Morrison." The next song was, *Hello, I Love You.* In between sets one of the guys from the table came up to me.

"Hey, man, you trying to move in on my girlfriend?"

"No, I'm not trying to steal your girlfriend." I said, smiling broadly, drawing him into my confidence, "I just wanna fuck her and then I'm leaving town." He laughed.

"Man, you're all right!" He said, slapping me on my back, "I'll buy you a beer."

"Cool, man."

"We're havin' a little party after the show, do you and your band want to come over?" You can get away with murder when you're in tune with the universe.

We went to their crash pad of an apartment, probably the first apartment of whomever's it was. There all ready seemed to be a party in progress when we got there. There were a few people sitting around a big round table in the middle of the room with a bong on it, surrounded by an old chair and sofa. Within leaning distance of the chair a top of the line stereo, with an equalizer, a professional turntable, while the rest of the furniture looked second hand. It was clear this was the center of the apartment.

After a couple of bong hits I noticed a girl standing against the wall watching every move I made. She looked more interesting than the others, she was wearing black-rimmed librarian glasses and had long dishwater blond hair that hung over her face like she was trying to hide, at least that's the impression she wanted you to have. At first glance you would think she's plain looking, but the more I watched her, the more I could see the beauty behind the glasses. She was pretty, but it was a forced perspective, the angular features of her face met to form a jigsaw of beauty, she could've been a librarian or a model depending on how she cleaned up. I watched her watching me, I could see stories in her face, like she was trying to explain everything that's happened to her, the histories and mysteries of her life. Then she would drop her head a little and seek temporary refuge, I knew once you befriended her she would show you the wilder fires that burned within.

"I'm gonna' get a beer." I went to the kitchen, she followed me, pinned me up against a wall, and started kissing me, my hand shot up her shirt like a snake after its prey. I stepped back and looked into her deep blue eyes. All I could do was stare into them and think of how I wanted to get lost in her eyes and other poetic clichés.

"What's wrong?" She asked.

"This feels too familiar. I could let myself be drawn into you so easily." I said, "but I can't!" I pushed her away. It would've been like getting back together with Deidre, "you don't know me, and what I'm really like. I can't help you, I'm Sorry," I said. No more compromises.

I went back into the living room where everyone was sitting in a circle on the floor very zoned out listening to *Led Zeppelin*, a whole *When The Levee Broke* feeling. The bong still sitting in the middle of the table surrounded by some very stoned knights of a round table. The night diffused into a hazy golden color. That's how I remember it, all of us sitting in a circle in that living room. Each of the boys smiling like he was in a golden halo, or maybe a spotlight in the surrounding darkness.

The Saga of Jimmy Stark Pt I

Merri Caldwell, the Hollywood Today! reporter, was sitting across from Sandra Wright the actress who had played Jimmy Stark's mother on Family Muse. They were in a living room of what looked like a mansion. In the background was a huge window with sunlight diffusing through the curtains, both sitting in highly polished expensive looking wood chairs, perhaps cherry or mahogany. Merri and Sandra were across from each other in the classic interviewer/interviewee pose. Sandra still looked attractive in her mid to late fifties.

"Good to see you again." Merri said.

"Good to see you, Merri."

"What was it like working with Jimmy Stark?"

"Well, I only worked with Jimmy for the run of the series, he was eight when it started and thirteen when it ended. He was very bright and had a great instinct for acting for such a young person." Sandra Wright spoke in the clipped tones, and formal enunciation regarded as a sign of erudition and breeding by the elocution coaches of the old studio system.

"What kind of instinct?" Merri asked.

"Even when he was young he just knew how to act, how to make a scene work."

"He did?"

"He was a very observant young man. I sometimes watched him watching everybody else. If he saw an emotion he could replicate it again and again, and I don't mean he was merely imitating people. I don't know how he did it, but there was more depth to it than that."

"How did the success of the show affect you?"

"Me? Well," she paused dramatically for the effect, "I got more money . . . eventually." She forced a laugh, "it really changed more for Jimmy, than me. The producers really didn't foresee how Jimmy would click with the public, but when they did, they worked that poor boy to a frazzle."

"There have been rumors you dated Jimmy while the show was on the air."

"That's really a popular myth. First, he was very young when the show aired. Secondly, his mother was always there during filming. I did date Jimmy about five years after the show ended, when he was eighteen and I was in my late thirties."

"How did it go?"

"We discovered our relationship was more of a mother-child relationship than either of us was willing to admit."

"Do you know what Jimmy's doing these days?" Merri asked.

"I heard he was living on the streets, but there's a lot of rumors that surround Jimmy. I've read he's a cop, he was killed in the Navy, that he became a Buddhist monk. I guess anything is possible with Jimmy."

Caitlin

During the first set of the night in Nashville I looked out across the smoke hazened bar. We were playing a real roadhouse, we were in the land of belt buckles and cowboy hats there were spittoons that I don't think were decorative. It was a large room with tables and chairs that filled the center, and lining the perimeter, on the walls were booths. People were coming and going out of one of the booths, like bees from a hive, including 'the girlfriends'. I wondered whose booth it was. A record industry executive's? A local bigshot? Or maybe a country western star? All I could see through the spotlight and the people gathered around were flashes of a beautiful red headed woman. In between sets, everyone backstage and at the bar was talking about this woman. All the interest was starting to piss me off, so I asked Alex about her.

"That's Caitlin Stewart, she's the daughter of Jerry Osprey." Alex said.

"Jerry Osprey?" I said, "*The* Jerry Osprey? The guitar player?"

"I knew that would impress you. Yeah, him."

I sauntered up to the booth, putting on my best Morrison pout. She had burnt red hair. Nothing of the carrot there but of the flame, it was the color of a dark fire, hot enough to burn. She was dressed the same as every other woman in the club that night, in jeans and a blouse but she had a sense of style that was far and above the taste of every other woman there, including the sequined 'girlfriends'. Her breasts were as nearly perfectly rounded as could be and were pulling the fabric of her blouse in interesting directions, her jeans seemed melted to her skin. She looked like the type of woman I was looking for. And if she really was Jerry Osprey's daughter, maybe she could help me. I just couldn't figure out why a girl like her would come to a place like this.

"I'm Michael Gray." I said, extending my hand, "are you really Jerry Osprey's daughter?"

"Really." She said. I examined her features, she smiled nervously under the scrutiny and a light entered her eyes as her face rounded to the familiar shape of her father's.

"Can I buy you a drink?" I asked. Before she could answer I saw the band milling around the darkened stage, "Oh sorry, it's time to do the next set." I sauntered back to the stage, making sure she got a good look at me.

After the last set, I walked back out into the club, into the glare of the house lights. A thin layer of cigarette smoke still hung in the atmosphere, and the sound of the band still rung in my ears and echoed off the walls. I could see the devastation of the closed club, cocktail napkins and cigarettes on the freshly beer stained floor. The waitresses silently milled about from table to table cleaning up the half filled glasses and overflowing ashtrays, and trying not to look interested in anything except what they were doing. The band and 'the girlfriends' stood in a circle around Caitlin and a guy who I hadn't noticed before that seemed to be with her. The bouncers stood around the edges in a looser circle trying to look cooler than the band. They weren't succeeding. I joined the inner circle.

"We're just doing this to get a little exposure," Johnny was saying to Caitlin, "and do our own songs."

"You have originals?"

"Yeah. We even have a demo tape." The other band members stood around shaking their heads in agreement.

"Really?" She said, "so what do you have to say for yourself Mr. Morrison?"

I smiled politely, "Michael, please." From the back the owner of the bar came up to our group, he was a good looking young guy in a silk shirt, with slicked back blond hair, constantly fidgeting with it, running his hand over the sides of his hair, or adjusting his sleeves. I wondered what he was doing, speed or coke.

"Time to go now. That includes you, Caitlin." I could tell there once had been something between them, and that he hadn't been the one who ended it, he kept glaring at the guy with Caitlin.

"I'd love to hear your tape," she said to Johnny, "why doesn't everyone come to our house for a little party and we can listen to it?"

Caitlin and I walked up the path to her house, it was a huge modern tri-level with windows that ran its length, it was surrounded by a copse of trees hidden by and meant to be part of the environment. Everyone else was lagging behind us.

"What kind of music do you like?" I asked.

"All kinds."

"Everybody says that."

"But I really do like all kinds of music!"

"Everybody says that too."

"I can prove it." She said as we walked up to the front door of her house. A warm light shone out into the night. We walked into the living room, everybody fanned out of the vestibule behind us, we were all taken aback by the sight that greeted us. The decoration, like Caitlin, showed a simple but eloquent taste. Lining the walls of the living room were record albums, wrapped in plastic, and neatly arranged on shelves that spilled over into the other rooms I could see.

"Wow." Was all I could say, breaking the awed silence.

"Start here." She said, pointing to the closest shelve in the room. I pulled out the album closest to me.

"*Abba.*" I said.

"They're arranged alphabetically." I pulled out the next album.
"*Abba, Waterloo.*"

"And in order of release," she smiled.

"How far to *AC/DC*?"

"Farther down."

"Impressive." I said, "how many are there?"

"Eight hundred." I ran my hand over the albums and walked about two feet before pulling out another album. It was *Black Sabbath.*

"You ever hear of CD's?" I asked.

"It's too late," she said, "I'm invested. I've been listening to albums since I was about ten, starting with my fathers."

Caitlin got out a bottle of Beaujolais Nouveau and we sat around the living room listening to the boys tape, and it kind of reminded me of the party at the apartment except on a much more prosperous level. I watched the interactions around me, the waitresses and bouncers from the club loitered around the room outside the hub of, me, the band, and Caitlin. Caitlin was sitting next to her boyfriend Jake, Jack, Jess. I don't really remember which it was, and sure enough the manager of the club took a seat across from Caitlin and displayed a certain amount of familiarity as he fidgeted from whatever stimulant he had taken, while she looked amused by him. I smiled at her and looked at her intently, trying to communicate.

"Michael, would you like a tour of the house?" She asked me.

"Sure," I said, glad for the chance to be alone with her. We walked through a couple of the rooms. She pointed out some delicate facet about a piece of furniture, or of the room before asking, "do you sing the band's original songs?"

"No, The Unknown Soldiers and Ghost Dance are two different things."

"You don't write the songs or anything?"

"I don't do anything creative, I'm the idea man." I said, as we strolled to another room, moving farther away from prying eyes of the group. "What do you do?"

"I'm a publicist for a small record company, low wage, menial, I don't know anything else except music, and love being around it."

"This house doesn't look like you're too low wage."

"Oh," she said, waving a hand, "my father has a lot of guilt and a lot of royalties."

"What about the guy?"

"Judd? He's my boyfriend."

"The nightclub owner doesn't seem to think so."

"Lance?"

"He's a loser." I said, cornering her against a wall. I could feel the heat pouring off her body.

"How do you know?" She said, softly.

"Because he's not me."

"Sure of yourself, aren't you?"

"I am the Lizard King." I said, grandiosely.

"You take that seriously?"

"It's my job."

"So, are you making a pass at me because you're attracted to me? Or because you think Morrison would act this way? Or because you think I'm vulnerable?"

"Does it matter?"

"I met him once you know." She said, pushing me away from her as she moved on to the next room.

"Morrison?"

"Yeah, my dad's band opened for *The Doors* once."

"Really?"

"Yeah, it was during one of the times when my mother felt like my father should be spending more time with me, so . . ."

"How were they?" I asked.

"OK, I guess. I really don't have a good reference point. When Dad opened for *The Doors*, I was backstage for a few shows. Usually just long enough to see him play and then back to the motel. I really didn't get to see that much."

"What was he like?" I asked.

"Morrison? I don't know. Cool, I guess. I was only about nine or ten, we were backstage and I scratched his head and did a little curtsy, it was filmed, I'm sure you've seen the film. It was all pretty innocuous." We walked a few steps more, "so, let's talk about you. It must be pretty interesting to be in a band, what else have you done?"

"A lot of things. I'm just tryin' this music thing out to see if it leads anywhere." I said, staring at her intensely.

"Be careful, you just may get what you want. Just ask my father," she smiled, "just ask me."

"What's it like growing up with a father who's a legend?" I asked.

"I don't look back much."

"I guess that's easy when you're successful, and have what you want."

"OK. Do you want the full length version, or the cheery, everything is roses version I use for magazine writers and fans of my father's?"

"Whichever is true."

"Basically, I paid for my father's Rock 'n' Roll dreams. I was conceived on tour, I was born on tour, and I think my parents even managed to stay together through that tour. Whenever my mother thought I needed a father figure she'd ship me off to be with him. I guess I did need a father figure, I ran away with a boyfriend who was nineteen."

"Nineteen?"

"When you're sixteen, nineteen seems a lot older. They seem, uh, cool, together, like an adult. He had this vague idea to go to L.A. we'd get jobs in a restaurant, and be discovered. I was this romantic sixteen year old, so we ran away. I thought we'd be together and be a famous couple. I thought someone would recognize me or find out I was Jerry Osprey's daughter and wouldn't allow me to live on the streets, but my father's career was well past its height, and no one cared if Jerry Osprey's daughter lived on the street." She smiled, it looked more nostalgic than wistful. "I got a lot of living done, waitressing, moving from city to city. We were living on Hollywood Boulevard, and . . ."

"You lived on Hollywood Boulevard?"

"I mean ON IT. Sleeping in the doorways of closed shops when we couldn't scrape together enough money for a crappy motel room. I finally realized he was more confused and screwed up than I was, so I called my mother and went home. My friends tell me I should write a book or an album, but . . ." She stopped and looked into my eyes. "I don't know why I'm telling you all this."

"People tell me all kinds of things. You'd be surprised." I said. "But what about now?"

"Now?"

"You get along well with him now, right?" She looked at me quizzically, "your father, I mean."

"Yeah, OK. He usually calls whenever he's in town." She looked at me out of the corner of her eye and smiled a little, "I don't understand why people would think my life is more interesting to them than theirs. Is that all you're interested in, my father?"

"No, uhhh . . ." I stammered.

"Don't worry about it, I'm used to it. One of the reasons I fell in love with that nineteen year old, he was the first guy I met that was interested in me and not my Dad. He told me I was beautiful, and for as big a screw up as he was, he only wanted me. Some of the guys I've meet, I've felt like I'm a collectible to them."

"A collectible?"

"Yeah, just another thing to add to their Jerry Osprey collection, like the authorized guitar, the special edition album, The daughter, wrapped in plastic and put on the shelf, the ultimate collectible." She looked uncomfortable and paused, "why don't you tell me about your dark history with your parents."

"What makes you think I have a dark history with them?"

"I don't know," she said, "you just look it."

"I don't know." I said, trying to decide if I could trust her.

"OK then, why're you so into Morrison?"

"I just always identified with him I guess."

"How?"

"Well, my father was military too, like Morrison's. We traveled around a lot until I was in high school."

"Well, that's you and several million other people." Then she paused. "Could it be you don't want to tell me because you just think Jimmy was a really cool guy? Conqueror of women, befriender of men and animal, the mystical shaman?"

"I guess Morrison fit my mood when I read about him. He showed me a way to get what I wanted."

"What do you want?"

"I just want, well . . ." I struggled to put it into words, "I want to know what he knew. He seemed like he understood a lot of things, a lot of the mysteries of life. I'm just trying to find out what that was."

"The meaning of life?"

"I never looked at it that way, but, yeah, I guess you could say that."

"All you may ever figure out is the meaning of his life," she paused, "what if it means nothing to you?"

"Then I've discovered something."

"Is that why you started the band?"

"Let's just say I heard the voices of the gods calling me." Which I thought was one of my better lines. She was unfazed.

"So, what it comes down to is, you find me interesting not because I'm Jerry Osprey's daughter, but because I once met Jim Morrison. God! That's a new one!" She laughed. "Hmmm, what can I tell you about Morrison?" She said, "nothing really. I met the man for perhaps ten or fifteen minutes which is forever imprisoned in time, captured on film. I never knew the man, but it seems to me he had a lot of problems, and delving into him might invoke those demons, or awaken your own."

"How do you know it hasn't, I'm dangerous." I said, leaning in for a kiss.

"Why do all men like to think they're dark and dangerous?" She asked. "What can I do for you, Michael?"

"What can you do for me . . . noone's ever asked me that before."

"You made such a production out of letting me know you wanted to be alone with me." I looked like I didn't know what she was talking about. "Maybe we should go listen to your band's demo tape?"

"It's not my tape." I said.

"You realize I'm not going to sleep with you, don't you?"

"That's all I have time for, sex, nothing else." She didn't look amused.

"Yeah, right." She said laughing as she pushed me away, again. "If you tried to see Morrison as a whole person instead of a hero, well, it doesn't matter, what you reflect of him probably reveals some aspect of you, more than of him." She looked into my eyes one last time, "are you sure there's still a you in there?"

Close Cover Before Striking

On one of our ever increasingly rare nights off, Tom and I were just hanging out in his room having a few beers, watching TV. He went to get a couple of beers for us out of the sink we had iced down. I saw his sketchbook lying on the bed I absently started flipping through it, it was filled with drawings of *Iron Maiden* album covers. When he came back into the room he stopped dead when he saw me looking through it. "This is what you've been drawing?" I asked.

"Are they bad?"

"No, they're great," I said. "But *Iron Maiden*? You hang out with a *Doors* cover band for a few months and all you can draw is *Iron Maiden* album covers? Aren't there any other bands with cool album covers?" Tom just shrugged his shoulders. "I expected caricatures of us, landscapes, or even sketches of truckstops. I haven't even seen you with any *Iron Maiden* albums, or play any *Iron Maiden* tapes." Then I realized, "you've been drawing these from memory?"

"Yeah, I just like the covers, so I draw them." Tom said.

"WOW!" I said, genuinely awed, "you ought to do something with that."

"Yeah, I know." Tom said, hanging his head down. I glimpsed some hurt of the past in the look. "I've been thinking about entering this contest." He threw me a matchbook. I opened it, there was a picture of a pirate and it said, 'draw and send in for a free evaluation.'

"And in about six weeks you'll get a letter back saying 'congratulations! You're a budding Picasso. And with some refinement of your technique you can make a living as an artist and we can offer you courses to help you attain your dream, for as low as . . ." I said, "the thing is no one fails. They prey on your dreams, charging you, promising fame and fortune, but all you end up doing is giving them your money. You have to consider what do your dreams cost?"

Wanda

Then things started getting weird, at the gigs I was meeting people who knew Morrison, or at least claimed to have known him. There was the woman from Oregon who said she met Morrison in a bar on Christmas Eve and they talked about the meaning of life, but the story sounded too metaphorical. Then there were those who claimed to be Morrison, by reincarnation. Those who claimed Morrison was communicating with them either by letter, possession, or from the spirit level. And finally, those who claimed to be Morrison in the flesh.

The first group, the reincarnates, those who thought they were Jim Morrison reincarnated, that was an easy one to solve. I just asked them how old they were, over twenty and it was "sorry, Morrison was still alive when you were born." That usually stumped them and sent them back to the drawing board, except for the hardier, more obsessed soul.

"No, dude, it was a transmigration of the soul. He knew he was dying a long time before he died, so his spirit left." For those people there really was no answer.

Then there were the possessions. Those who claimed Jim was possessing them either full time or only on occasion, and Jim was dictating a new book of poems to them, or was collaborating with them on a book for the purpose of clearing up the misconceptions of his life. And, lastly there were the guys who said they were Jim in the flesh and were just waiting for the right time to reemerge.

One night there was a conversion or collision of the types that presented what I thought was a unique opportunity. Between sets a guy came up to me and told me he was Morrison, this guy had long wild hair, a beard, wearing a plaid workingman's shirt, and jeans he'd been living in a little too long. His face was ruggedly lined like he'd been living outside. I thought he looked more like John The Baptist, maybe he was Morrison after all.

"Where you been man?" I asked.

"Living out in the wilderness where nobody can find me."

"What're you doing here?"

"Making sure you don't sully my memory."

"Sully?" I said, dropping my jaw, "I haven't sullied in years."

"Don't tell anyone I'm here."

"No problem, man." Not two minutes after this encounter, a woman came up to me and told me Morrison possessed her every now and again and that he was glad I was helping keep his memory alive. I saw that an opportunity like this wouldn't present itself again so I decided to have some fun with it when I went back on stage.

"Ladies and gentlemen we have a special guest tonight." The band looked at each other, then looked at me, perplexed. The audience murmured. "We have a confluence tonight, as it were, a strange alignment of stars!" I had the hook baited, "we have Jim Morrison in the audience tonight!" There was a hush. The crowd didn't know what to make of this pronouncement, "we have a gentleman here with us who says he is Jim Morrison," at this point the guy claiming to be Morrison got up and scurried towards the door, "and a young lady who says Jim's spirit visits her nightly!" The audience cheered, the woman actually stood up to take a bow.

Then there was Wanda. That's when it started to get seriously weird. The thing was, she was for real.

"I'm Wanda the Witch."

"You're kidding, right?"

"No, I knew Ray and Jim at UCLA." She looked to be about the right age, "I was a theatre student and I wanted to be an actress. I was in Ray's movie and I've been into Wicca forever. I may have been the first person to get Jimmy interested in witchcraft." She looked at me with such a look of desire, "I could tell you a lot about Jimmy," she said. She seemed pretty drunk, slurring every word she uttered, but I was morbidly interested.

"What'd you talk to Jimmy about?" I asked.

"We talked about a lot of things, like poe-ahhh-tree and Artraud."

"Artraud?" I said, taunting her about her pronunciation.

"Yeah, Antonin Artraud, the French theater guy or something." She said, waving it off.

"Tell me something else about Jimmy."

"Jimmy was a tabula rasa. He could be an altar boy, or a murderer. He was a mirror, get it!? You got what you looked for, he was amazing at reading people."

"What did you see?" I asked.

"A lover." She said, eyeing me lasciviously, "wanna go to my car?" She was in her early to mid-forties, gaudily dressed in tight jeans, denim jacket with fake fur at the collar and cuffs, a low cut blouse with more than a hint of multicolored bra sticking out. Her face was lined, and portions looked like they were about to drop, her make-up was applied thickly. She was working hard to look sexy. She was right at my break-off point, but her sleeping with Jim Morrison added another dimension and tipped the balance. It was still worth a plunge into the pool. I mean how many chances in life do you get to make it with a woman who made it with Jim Morrison?

We were in her car making out and suddenly I was roaring drunk. I was seeing things in swirling disconnected images. But how had I drunk too much? I had a couple extra drinks to make it easier to make it with her, but I had drunk more than this before, without such a dire turn of sensation. Maybe it was the synergy of the beer

I drank and the whiskey on her breath. I opened the car door for some fresh air. As soon as it hit me, I felt a rush from my stomach. I threw myself out of the car onto the gravel parking lot and started throwing up. As I lay on the ground I heard Wanda get out of the car and walk around to the side of the car I was on. I looked up and saw her leaning against the side of the car smoking a cigarette, hovering over me like an animal protecting its kill. I heard the crunch of gravel as someone approached.

"Is that our mini-Morrison?" A voice I recognized as one of the boys, appeared in my mind as an island out of the mists, but I couldn't tell who it was. I reached up towards the voice saying "ha, he, hel . . ." I was trying to say help, but in my state, couldn't.

"I'm going to make out with him some more when he stops puking." I heard Wanda say.

"Yeeeeech, gruesome." A female voice said.

"Live the lifestyle Mikey," the boy's voice said. "You can have him lady, just make sure he's back to the motel by eleven AM tomorrow, or we leave without him." And they laughed.

Wanda pulled her car into the parking lot of her rooming house. I was laying in the backseat, tattered vinyl and used wrappers floating with me in virtual zero gravity. She pulled me out of the car, dragging me towards the house, my boots pushing on the gravel, the best mime of walking I could muster, one arm draped across her shoulders, it was a minor crucifixion. The landscape was bleak the wind howled around me, everything washed out to the color of bone, the moon. It was a tundra of a parking lot. I managed to pull the house into focus, it was larger and somehow harder looking than the surrounding family homes. Maybe it was because the house, as well as the people that inhabited it weren't as well taken care of as the people in the family homes.

Once inside, I bounced off the walls of the communal kitchen. Wanda guided me up the hallway stairs, passed padlocked doors. It reminded me of a prison. We came to the last door down the hall, she opened the padlock and we fell into her room. I stood in the middle of the room, swaying, trying to comprehend. I saw all the possessions of a lifetime that were stuffed into this ten by twenty room. There was her girly dressing table covered with combs, a skirt of ancient chiffon ran around the outside of it. Sticking out of the frame of the mirror, a photograph. I plucked it out and tried to focus on it. It was a picture of her with Morrison. The colors separated, turned yellow with age. It was ancient sepia now. It must have been taken early in *The Doors* career, or maybe they were still at UCLA, they both looked achingly young, Morrison was still in his cruel handsome youngboy looks. I matched the face of the girl in the picture and Wanda. It was her all right, without the wrinkles, and without the feral look in her eyes. Their clothes were almost antique looking even to my sensibilities, even though I remember people dressing like that. I remembered dressing like that. It wasn't like the other photographs of Morrison I was used to seeing, Morrison, in his natural state, relaxed and in the moment, he'd always looked like a modern among the primitives to me. When I was a kid, I thought all the adults were in their fifties, they all had short hair, black rimmed glasses, and because the clothes they wore were dull and lifeless they, and appeared to be in black and white. Morrison looked more like me, and the people I hung out with, alive and in color. The picture of Wanda and Morrison was a typical posed photograph. The body language of both spoke volumes. She was trying to be close to Morrison, and he was standing rigidly, waiting for the moment to be over so he could pull away. I dropped the picture down on the table.

"Where's the bed?" I asked turning around. Tucked away in the corner of the room was her bed. I fell straight down on it and for a minute everything swirled around me, then I passed out. During the night I remember her waking me up for sex. I responded out of some sense of duty, either to legend or my own ego. I noticed the longer I was with her the older she looked. All I remember was a flash of tit and pussy as I escaped back down the darkened swirl. It didn't matter I was unconscious anyway.

Some time after that I woke up, it was still dark out, it seemed like the night was lasting forever. At least I felt like I was sobering up. I looked at the other side of the bed. Wanda was awake, watching me.

"Do you have a girlfriend?" She asked, running her hands over the skin of my chest

"No, why?" I asked.

"I can be your girlfriend, and follow you to all your gigs. I can be your lover and tell you everything I know about Jimmy."

"What makes you think I'm that into Morrison?"

"Look at you. Dressed like him, you act like him, and you even fucked me because of him."

"No. We don't need any more camp followers." I said.

"Camp followers!" She bellowed. "Well, that's the difference between you and Jimmy. He was an original performer he brought life to the stage. All you bring is a ghost and that's why you'll never be anything but a cheap imitation!" She rolled over and went to sleep.

I woke up early the next morning. Light was finally starting to pry its way through the lone window in the room. Wanda was snoring next to me. I pulled on my pants and shirt. Next to her bed was a scrapbook, one of those huge old-fashioned kind where you can keep adding more pages. I sat on her dressing table chair and looked through it. It started with typical childhood photos, proud mother and father holding the baby, growing up modeling different chiffon dresses and Wanda smiling broad toothless smiles, first communion. Then there was a newspaper clipping of a little girl, Wanda in a tutu, a production of Swan Lake. The caption gave the little girl's name as Stephanie Mulgrew, but it was Wanda. I could still see the little girl in her face. I turned the pages, there were more pictures and reviews; from high school plays, the perennial production of *Our Town*, followed by pictures of her in college at UCLA, the plays now Ibsen and Beckett. Then some reviews and programs from small L.A. playhouses, this was her rise to stardom! I noticed a few early *Doors* reviews interwoven. There was an early connection. Then a movie ad, I read it over carefully, her name wasn't anywhere on it. But she must have had a part in it, or else why would it be in her scrapbook? Then it became a scrapbook about Jim and *The Doors*, culminating, of course, in Paris. Then there were a couple of blank pages. They were yellowed and brittle like the pages before them. When it resumed the pages were newer, cream colored. It became a diary and there was a ferocity in the entries until towards the end they became manic. I realized I had been wrong it wasn't a scrapbook chronicling her rise to stardom. It was a scrapbook chronicling the death of her dreams. How many years did the blank pages represent? Where had Wanda come from? A character she carved out of, perhaps, her conversations with Morrison, like Alice Cooper in Morrison's conversations with a young Vincent Furnier. When did she go from being Stephanie to Wanda? When Stephanie became powerless in life and Wanda offered her that power and control again? In the clarity of the morning light, and my clearing head I realized the look of want I had seen on her face the night before wasn't for me. What I had mistaken as desire for me was really a desire for what I represented and the desire to try and rewrite history. A desire to change this leaden reality of her life and restore the golden dreams of her fantasies. Maybe she and I weren't that far apart. She looked deep inside for the simmering essences of truth; she had found madness. She moved a little in the bed, even asleep she didn't look at rest. I pushed a lock of sweat matted hair off her forehead, I could see the hurt child with dreams that was in her, that had made her this madwoman.

"Peace, Stephanie, peace." I said, softly.

I stumbled out into the cold morning air I pulled my leather jacket tight around me against the cold. The wind still tore through me, the word mourning bouncing around my hung over head. I looked around trying to get my bearings. I seemed not to be too far from the bar and motel. I started the cold trek back in the direction I thought I should go. By the time I was at the end of the gravel parking lot, Wanda was out the back door yelling at me.

"Just like Morrison, asshole!"

The Saga of Jimmy Stark Pt II

Merri was standing in an office, there was a desk, and the walls were covered over with fake plywood. With Merri was an older looking gentleman wearing a golf shirt and sansabelt pants in some bad pastel color. He looked like he'd just come in from the golf course, or the clubhouse, I imagined that just off camera smoldered a cigar one end chewed, I could almost smell the tobacco on his breath. At the bottom of the screen it read, Max Springfield, "we're here with Jimmy Stark's agent of thirty years," Merri said, "Max Springfield. Max, you're the one who discovered Jimmy Stark, and have stuck with him through the years."

"Well," he said, with a bit of wet lisp, "that's because of Jimmy himself, he's a very special person. I remember when his mother first brought him into my office I think she had him dressed like one of *The Beatle's* in a *Sgt. Peppers* era costume. I wasn't that interested, but as I was talking with him I saw something. I convinced his mother to stop dressing him in costumes, which was a lot harder than it should have been and we sent him out to auditions. And the rest you know, as they say, is history."

"How did Jimmy get the role on Family Muse?"

"That's almost as legendary as Lana Turner being discovered at Schwabs Drugstore. One of the producers saw him on a commercial, and at the time I was one of the two or three biggest agents, and I was the first call he made."

"After Family Muse Jimmy's career hit a snag."

"Jimmy hit the wall most child actors do when suddenly they have to have a talent other than looking cute. If he were coming to us today, there's so much more we could do with him, but in those days we were pretty much limited to the cute kid or the precocious kid roles. Luckily, Jimmy could play both."

"Jimmy developed a reputation as a party animal early in his career."

"He loved to play!" Max exclaimed, "he thought acting was playing, that's why he was so good, he was just playing. So when he discovered what he took to be adult playing, he was a natural at it."

"It seemed at one point Jimmy was deliberately trying to sabotage his career?"

"That was later, in his twenties. Nevertheless, I got him some very good roles, roles that still hold up. Tender Fury comes to mind, of course, for which he got a best actor nomination."

"We've been trying to track Jimmy down to let his fans know how he is. Have you been in contact with him?" Merri asked.

"Of course, hardly a month goes by that I don't hear from him."

"Could you put us in touch with him?"

"Well, I haven't heard from him in a while, but when I do, I'll be in touch."

"Thank you Max, for setting the record straight." He nodded his head, and then they cut back to Roger Hudson in the studio, I turned the TV off.

Breaking Up Is Hard To Do . . .

One afternoon I was sleeping when someone started pounding on the motel room door.

"Go away!" I yelled as I rolled over, the room was dusky, I had pulled the drapes tight to keep the light out. Someone pounded on the door again. I got up. I padded over the matted brown carpet, and opened the door, Tom was standing there without a shirt on. The light assaulted my sensibilities, it took me a minute to comprehend why it should be light out while I was sleeping, there really is something vampiric about the lifestyle of being in a band, if you see daylight you either shun it or you know it's been a late night.

"Yeah." I said, sleepily.

"You gotta come to the other room, we have an emergency."

"What kind of an emergency?" I asked.

"I don't know man. Ian says he's quitting the band and going back home."

"Shit." I said, "does anybody know why?"

"No. He's been babbling, but not making any sense. Just something about the price being too high." I threw on a shirt, and ran hot footed across the cold concrete sidewalk to one of the boys rooms. All of them were sitting around Ian who was sitting on the bed sobbing while the TV blared in the background.

"What's going on?" I asked.

"He broke up with his girlfriend."

"Or she broke up with him."

"That's all?" I asked, sitting next to him. He was pale, his face was all washed out from his tears, "c'mon buddy you can't let something like this knock you down." No reaction.

"We've been telling him that for like two hours now." Johnny said.

"Ian, can you tell us what happened?" I knew if I kept asking questions that as soon as I broke through and got an answer the rest of the story would come flooding out.

"I, I can't live without her!" He sobbed. I could see he was making an effort to contain himself.

"Of course you can. You were able to exist before her, right?"

"Uh-huh."

"OK, now listen carefully and do everything I tell you, OK?" He looked up and shook his head 'yes', "I learned this a long time ago, cry." I said. A couple of tears ran down his cheeks, "C'mon cry!" I yelled. "Didn't you love her?"

"Hey, c'mon, man." Brian said, "don't be so cruel he's had a rough time of it already."

"You gotta get her out of your system." I said to Ian, and for the benefit of them all. "OK, now think of everything you did with her," I looked at him, he was trying to fall back into self-pity, "you thinking about her?" He shook his head a weepy yes, "think about every place you saw together, every candlelit dinner you had, the jokes you shared, the kisses you stole, the plans you made. Cry them out until there's nothing left."

He started sobbing loudly, "why? Why? Why, doesn't she love me?" It was the heartbreak of the unanswerable question we all have one time or another. I knew that pain in the past, but steeled myself against it, in the present.

"Let the band be your armor against the loneliness of those feelings. Do you wanna be a rock star or not? Is it just a dream, or your destiny? You're out here on the road accomplishing something. Most people aren't doing that in their lives, you can't let such things alter your journey." Tears were streaming down his cheeks.

"I'm tired now," he mumbled, "I jus' wanna go to sleep." He laid on the bed in the fetal position, subdued.

"How long until the show tonight?" I asked, suddenly sleepy again.

"About four hours."

"He'll be OK. Maybe a little vulnerable and raw for a while, but he'll be OK." That night we had one of our best shows because Ian had a little more emotional intensity in his drumming. A few weeks later the hole in the girlfriend troupe was soon filled with a new member, Cassandra, of all things.

Sibling Rivalry

We were playing in Austin, and like Madison was the state capitol, and a college town on top of that. It was like a homecoming. It had a strip of bars that mixed the nightlife, there were students and an intermingling of people in business suits trying to fit in, they were the mirror reflections of each other, the students looking ahead to see what they'll become and the professionals dabbling in shallow nostalgia. Looking down the strip the neon gathered above the buildings, a reddish aura that hung just above the city. Swifty's strategy was to play a night or two in a club, then another night or two at a club farther down the strip or in the outlying areas and then another couple of clubs in Austin, and so on until we had maximized our presence at the clubs, as Swifty had put it. The clubs were packed, hot and sweaty, smoke filled. We played some of our best shows, the boys were learning how to play better, before they played well, but now they were mastering the intricacies. On the third or fourth day there was a knock at the door of my motel room. I thought it may have been Tom or one of the boys seeing if I was ready to go to lunch, a movie, or something. I opened the door and there stood my brother and sister.

"Ah, the infamous committee of two. No doubt sent by Dad to straighten me out."

"No, Mike, we saw your show last night." My brother said, in the practiced kindly bedside manner of a doctor, which he is. He still looked the dashing athletic college fraternity brother I remember growing up. "It's been a long time since I've been to something like that."

"How'd you find me?" I opened the door and they walked in, "have a seat." I said, pointing to the chairs in the room. I sat on the edge of the bed.

"When you're a member of the local chamber of commerce, you can find things out."

"I forgot I was in your home territory."

"We really enjoyed your show." My brother said.

"I wish I could do something like that." My sister said.

"You're not the adventurous type." My sister was shrill, her reasonable demeanor at the moment was a mystery. She was the oldest and quite a bit older than me, she always bore a motherly authority instead of a sister. She had long stringy black hair, a thin face and a thin body despite having two children, she was almost always dressed in black, and as a child, she conformed to my every expectation of a witch.

"Boy, I remember when I found you listening to my *Sgt. Peppers* album," my brother said, "I didn't think anything of it until you listened to it over and over again, and then proceeded to go through the rest of my record collection. You were a hip little kid."

"But then that interest just drifted away, like it always does." My sister said. My brother shot her a look, saying 'you brought that up too early.' He was forced to adjust his tack.

"And suddenly you just quit, what was that?"

"Because I knew I couldn't create anything as elegant or eloquent as that, it seemed everything had been done, everything had been said, better."

"Maybe," he said, "but you still try." He took a breath to think and I knew a speech was coming in his well modulated, well practiced bedside manner tone of telling a patient he has cancer. "Mike," he said "maybe that's the point. Your interest has always focused on one thing until you master it, but then your interest always does falter and drift until you find the next thing. Look, when I was in medical school I realized the world doesn't need another doctor," he paused for dramatic effect, "you have to make them want you, I didn't have a practice I didn't know how I would build one but I did, and maybe the world doesn't need another doctor or lawyer, or another Jim Morrison, but it just might need a Mike Night."

"Mikey," my sister said without trying to modulate her tones at all, "with your degree you can teach, get something that has a future. And if you're really interested, you could even do something in the music field."

"When are you two ever going to learn?" I said, shaking my head sadly. "You were always Joe college cool guy," I said to my brother. I got up and started to pace the space between the bed and where my brother and sister were sitting, "and you two were always the favorites, tittering little secrets between you. I looked up to you, and it was always thrown in my face how different I was from you two, and how I should strive to be better. So I read and read until I became the smartest kid in class. And whatever I took up as a hobby, I worked at it until I perfected the skill. Most people get good at only one or two things in their lives. I'm good at everything I do."

"Mike, everyone knows all the hard work you've put in. We're just worried because someone as intelligent and gifted as you are can have so much more in life."

"You've never approved of anything I've ever done." I said.

"Michael, look, I had my wild and rebellious days, I just didn't rub it in Mother and Father's faces." My brother said, "and if you truly believe in what you're doing, what do you need any of our approval for?"

"At least get a trade," my sister said, "this can't last forever. I mean how much demand is there for a Jim Morrison impersonator?"

"I know it won't last, but by then I'll have used it as a stepping stone."

"To where?"

"I'm working on it!" I yelled and scared myself at the sudden defensiveness. "I don't know yet, I've made some connections. I just don't know how it's going to pan out yet."

"Do you and that band have any original songs?" My brother asked.

"They do, the band does."

They both looked at me, "are they any good? Do they have a future?" I shrugged my shoulders. "Do you have any originals?"

"No."

"You can't record an album of *Doors* songs."

"I don't want to be a singer." I said petulantly.

"Then what do you want to do?"

"I don't know. When this is over I'll probably go to L.A. and see what opportunities come up."

"That's it?" My sister said incredulously, "you're going to L.A. to see what comes up?"

"I met Ray Manzarek. Who knows, maybe he'll come see me and I can go on tour with them as Jim." By the look on my sister's face it was clear she didn't know who Ray Manzarek was. My brother, looked skeptical at this obvious fantasy trying to be the voice of reason, he decided to employ his world famous technique of Socratic questioning to prove his point, "what are you trying to create here, Mikey?"

"An experience." They looked at each other.

"An experience?"

"Something where everybody can say I was there, I saw that."

"And while you're creating an experience," my sister said, cutting quotation marks in the air with her fingers, "they're creating a career and building a life for themselves."

"It's my band, they'll do whatever I want." I said.

"At least until they get what they want, or get fed up with you."

"It seems to me they're using you more than you're using them." My brother said sadly.

"Michael," my sister added, "you could disappear from music tomorrow and it wouldn't be missed. There's no market to support you." As soon as she said it I could see she regretted it, but still, she had said it. I tried not to show my hurt.

"Sure, I could disappear tomorrow and no one would miss me, as you put it, but the world would never know what it missed."

"Mikey, if you don't protect yourself, they're going to end up with a career and you'll be left out in the cold."

I paced the room more frantically. I looked at them and looked away. My feelings were running wild within me until they burst out, "I never felt like I was part of your family."

"Mikey, that's not true!" My sister said, "we treated you better than a sibling. We treated you like a child of our own. We've helped you, given you advice, nursed you along. We probably did more than we should have."

"It probably isn't true," I admitted, "but it's how I felt. I didn't fit in the mold of the rest of you. I felt like I was someone different and that I'd been placed there by mistake."

"A mistake?"

"You know, like something outside of us all placed me there to be raised by Mom and Dad, but not of them."

"Mikey, that's ridiculous. It's almost crazy."

"I was an accident. Mom and Dad never paid that much attention to me. And you two were off at school, I'm more a product of the books I read and TV. This band will change me. It'll get me what I want." I looked at the both of them, they still didn't understand, "sometimes I did things because that's what I thought was expected at that moment in time, I guess like an actor, I don't want to act any more, I want to be, it's like from lead to gold. I don't expect you to understand. Morrison had the same thing with his parents and family."

My sister looked aghast, "let me get this straight Mikey, you're nursing some resentment against Mom and Dad because Jim Morrison did? Is that what you're saying?"

"Oh, Mikey," my brother said, "who knows what the real situation was with Morrison and his parents. Maybe even his family didn't know what the problem was, no one may ever know for sure. Maybe it was nothing more than a misunderstanding of youth, as I get older I understand why parents have to do some things that children don't understand. I realized that a while ago and I've made my peace with Mom and Dad."

"You've forgiven them?" I asked.

"Maybe forgiven isn't the right word, but understanding that led me to making my peace with it."

Suddenly they both looked sad. They realized they'd done their best, but nothing would be accomplished. There was nothing else they could say except what would be regretted by everyone concerned.

"This mess is your doing and it will be your undoing." My sister said.

New Orleans

Our next stop on the tour was New Orleans for the Blues and Jazz Fest, which was a pretty prestigious gig for a small club band like ours. We, of course, were a warm-up act. More like the warm-up for the warm-up act. The headliners were supposed to go on at ten, we were scheduled to go on at seven. Two or three full acts before the headliners.

I woke to the warm moist gulf air, speeding down the highway towards the French Quarter. This gig was a bit of a treat for us, we were going to stay in a real hotel room in the Quarter, as opposed to some motel off the highway. It was still early morning and as usual everyone in the van was quiet. During the drive I hadn't said much, brooding. My brother and sister were right about one thing, I could find myself standing on the side of some windswept road while the band could go on to find themselves on the threshold of a career. I busied myself watching the fleeing scenery to distract me from my thoughts. Even though Texas and New Orleans weren't that far apart, you can tell Texas is part of the southwest, dry, hard, and the vegetation is scraggly, while New Orleans is verdant. Every quarter mile was looking more and more stereotypically like my conception of Louisiana. There were the trees with moss hanging off them. From the back, Mitchell read a monologue from a guidebook.

"The moss are actually lichens with white flowers that are slowly killing the tree." We passed an ancient ruin covered with moss, its cement wall blackened and weathered. The way the window was shaped, in a cross, made me think it had once been a church, or maybe a Spanish fort replete with ghosts, guns and gold. I let all the images burn in my romantic imagination where they glowed with a pirate light. There were some mausoleums on the right, and more guidebook discourse from the back, "all the graves have to be above ground because New Orleans is six feet below sea level." The van rounded a curve as we whisked passed the Superdome, thoroughly ending my romantic visions of the past.

"The Superdome . . ." Mitchell read.

"Hey, let me see that guidebook." I said. Mitchell passed it forward and I leafed through it. "It looks pretty complete, chock full of information."

"Yeah, it is.." he stopped as I rolled down the window and threw the guidebook out. "And boring. You act like a tourist and you are a tourist."

"*You act like a tourist and you are a tourist?*" He said, mockingly, as if the words were something alien. "What is that supposed to mean?"

"We're explorers, not tourists."

After we checked in at the motel, the boys went to take showers and get cleaned up, I went to the bar to have a beer, it was cold and one of the best beers I've ever had. We were supposed to meet 'the girlfriends' for breakfast later. 'The girlfriends' didn't travel with us to all the gigs, just the bigger ones, or when the boys got lonely, they'd never been to New Orleans before and they all were excited about seeing the city. Of course they couldn't travel with us in the van, so they were coming separately.

New Orleans was like Jim Morrison, swampy mystery and a controversial history, like the flowers slowly killing the trees. But New Orleans was a double-edged sword for Morrison. After one trip he said he enjoyed the city's sights and sounds, and visions of Victorian spaceships. But it's also where *The Doors* had their last concert, where Morrison pounded the microphone into the stage until it splintered and Ray Manzarek said he literally saw Jim's spirit leave his body.

I wanted to see the Mississippi before anything else. I wanted to lose myself in its mysterious waters, to stand on its shore. As I wound my way through the French Quarter it occurred to me that these were the stones of the steps that Indians and pirates had walked, where Jean Lafitte and Andrew Jackson had made war plans, the same quays where Abraham Lincoln landed and watched the riverboats load and unload cotton, and of course where the darker history of slavery was plied. I went over the top of a rise and before me lay the Mississippi. It looked like quicksilver from where I was. I watched the boats skating across the water like insects that never break the tension of the surface or they're engulfed and drown. There are certain geographical sights that impress upon you their sense of history. Iconic locations, that when you mention them they conjure concrete images in people's minds, triggering a sense of awe and adventure, which have been drawing people to them for centuries. Places like the Amazon, the Seine, the Alps, the Nile, the Rhine, and the Mississippi. It's dark, lapping waters that flow through America from top to bottom, the waters that inspired Mark Twain and Tennessee Williams. I wondered, do these places naturally inspire awe in us, or is it the history we inscribe on them?

I'd told Ian that being out on the road touring was accomplishing something. But was it true for me? I knew it had been at first with the rehearsals, then the gigs at 'The Place,' I knew I had accomplished something, but the night after night routine without anything new happening? I could see the far away end of the tour, the proverbial light at the end of the tunnel, but where would that leave me? In whatever city the tour ended in? Or wherever the very finite money I would have left over would take me? Or with no prospect except to return to the life I'd known before. That would be nowhere. Could I somehow become part of the band? Or would it become every man for himself? The waters of the river lapped at these murky thoughts.

I found the boys waiting for me outside *The Court of Two Sisters*. 'The girlfriends' had caught up with us, and they had all glommed together in the correct couplings. We walked through the wrought iron gate of *The Court of Two Sisters*, a large courtyard opened in front of us. There was a ceramic and iron fountain in the middle, musicians were wandering from table to table.

"It was a courtyard society." Mitchell said, reading from a new guidebook.

"Where'd you get that?" I asked.

"Store next door, a dollar and a quarter." He said, smiling broadly. I just shook my head.

As we looked over the menu, we were awestruck by the diversity and the quality of the food, omelets, quiches, aspic, mousses. We became instant epicureans, aficionados of food, detailing its lore and our favorite dishes. It was the first time in a long time we had eaten well. The boys loved the pate and aspic. The violinists, seeing a table of mostly couples, came over and serenaded us. It was the kind of gracious living I could get used to.

After brunch we were right back where we started, on the street in front of the restaurant. By now the quarter had awakened. The streets were crowded with people, alive and in motion. Bourbon Street was like the river itself, currents of people ebbed and flowed into sight and out. Swirls and eddies in front of the bars, strip joints, restaurants, and curious shops that lined the streets. There were mimes and shills trying to pull you into the strip clubs, while the main current pushed you farther down the street. The buildings were close together and ancient, with fancy iron railings surrounding balconies that were decorated with plants and beads. We moved down the street as a single entity with twenty eyes and arms reaching out from every direction trying to see everything, to experience everything, and absorb all the sensations at once. We followed the current down the street. Digging the sights, sounds, and smells as a group. We were a band that day.

"Let's get a beer." I said. I'd seen a few storefronts that sold twenty-ounce beers for a buck and a quarter. We each got the local favorite, Jax beer. I took a sip and almost immediately spit it out, "that's terrible." I said. I saw a homeless woman trying to cadge money for a drink from passersby "here baby," I said, handing her the beer.

"Thanks, honey." She said, her eyes lighting up at her new found bounty. She hooked her arm through mine, "want some company, sweetie?"

"No, thanks." I said, tearing away from her grip.

The good thing about the French Quarter, if you walk six feet you'll find a shop that has whatever you want, need, or desire, including Voodoo, luckily I saw a shop that had a hand lettered sign in the front window d-a-i-q-u-i-r-i. The lettering seemed deliberate, unsure of itself like whoever wrote it wasn't quite sure how to spell daiquiri. Inside the shop there were about twenty soft serve ice cream machines. Each had a different flavored daiquiri stirring in it. From the relatively innocuous sounding, fuel injector to the more exotic like flaming-gorilla-tits. We quickly replenished our twenty-ounce beers with daiquiris. The boys were walking down the street, a daiquiri in one hand, their girlfriends in the other. Everybody was happy. I saw a couple of lesbians walking down the street and became enamored of young love. In the next instant I saw a group of women, each wearing a solid pastel colored dress with a silk ribbon sash slashing across their bodies, beauty contestants! I ran up to them and bowed, over exaggeratingly courteous, stepping easily into Morrison's persona.

"Hello, ladies!" I said, "where you all from?"

"All over!" They all shouted enthusiastically.

"All right!" I said. "You ladies wouldn't be going to the Blues and Jazz Fest tomorrow night, would you?"

"We are!"

"Come and see us," I said, pointing to the boys "we're a band, and we're playing there tomorrow. We're the opening act." They made some vague promises to come and see us and we continued floating down the street like flowers in a stream.

After another daiquiri, we had started running relays for more daiquiris. I found myself standing in front of the open door of a strip joint staring at a beautiful girl on stage dancing. I looked around, I was alone, people flowing around me. The band was gone I'd become separated from the group.

"Come on in!" The shill said, "all the girls, all naked!"

"Do you like that?" A voice asked. I looked around. Alex had come out of the crowd and was standing next to me.

"Huh?" I looked around realizing I had been staring.

"I said, do you like that?"

"Sex is all I have time for" I said, smiling. She walked away shaking her head, and I went inside for a while.

When I came out it was late afternoon and I soon caught up with Ian and Alex, they too had become separated from the rest of the group.

"Should we look for them?" Ian asked.

"No, when lost in a wilderness the first rule of survival is stay where you are. Besides, it looks like this guy is going to be doing something soon." We had stopped in front of a big guy wearing a beret, a blue vest with a pack of Kools in the pocket, and a saxophone. He was messing around with his equipment, muscling some big amplifiers into position. He hooked up his amps into a ghetto blaster tape deck that had a stack of tapes in front of them. We sat on the curb to wait for the others, watching the jazz guy set up his equipment. On the sidewalk across the street a shoeshine boy seeing the growing crowd, stopped and was hustling passersby for business.

The day was starting to melt into evening. Cool breezes were blowing in off the Mississippi, as the jazz guy started blowing his sax, an electric fuzz filled the air, or was it because of the steady stream of daiquiris? The music bopped and hummed in our ears. The crowd started to grow. Ian, moved by the music, cupped his hands and started jamming on a harp with the guy. He bopped and danced, sweating, following and filling in the jazz guy's leads. We were all into it, grooving, clapping, and laughing at Ian's exaggerated movements a satire of a rock star. The jazz guy seemed to be into it too. He bopped to Ian's playing and even gave him space for a solo. In the middle of it, the rest of the band appeared, apparently resupplied and re-energized with alcohol. When the song ended Ian uncupped his hands, they were empty. He didn't have a harmonica!

"Wow! You were great!" We enthused, crowding around him. Almost leaving the jazz guy out of our praise.

After the jazz guy had finished his street side concert, we all dropped a few bucks in his sax case as he was taking down his equipment. It had gotten dark and the streets had changed. People were now dressed for the night, gone were the gawking tourists. The air had become chilly we ambled along letting the current of the crowd still carry us farther down the river, until we found ourselves in a darkened end of the Quarter. We realized we were all lost and didn't know how to get to more friendly environs. We found a well-lighted oasis and stopped to rest while Mitchell consulted his guidebook. Everyone was relieved it finally came in handy and that he had it. Ian noticed some street musicians playing under a street lamp, dressed in leather jackets, and strumming acoustic guitars an open guitar case in front of them for people's 'contributions' and 'donations'. They looked harder, more street worn than the saxophone guy. Ian went over to talk with them, I leaned against a street lamp farther down the street. I was tired and hungry.

"You kind of have the Morrison swagger." Alex said, sidling up next to me.

"I'm borrowing it, since he isn't using it."

From where I was standing I could see the whole intersection. On a side street I saw a drunk approach a cop, their body language was so distinct it was like a pantomime. The story wasn't that hard to discern. The drunk stumbled towards the cop. His lips, from this distance looked like they were moving in silent movie fashion, trying to make some point to the cop. The cop faced him and pointed in the opposite direction. The drunk submissively turned back the way he had just come. Ian and his 'harmonica' were jamming with the street musicians. Alex was talking with a couple of guys in biker jackets and the rest of the band sat on the curb, too tired to move. The drunk across the street was stumbling back towards the cop. Again, the cop warned the drunk off.

"What did they want?" I asked as Alex came back by me.

"Just some local creeps." I watched as the drunk approached the cop for a third time. The silent movie playing itself out, the cop turned around and knocked out the drunk with a single punch. The night suddenly had a surrealistically violent undercurrent. The guys who Alex had been talking to were hovering nearby sizing me up trying to figure out if I was her boyfriend and if they could take me. Alex was clinging to me, trying to look like she was with me as much as possible. The musicians weren't as tolerant of Ian's faux harmonica as the jazz guy was. Something in their demeanor was malevolent. Everybody could see it, except Ian.

"You better get him out of there." I said to Alex.

"What should I tell him?"

"You're tired and want to get back to the hotel, anything." Alex went over and whispered in Ian's ear while I kept my eye on the creeps watching Alex, and making sure the musicians didn't jump on Ian before Alex got him out of there.

The night ended sitting on a picnic table at the Cafe DuMonde, sipping hot chocolates and munching on beignots. The dark shore of the Mississippi only a few hundred feet away, those mysterious waters gurgling on, a void right in front of us.

The New Beginning

The next morning, I joined the band for breakfast at the local Denny's, something I rarely did. They all stopped talking as I sat down at the table. I was overwhelmed by the clatter of silverware on plates, the smell of eggs, sausage, toast, and pancakes. The table was a collection and confusion of plates, cups of coffee, glasses of soda, and syrup.

I watched a father and his children. He was letting the kids try some of his breakfast he put a little something on his fork and reached over to put it in a child's waiting mouth. The gesture reminded me of a bird feeding its young. I remembered the warm morning at the breakfast table at the house the day after playing 'The Place'. It was the beginning and maybe this could be a new beginning for us. Out of the clinking and clanking of the dishes I said, "HEY!" A little too loudly, my actions seemed jumpy, even to me because I was trying to act normal and everything just seemed out of proportion. "I have an idea."

"About what?" Brian asked.

"Well, uh, I think I can help your band out."

"Ghost Dance you mean?" Johnny asked.

"Uh, yeah," I said. I tried to smile as nonchalantly as I could manage. "How?"

"I was thinking my voice has gotten really good and you know I can do a good show. What I'm trying to say is I could be your lead singer. I could, well if I was the singer that would free up Johnny to play more complex and intricate leads." They all nervously looked at each other, I looked to see if I could see the communal mind at work.

"Your voice doesn't really fit the sound of the band, or the music we play." Brian said.

"You make a fine Morrison," Mitchell said, "that's fine for the cover band stuff . . ."

"Well, maybe I can do something else then."

"All the positions are filled." Ian said.

"Look," Johnny said, "you've done a lot for us, getting us out on the road, and we're having a lot of fun, and we don't even care that you cut yourself a better deal with Swifty, but you're not letting us play our songs, we're not getting any exposure, when this is over we're right back where we started."

"Yeah, why couldn't we have played one or two of our songs last night?"

"That would've been major." Brian agreed.

"What else do you have to offer us?"

"I know we haven't been playing your songs in the sets but maybe we can start working that in now?" I sounded as desperate as I was.

"It's a getting a little late isn't it?"

"Then I can manage the band when we finish this tour. I can show you things you don't understand or don't have a lot of experience with. I know about the music business."

"What's this knowledge and experience you keep talking about?"

"I've read a lot of books about the music industry."

"The music industry you read about is twenty years gone dude."

"Uh, yeah, I see." I said. I went back to my room.

New Orleans Times-Picayune Review

Raitt, Thunderbirds Fabulous

by Jess Armstrong

Bonnie Raitt and *The Fabulous Thunderbirds* did fabulous sets last night as the headline acts at The Jazz and Blues Fest. Raitt was the consummate professional delivering her songs. *The Thunderbirds* played their hit songs, including *Tuff Enough*. After *The Thunderbirds* set, Raitt and opening act John Lee Hooker joined them on-stage for a memorable extended set that lasted well into the night, Jimmie Ray Vaughn playing a purer blues, a harder rock edge than his brother Stevie, who history may show as nothing more than a Hendrix imitator. Speaking of which . . .

In a departure for 'The Jazz and Blues Fest' the opening act for the evening was *The Doors* cover band 'The Unknown Soldiers' who

played a lackluster set. It seemed like the band wasn't talking to the
lead singer, who was drunk and drinking and seemed more interested
in trying to pickup beauty pageant contestants who were at the show,
than in giving a show.

Planes Are A Problem . . .

The next big gig we had was Milwaukee's Summerfest. Swifty
must have had a lot of connections in the Milwaukee entertainment
industry. He'd managed to finagle us a spot in Summerfest's lineup. I
didn't know if there was an open spot until the last minute, or if we
were a last minute replacement for a band that canceled. Whichever
the case, the problem was we were nowhere near Milwaukee. We didn't
have the time for an overland haul across the Midwest. Everyone
and everything squeezed into the van for a prolonged period. Fleeing
the scenery, the only breaks long enough to fill the tank, empty our
bladders, and grab a sandwich, all to arrive at the gig tired, smelly,
and more pissed off at each other than the normal road irritations.
It would've been the Battan Death March of Rock 'n' Roll.

The airplane lumbered onto the runway. As we taxied, Mitchell
started one of his informative travelogues.

"Did any of you guys ever see the movie *Alive?* Where the
plane crashes in the mountains and they have to eat each other?"
No response. Everybody had become used to Mitchell's musings.
Recitations that had pretty much had become part of the background
noise. Undaunted, he went on, "I read somewhere that landings are
controlled crashes."

"Shut up!" Brian snapped, "what are you the bearer of glad
tidings?" Mitchell picked up the sarcasm in the comment. It was true,
the track record wasn't very good for rock bands in airplanes. Just
ask Buddy Holly, Richie Valens, Lynrd Skynyrd, or Ricky Nelson.
Most of the big bands rely on them for touring, smaller bands use
them infrequently, except for emergencies like we had. With every
bump and tussle of the plane, all I could think of was Buddy Holly,

The Last Stage   135

and the little splatter of a footnote we'd make in the annals of Rock 'n' Roll if we crashed. Not even an answer to a trivia question. We couldn't pass up playing in front of an audience that size. The payday was a little better than we were used to, which justified all the effort. Swifty had rented a plane, and like the van, it was just big enough to fit all the equipment and us, and fulfilled a rock truism, the smaller the band, the smaller the plane. I just hoped the plane was in better condition than the van. I sat looking out the window imagining I was a real rock star on tour. Then the engines throbbed with pent up power and the plane jumped and raced like an animal that had remembered its purpose, speeding down the runway until it pulled itself into the air.

Summerfest

Swifty had rented a van from the airport to the fairgrounds, we were driven straight to the backstage area. The backstage was all skeleton scaffolding that our equipment needed to be lifted onto, but the boys and the backstage crew would see to that. As I walked onto the grounds I felt like it was my triumphal return to Summerfest, though it played only in my head. It had been a long year since Deidre and I were here together. There was a row of bikers sitting on their bikes having a couple of beers. I crossed their gauntlet to jeers and catcalls.

"Lookit here, it's Jim Morrison." One sneered.

"Faggot!"

'Uh-oh,' I said to myself, not a very auspicious beginning for my triumphal return.

As I climbed the stairs to the backstage area my fears were allayed. Summerfest was a big ticket production, there were production assistants and gofers rushing around with walkie-talkies showing the bands where to set up. After talking with the stage manager they had a PA show me where the dressing room was.

"Wait here, one of the production assistants will come and get you five minutes before you go on." I finally felt like I was making it to the big time.

I sat in the dressing room in a studio chair in front of a theatrical mirror, listening to all the hustle and bustle happening around me, running footfalls on the metal scaffolding, someone yelling for someone or something. But I was in the calm eye of the storm, I wasn't nervous, I couldn't even remember the last time I was nervous. I reflected on how far I'd come from being part of the milling crowd to literally setting myself above the crowd, but I was also aware of how far I still had to go. I wondered if Deidre was somewhere out in the crowd. There was a knock at the door.

"Yeah?" I said. A woman peeked her head in the door.

"Make-up?" She asked, "you want a little make-up it'll make you shimmer and the people in the back will be able to see you."

"Sure." I said.

"OK, just sit back in the chair and close your eyes. I did as she said, and I heard her put a few things down on the table and then I felt the make-up caressing my face, and she continued to talk, "I have to kind of sell the idea of make-up to the male bands even in this day and age it's hard to get men to put on a little base, if only they realized Elvis wore make-up." This was part of the seduction and I knew it, the woman running her hands over my face, an intimate act one that you could get used to very easily. There was a knock at the door.

"Ready Jim?" A woman's voice asked, as she opened the door.

"Lets go!" I said jumping out of the studio chair. The PA led me through the maze of the backstage area until we, at last, arrived in the wings of the stage. From where I was, I could see the band's equipment was already on stage. It looked woefully small on a stage out in the open, not enclosed in a club. I wondered if the amps were big enough to pump out a loud enough sound. The boys were nowhere to be seen.

"Is my band here yet?" I asked the PA. She whispered into her walkie-talkie before saying,

"They should be coming up on the other side any second now." And as I looked across the stage to the other wing I saw the boys come up the stairs.

"There a lot of people out there?" I asked, trying to make small talk.

"Uh-huh." She said, distractedly. Then I heard the stage announcer say,

"Ladies and gentleman, The Unknown Soldiers!"

The PA said, "go."

"Thanks." I said. As I walked out onto stage the band came out from the opposite wing and took their places at their instruments. I took my place at the microphone and for the first time I was able to see the whole audience. There was literally a sea of people in front of me. It was then that I truly understood what was meant by the phrases 'a sea of humanity', and 'an ocean of people.' They ceased to be several thousand individuals they became one thing, a new creature to do with as I pleased. Suddenly, I knew what Morrison knew. You become part of a crowd, faceless, anonymous. The individual becomes lost, you lose your self in a crowd, free to do as you please, free to live your dreams, free to enact your nightmares, all bets are off, there are no limits, no laws. People do things in a group they ordinarily wouldn't do. There are no witnesses, there's truly safety in numbers. I could make them do whatever I wanted, I could make them wave, I could make them dance, I could make them riot or I could throw them away. It was the door to power, the power that despots and rock stars know. There's always been something of the fascist about Rock 'n' Roll, that's probably why every rock opera is about exactly that, a charismatic leader with a small band of followers to assist. *The Who* understood this with *Tommy*, *Bowie* and *1984*, hell, even *Styx* understood this.

Arguably, one of the reasons Morrison may have wanted to start a rock band was to prove some of his theories. Morrison thought crowds, like individuals, could be neurotic and like individuals, they could be cured. In college he tried to enlist some friends in an experiment to see if they could make a crowd riot by placing his friends throughout the crowd and shouting slogans at appropriate moments. His friends thought he was crazy and refused to participate, so he couldn't prove his theories until he was in *The Doors*. Morrison saw music, theatre, poetry, film, and the neuroses of crowds as a crossroads. The crossroads is the place where magic is practiced, the crossroads is the place you can sell your soul to the devil to play the blues, the crossroads is the place where a cure can be effected. Morrison consciously provoked riots. Later rationalizing it, by saying, 'I thought we ought to have a riot. Everyone else did. So I tried to stimulate a few little riots.' But later saying, 'it got to the point where people didn't think it was a successful concert unless everybody jumped up and ran around a bit.' I decided to see if I could do it. Finish the experiment to see if it was something inherent in Morrison, or if it was the neurosis of the crowd. The crowd was the right size and temperament, and they were ready for it, maybe I could cure them, maybe I could cure myself, I discovered power.

Milwaukee Journal–Sentinel Review

NEAR RIOT AT SUMMERFEST

After years of rock bands playing at Milwaukee's Summerfest, a minor incident has slightly marred this summer's festivities, and the event's pristine track record.

The *Unknown Soldiers*, a *Doors* cover band which was a last minute addition to the roster, in an all too good emulation of the sixties classic rock band. The lead singer exhorted the drunken crowd into a reenactment of the worst elements of a *Doors* concert. It's unclear if the audience reacted the way they did because they thought that's what was expected from them, or if they were genuinely moved by the band and the antics of lead singer Michael Gray. Most of the crowd was seemingly oblivious to the danger, and no one was hurt. Otherwise, a good time was had by all.

Fallout

By the time the bad reviews and fallout of the show came out, we were already back on our scheduled itinerary. Swifty forwarded the reviews to us. Despite the initial bad review of the Milwaukee paper, the 'riot', as they termed it, was nothing more than a few people near the front rushing the stage. The reviews from the outlying areas offered a bit more of a balanced look at the events and put them into perspective.

Afterwards the band became more distant. None of them said a word to me until they decided to confront me between sets of a show about a week after the Summerfest reviews came in. I was sitting in the backroom of the bar we were playing when all of a sudden all four of the boys came piling into the room.

"Are you trying to sabotage the shows?" Brian asked.

"What are you talking about?"

"Your little riot." Johnny said, flinging the reviews at me. "We gotta talk about working some of our songs into the sets."

"I thought we did already?"

"No, you never bothered to answer us, you just mumbled something and walked off."

"You're not ready and neither are your songs." I said, dismissively.

"What!" Brian said, genuinely incensed, "you can't even name one of our songs!"

"It doesn't matter, I can tell."

"What do you mean, you can tell?" Johnny asked. "You can't even tell us how to play your damn *Doors* songs and you have the nerve to tell us we aren't ready? We've been riding in that van for months now, practicing your *Doors* sets, then practicing our songs. Did you ever listen to the tape I gave you when we first met?"

"No." I admitted.

"And you managed to disappear with Caitlin Stewart when we played it for her."

"So?"

"Did you tell her something to discourage her from calling us?"

"Did she contact you?" I asked.

"Obviously no!" Johnny said.

"Then she won't."

"How do you know that?" Mitchell asked.

"Because that's how things work. If she was interested she would have called."

"We just played in front of the biggest audience we're probably ever going to be in front of." Johnny said, "what good does it do us to tour if people don't hear our songs?"

"You couldn't do your songs at Summerfest because we were booked as a cover band. And cover bands don't do originals. And you're right again," I said, "I can't name one of your songs, but I've listened to your rehearsals. You've never availed yourselves of my opinions and rebuffed my offers to help. I know a lot about this business and I can help you."

"Like you've helped us so far?" Johnny said, "all you've done so far is take advantage of us. You cut yourself a better deal with Swifty while it's us that's carrying the burden of performing. You treat us like roadies. You've never moved a piece of equipment that I'm aware of and your drinking is affecting the shows."

"All the reviews Swifty sent us are all about you and your 'antics'," Brian said. "How're we going to get more gigs if word is out about you?"

"I got you this far didn't I?"

"You've lucked our way this far. You only got us that first gig because you were friends with the bar owner."

"And this tour because he was friends with Swifty." Brian said.

"All right." I said, straining to rein my temper in. "You wanna do one of your songs?" I asked rhetorically. "At the end of this set you can do a couple of your songs." I smiled, as I walked out the door and back to the stage. I was going to use everything I'd learned to make the audience do what I wanted. An exercise of power, if you will.

When we got on stage I stood off at the far end, doing my best Morrison scowl as the band plugged in their instruments. When they were in place, I walked in front of them and said.

"*When the Music's Over.*" They started the song. I hung back listening as the music built, until it got to the part where I was supposed to come in, but I didn't and they had to start over and they played it louder, but this time I wasn't missing the cue because of nerves, it was on purpose I wanted the pressure to build until no one thought they could take it anymore, they hit the cue again and sustained the crescendo, I jumped at the microphone screaming "Yeahhhhhhhh!" And did the best show I knew how. I used every trick Morrison knew to whip crowds into a frenzy. I screamed, writhed, fell to the stage, jumped, until the audience didn't want to hear anything except another *Doors* song. I saw the band exchanging looks between them, asking themselves what the fuck I was doing, but they knew what I was doing and it was too late. Then I went into a Morrison rap.

"We have a special treat for you tonight!" The audience cheered, "right on! All right!" It was easy to manipulate them. At the very least their reaction was predictable.

"The band wants to do a couple of their songs!" I walked off the stage and Ghost Dance was received to a thundering silence. I watched the rest from the bar. Johnny and the band played loud, hard but it was empty, an empty gesture, the audience didn't move. A sea of blank faces staring back at them.

"*Light My Fire*, motherfuckers!" Somebody screamed.

'That'll show them who runs this band.' I thought.

Kansas City Star Review

Last night a new type of act passed through town. A cover band, of *The Doors*, to be concise. Since the act focuses on the lead singer as rock legend Jim Morrison, it is fair to single out his performance. Michael Gray does tend to resemble Morrison when a light hits him right during a pose, but up close the wrinkles and extra years that Morrison didn't get are apparent. The singer's voice tears into a song differently than Morrison's, but the spirit is there and the intent is right.

The first set was good, but lackluster compared to the second set. The band came out burning. The music was taut and powerful. Gray added a lot of emotion to *When The Music's Over* that was missing during the first set. I don't know if this was done by design to emulate the feeling of *The Doors* experience or not, but whatever they did between sets to get that edge they should be doing all the time. The original songs the band closed the show with, shows they have promise if they want to embark on a recording career.

Mutiny on the Vanity

We were crossing a bridge, it was about three in the morning. The boys were asleep in the back of the van. Tom and I were the only ones awake in the front. We could see the lights of refineries in the industrial haze generated by factories, across the fog on the river. The stars glistened in the crisp night it was beautiful. We were about a quarter of a mile from the end of the bridge when the van choked and sputtered to a stop. There was nowhere to pull the van off. We were stuck in the middle of a lane and there were no other cars on the bridge.

"What do we do now?" I whispered. Tom looked out the windshield like a navigator trying to shoot the stars to get his bearing, "I know a guy who lives about an hour from here, I can call him."

"That sounds cool."

"But we gotta get the van off the bridge. If John Law comes along he's gonna' hassle us about that."

"How're we going to do that?"

"Gotta' wake everybody to push." I leaned back in the seat.

"Wake up!" I said in my Morrison baritone. There was a little movement, but no rousing. "C'mon, wake up!" I said more forcefully. I banged my fist on one of the amps. Brian raised his head.

"Huh? What's going on?"

"Are we there?" Johnny asked.

"No, we're not there, dude. We're stuck." Tom said.

"What?"

"The van's stalled out and we're stuck on a bridge."

"What!" They all lurched forward to look out the front windshield.

"We gotta' get out and push," Tom said, "and get the van off the bridge. I know a guy who lives near here, we can call him."

"Shit." Brian said. They all muttered, but they got themselves together, put on shoes, another shirt, a jacket. Within a couple of minutes, all were outside stretching and warming up. Tom looked over at me and I looked at him.

"What?" I said.

"Get out and push."

"I'm not pushing."

"Dude, the van is weighed down with equipment, we need everyone to push."

"Morrison wouldn't."

"You're kidding, right?" He asked.

"No."

"Why do you do this kind of shit?"

"To maintain the illusion."

"Man, this is backstage, there's no illusions just a harsh glare." Then for the first time since we met, the look on his face changed to anger, "fuck, you're not Morrison, and this ain't *The Doors*. Get out. At least they won't have to push an extra two hundred pounds." I got out of the van and walked even with the front of the van as they pushed it the quarter of a mile off the bridge.

From that point on the situation with me, and the band deteriorated. It was a race to the end, to the last gig, which was literally a battle of the bands. There were sullen looks and thrown equipment barely missing me. On stage, the band occasionally tried to sabotage my show, a song would end early, or they wouldn't hit the vocal cue they would just keep soloing. I'd look over to see what was going on, to see one or all of them laughing. Traveling in the van was a dour experience, sullen and silent. It was only the contract with Swifty that kept the whole thing together. I fell into old habits. I drank more. The women I picked up tended to be the girls wearing leather pants and purple hair. I had left my life behind, my family, Deidre, I could leave them behind too. All that was left was the end.

Calling Caitlin

I put about three dollars in change into the pay phone and dialed her number. It rang, I felt nervous. It rang again I wanted to hang up. I had the phone half way back to the receiver when I heard her say,
"Hello?"
"Uh, hello, Caitlin?" I felt like a seventh grader calling a girl for the first time. "This is Michael Gray, please don't hang up."
"What a silly way to start a conversation." Her voice was soft, mellifluous, dulcet tones, or maybe I was romanticizing it, a soft harbor from the asphalt realities of the road.
"I, uh, just wanted to call, what I said that night, I was kidding, it was a joke."
"What'd you say?"
"About not having the time for anything but sex."
"Jokes aren't usually very far removed from where our hearts are." She said.
"I don't really know what I called for." I said, looking down at the ground.
"Sure you do. What can I do for you?"
"Everything is going wrong,"

"I'm sorry."

"We just had a bad gig. I guess they really weren't into what I was doing. The band hates me, the fucking van broke down"

"It can't be all that bad."

"But on the upside I did meet a woman that knew Ray and Jim."

"Oh, yeah," silence, "she must be getting up there."

"Late forties, I guess." I didn't know what else to say, "I'm meeting the wrong women."

"What're you telling me this for?"

"I thought you would understand, you know, what it's like being on the road."

"I do understand I just can't help you. Michael, I don't know what you're asking me and I don't think you know what you want."

"I just wanted to hear a friendly voice I guess, and . . . I needed to talk to someone. Friends are few and far between on the road. You're the only person I've met I thought I've become friends with and I didn't want to leave it the way I did. I wanted to tell you how much I enjoyed your company."

"That's sweet Michael, thank you."

"You have all this style and class, I can understand why you wouldn't . . ."

"Michael, it's not that."

"If I were Morrison you would come with me . . . I have to go." I hung up.

The Saga of Jimmy Stark Pt III

Hollywood Today! Came out of a commercial, Merri was sitting in a very open room with bright natural sunlight filtering in. There was wood paneling, and in the background the wall space was filled with pictures of the famous all posed with the man sitting behind a huge desk. Physically he was a small man, the desk was an actual contrast, a statement on the man's stature. Everything about him said money, from the perfectly shaped haircut, to his store bought tan, and right down to his manicure you could see when he fidgeted his fingers on the desk top. He wore a huge pair of black framed glasses that looked like he'd stolen them from a maiden aunt. I remember seeing him in some B movies from the fifties, He was sitting back in a large leather chair.

"We're here with legendary producer Paul Derek," Merri said, introducing the man, "among his successes, Family Muse. Paul, at the time Family Muse was a rarity among TV programs, some have credited it with being the first of its kind of modern sitcoms."

"Merri, it was more than that, Family Muse saved the studio. That is in no small part due to the talents of Jimmy Stark."

"Your ideas revolutionized the industry."

"I was one of the first people to merchandise lunch boxes, thermos', records, dolls, personal appearances and, of course, the novelizations of the episodes. It really put me on the map, and changed the way the industry looks, and gave me the power to develop the projects I've been interested in."

"Will there be a Family Muse reunion?"

"Well, Merri, we tried a few years back, but it was at the height of Jimmy's, shall we say, 'problems.' He showed up drunk every day and was horrible to everyone on the set, especially Sandra. I didn't find out why until later."

"We've heard that your studio is in the process of developing a movie about the life of Jimmy Stark?" Merri said.

"That really is still in the initial stages of development. One of the drawbacks of doing a biography is that it always ends in the death of the hero, but since Jimmy is still alive, somewhere, we feel confident we can provide a story with a happy ending. We'd, of course, like Jimmy to participate in the production so if you find him, have him contact us."

"Thank you for talking with us today." The interview ended and cut back to Merri in the studio.

"In the last of our reports we'll be talking with Jimmy's mother."

My Miami

The van pulled up in front of the bar, it looked like a shack with about fifteen Harleys parked in front of it. The only reason we'd found it was because there was a portable sign on the curb that read: Tonight The Unknown Soldiers. Everyone got out and stretched, it was pretty much the one thing we could still agree on and do as a group. I could hear the sound of pool being played, above the sound of raucous conversation. Tom held open the screen door and we walked in. We weren't a couple of steps inside the bar when everything stopped, everyone stopped what they were doing and they were looking at us like we were some strange delicacy placed before them, you just knew they were going to spit out.

"Oh, shit." I said to whoever was standing next to me.

"This doesn't look good." I heard whispered back.

"I thought this only happens in movies." The bikers got a good look at us, and we of them. Then the moment was over and they went back to whatever they were doing the moment before. The sound returned to the air like a needle dropped onto a record. Tom sought out the owner of the bar, while we stood there. I didn't see where we were going to setup there was no stage. Tom came back a moment later with the bartender.

"This is Hildy, the owner." Tom said. She was wearing a bikini top with a midriff thrown over it, a more than an ample amount of skin rolled out from under the midriff. I noticed some of the exposed skin looked scarred over from a fire.

"Hi boys, boy you sure look the part." She said to me, "where do ya wanta setup?"

"How about there?" I said pointing to the far wall of the bar, it was close to the back door, easy access for bringing in the equipment. It looked like the natural area to have a stage, if they had one.

"That's where most of the bands pick." She said, "go to it. We don't have anyone to set up for you, so you'll have to do it for yourselves." The band started to clear away the tables to make a stage. Luckily the tables weren't filled because most of the bikers were at the bar, or playing pool. I went to the bar and got a beer, while the boys started bringing in the equipment. There hadn't been any griping about my not setting up the equipment. There was mostly no talking of any kind when I was around. There was of course no back stage area, or dressing room. After the band set up they retreated to the farthest corner of the room, nursing beers and keeping as much space between them and the bikers as they could. We had a few hours before we were supposed to start playing, so I killed the time playing pool with some of the bikers, or sitting at the bar flirting with Hildy, getting every other beer free. I noticed behind the bar was a Playboy Guide to Party Drinks, it didn't look like it got much use, this was a strictly beer and shot crowd. I doubt many were coming in and asking for a pina colada. Hildy was holding her own with me drinking. She was a biker chick who had won a settlement and decided buying a bar was more stable than a life on the road.

As the afternoon meandered into evening, more bikers started filling the small bar. It started getting hot in the bar. I was playing pool with one of the bikers when I noticed his girlfriend had taken an interest in me.

"So, you're with the band?" She asked in a seductive voice. She was dressed in jeans, a bikini top overflowing with waves of cleavage, and a denim jacket pushed back on her shoulders by the size of her breasts.

"What's your name?" I asked.

"Rikki." Her boyfriend noticed she was paying an inordinate amount of interest in me. I wasn't so drunk that common sense failed to prevail. Bikers are strange, they'll give you their girlfriends and let you fuck them, but if you show any interest in them they'll stomp you.

"Uh, Rikki, I have to do a sound check, I'll see you later." I said, extricating myself from her. I went over to the band and pretended to be concerned with some aspect of the set up.

I continued to drink as the atmosphere changed from hot to muggy. I could feel the humidity pressing in on me. I should have seen the elements of disaster falling into place it was starting to get ugly. The bar was crowded with bikers and at least one fight had broken out. It brought to mind *The Doors* playing in Miami under similar conditions. A hot sultry night, an overcrowded venue, and a drunk Jim Morrison who had decided to alter the parameters of his stardom. It ended in Morrison allegedly exposing himself, after which lawsuits and court appearances became the main venue for seeing *The Doors* live for most of the rest of their career. Miami was Morrison's experiment in crowd psychology that succeeded all to well. I saw Hildy talking with Tom, then they came up to me.

"Can you guys start playing early?" She asked. "I'll pay extra." I guess she hoped the music would cool the crowd out. Music doth have charms to soothe the savage breast, and all that.

By the time I took 'the stage' I was pretty drunk, but as the music started and I was waiting for my cue. The bikers started taunting me, calling me "faggot!" and "rip-off!" It surprised me. I had been getting along with them all afternoon. At least you knew where you stood with suburban kids. They got drunk and all they wanted to do was jump on-stage and dance around a little, or sing, and pretend to be Jim Morrison for a minute or two of their lives. But bikers get WILD and play rough. The club was jammed with bikers and it was like some synergistic effect had taken place. The bikers that arrived later added to the community blood alcohol content and everything seemed to escalate and accelerate. When they got together in large groups they pushed each other to ratchet up the good times into the rose of violence. It was always hard to gauge biker's temperament. It was all test and bluff. They pushed you to see if you'd run, or push back. The trick was not to push back so hard you pissed them off. They were throwing bottles and I wished they'd had a mesh fence barrier in front of the stage. I don't know if their aim was good or drunken, I only got clipped once by a bottle, and I think I walked into it. I saw Rikki come out of the crowd to the front of the dance floor. I was drunk now too. "*Light My Fire*," as the bikers recognized the opening they went wild! I grabbed the microphone from its stand, As the music started to build, I crouched down, and waited. Morrison frequently did this in the early days. When the music hit its pitch I jumped, as I straightened out the microphone momentarily extended like an exposed penis.

"Is it really that big?" Rikki shouted, "let's see it!"

"You wanna see it baby!"

Then one of the bikers lurched towards me, "that's my old lady asshole!"

"Knock that shit off!" I yelled, staying in character. Tom, who was standing nearby and could see what was going on, came up from behind and whispered in my ear, "uh, dude, you better lay off, some of these guys aren't looking to happy."

"Aw, they're never happy," I roared into the microphone, "it's part of their act man." So I grabbed for my pant's zipper and I heard from behind me,

"Stop him! Stop that asshole!" Someone tackled me from behind, we tumbled into the crowd, and the brawl was on. I was pushed, punched and kicked all the way out to the parking lot.

A Cosmic Mating

I looked out across the room. There was the usual contingent of waitresses, especially in the smaller towns there seemed to be an age gap in the waitresses, the younger women left at a certain age, and those left behind just aged. So, there rarely was a waitress that was roughly my age. Then I saw her from the stage, one of the waitresses. A brilliant blonde, her hair was almost devoid of color. She was wearing a low-cut, skintight red T-shirt and black shorts that seemed to merge effortlessly with her legs. As soon as we finished the song we were in the middle of I turned to the band and called for, "*I Looked at You.*" As the song started, I looked for her as she made her rounds in the bar. As my cue came up I caught her eye, "I looked at you, you looked at me," I sang, "I smiled at you, you smiled at me." She smiled. "And we're on our way! Yeah! And we're on our way!"

As I walked off the stage at the end of the set she was waiting for me with a beer and shot at the bottom of the stairs.

"Hey Morrison!" She said, "here's a drink on the house."

"Thanks." I said, drinking the shot. "I think I love you."

"Really?" She said smiling, "you can tell that from across the room?"

"Sure." I said, smiling, not letting myself be thrown off by her questions meant to embarrass.

"You can tell that by watching the way I walk?"

"Why not?"

"You can tell that by looking at the size of my tits?"

"Definitely." I said.

"Oh, what happened here?" She asked, touching the side of my face where I still had some cuts on my face from the debacle of the biker bar.

"Oh, you know, critics."

"You remind me of Morrison."

"I'm supposed to, that's the whole idea." I said.

"No, there's something about you that's the same. He's so sexy." She enthused.

I smiled. It wasn't the first time I'd heard that. "If he were alive," I reminded her, "he'd be old enough to be your father." She smiled a little awkwardly. "What's your name?" I asked.

She pointed to her name tag over her breast, and said, "Pam."

"Paaaam." I said, drawing the word out to the southern drawl Morrison affected when he wanted to impress someone with his charm, "I don't know how I missed it."

"Pam, the same as Jim's wife's name." I turned my head at an angle, another Morrison simulation, then smiled broadly.

"Indeed."

"I'm the biggest *Doors* freak ever," she said. "I can tell you anything about Jim you want to know. What're you doing later?" I could tell she was aching for a way out of this town and not end up stuck, one way or another like the older waitresses.

"Going to your apartment." I said.

"Good answer. Do you use it at every gig?"

I smiled. "Do you ask that of every lead singer?"

"Pretty cocky." She said.

"Well, am I?"

"You wanna do some 'shrooms?"

'Shrooms. Magic mushrooms, psilocybin, was a natural psychedelic. You eat a few and see visions. Indians have been using them for centuries in their religious ceremonies. She brought out a baggie of mushrooms. They looked just like your average desiccated mushrooms that you find on your pizza. I leaned back on the floral print couch in Pam's apartment studying the baggie of mushrooms.

"You just eat these?" I asked opening the plastic baggie and sniffing. They smelled terrible.

"Sure." She said. I popped one in my mouth and chewed it, "or I can make a tea from it."

"It tastes like shit!" I spat it out.

"Tea it is." She said, plucking the baggie from my hand and took it to the kitchen. The apartment was filled with pillows and soft colors, pewter framed pictures of family and friends. It was a girl's apartment. She came back a few minutes later with a very delicate looking porcelain teapot and teacup. We settled into having a joint while I sipped the tea, which for how bad the mushrooms tasted in their natural state, tasted like any other tea I'd had. Aside from the joint, we could've been maiden aunts gossiping.

"How'd you get so into *The Doors* anyway?" She asked.

"Well, I was in college or rather should have been in class. Anyway, I was in my room getting high and listening to their first album. And during the instrumental of *Light My Fire*, I found myself caught up in the trip. You know it felt like I was traveling. I'd never been moved by anything in life like that before or since. It was an amazing experience."

It was about twenty minutes later I took a hit off the joint and knew something was happening, The room turned orange. I was seeing tracers, little comets streaking across my field of vision. I knew it wasn't from the pot.

"Whoa, I don't think I need this anymore." I said, handing the joint back to her.

"What happened to pushing the boundaries?" She teased. "Don't you want to break on through to the other side?"

"I think I just did."

"What happened?"

"Uh, your apartment just turned orange. It was like a door opened, you know? Everything is orange."

"Cool. You know what's really fun to do now?"

"No." I said, watching silvery comets shooting past my eyes.

"Going swinging! C'mon there's a swing set right out back." She jumped up and started pulling me towards the patio doors. The night seemed to have turned into a wild, wicked world. The wind whipped at my hair and clothing. I wondered if this dramatic world was real or because of the tea. I turned back to her apartment. It was warm and inviting looking inside. Some part of me didn't understand why we had to come outside, while another part of me knew she wanted to go swinging. Out back was a rusting swing set with two well-worn ruts under the rubber and chain swings. We each grabbed one and started pumping our legs towards the stars.

"Higher!" She yelled, "isn't this fun!" We pumped our legs urging the swings higher. We were laughing as the stars drew close and fell away, we couldn't stop laughing. I let go and was rolling around in the cold dewy grass. I was still laughing when I saw a silvery spider web. Suddenly I felt like I was in a box, silvery spikes splintered through the top. It was a coffin! I was cold, and I was crying.

"I'm dying! I'm dying!" I grabbed my stomach and rolled over on my side. I felt empty. "I'm alone, I'm all alone." I cried.

Suddenly Pam was at my side. Where had she been? Or had only seconds passed? She cradled my head, "what's the matter?" She cooed, "what's the matter, baby?"

"Nobody loves me, nobody loves me! I don't know who to be anymore."

"Just be yourself, that's all you have to be, yourself."

"I think I'm losing myself."

"It's all right, you're home now, I'm here."

"Just love me."

"I do, I will. It's all right, it's all right baby! It's just cold out here. Come on, let's get you inside."

I woke up the next morning feeling raw and vulnerable. Exposed to the world. After what I told Pam last night, I suppose I was. Lying in a big overstuffed bed, I sunk into everything, the pillow, the mattress. I was covered with a white and pink comforter. I looked under the covers to discover I was still dressed, except for my shirt and shoes. I felt like every nerve had been exposed, like I had touched an open wire, myself, and held on for a minute longer than I should have. I was still cold. I pulled what blankets I could around me tighter. Pam woke up and rolled over.

"Good morning!" She practically sang, "how're you this morning?"

"Worn out."

"I always feel horny after tripping." She said. "You want to have sex?" She started digging through the covers.

"No, I can't." I said, pushing her hand away, "I don't want to ruin anything."

"No sex? Are you kidding? You mean this isn't even a one night stand?"

"Things haven't been working out well for me. You just may be another . . ."

"Bad choice," she finished the thought for me. I shrugged my shoulders looking a little guilty at the admission. I was still exposing myself. "Are you OK?" She asked. "I mean, we were laughing and everything. Then you fell, and all of a sudden you were crying. I mean it was exactly from one moment to the next."

"I'm fine. I hope I didn't scare you. I don't even know where all that stuff came from."

"It's all right. You shouldn't be afraid to reveal yourself to people, especially me. But you pretty much do that on stage every night."

"Not really," I said, "I expose Jim Morrison. I go out there night after night 'being' Morrison. Everyone thinks I am him. So much of this cover band thing falls on me, the band wants to do their original songs and they don't want to do the cover band thing anymore. They laugh at me every chance they get. They just don't understand everything I'm going through. So I try not to show any weakness. A king cannot appear to be as the common man."

"See, you are him!" She gushed and threw her arms around my neck.

"No one's gotten that before. I've tried explaining it to the band, but they don't seem to be able to understand that."

"You can explain it to me," she said.

"I've told a lot of people, a lot of different things."

"Which is true." I heard echoes of Caitlin.

"I started this, the band, to accomplish certain things. In certain respects it was a search for love." I heard myself saying. I wondered if it were true? And if I meant her, or someone else?

"A search for love?" She repeated the words to herself, softly. "So, why do it?"

"It showed me a way to be greater than myself. I was drifting, as everyone likes to point out. It was my seven years of exile, I guess."

"But you found the guts to leave that life behind, right?"

"I wasn't leaving that much behind. This band has been my tribute to *The Doors*. But it's an end to fandom. I've given so much to it already now. When this tour is over, I'm moving to L.A. I'm going to parley this paltry little cover band into something."

"What?"

"I don't know, I want to find myself . . . uh, what I mean is I don't want to find myself living in a trailer again. This whole *Doors* thing is going to open up. Maybe I can even pick up another band, and it'll be L.A. so maybe someone will notice my resemblance to Morrison. And this band experience can't hurt, right? Or maybe I can get together with *The Doors*, and I can sing and do my Jim act and they can do a reunion tour, or maybe even play Jim in a movie or something. Anything. I've even met Ray, maybe that'll help."

"It'll happen." She said confidently.

"How do you know?"

"It'll happen if you believe it will." She looked shy for a second.

"You know that's all I've been looking for from the band, a little belief.

"I love you!" She blurted out. In her eyes I could see the light of true belief burned.

"Come with me," I said. "No one has ever believed in what I want to do like you do."

"What about my job?"

"Quit, forget it. I left everything behind to be here." I said.

"There's one little problem."

"What?"

"I have a boyfriend." I looked at her, stunned. "But I want to go with you."

"Then what has this been all about? Is that what you wanted, a one night stand with a rock star?"

"An almost rock star." She chided. "Sure, I have a boyfriend, for a little security and to keep all the goons away. I've been like the prettiest girl in this one horse town ever since I can remember. I deserve something better than these guys I've grown up with around here, and a few more years of this shit and I'll be some fat, toothless waitress trying to decide which worthless candidate to settle for. You don't want that to happen to me, do you?"

"I can't. You have something here, I don't have anything to offer. You can't love me, you don't know who I am or what I've done."

"Do you think I like being promiscuous? Sure, I've slept with some of the bands that have played through here, but only with guys who have promise."

"Isn't that the plot to *An Officer and A Gentleman?*"

"Funny, you think I'm making this shit up!" I didn't know what to say or even what to think about it so I didn't say anything. "Fine!" She shrieked, pushing me away. "Don't take me with you. And the next time you're through here, probably on your way down, and these tits you are so fond of, are hitting the ground, see if I sleep with you!"

The Last Gig

The last gig Swifty had lined up for us was a battle of the bands with another *Doors* cover band that had sprung up. Our philosophy in the competition was going to be the same as *The Doors* when they were the house band at the *Whisky a-go-go*, 'blow the other bands off the stage.'

The club had formerly been a warehouse that was converted into a one stop fits all bar, nightclub, arcade, and dining area. Before the doors opened I was wandering around the huge club trying to get the feel of the place. I was alone except for an occasional bar-back lugging a case of something from one end of the building to the other, or a waitress, or a bartender setting up their stations. Each area was huge, having at least one bar in it. The nightclub, where we were going to be playing was huge and open with concrete floors and somewhat unusual in that it had two stages. 'It's going to get loud in here.' I thought to myself.

I went backstage to see if Tom and the boys had finished unloading the van. Instead, I found the competition. The other band in the battle of the bands unloading their truck, I watched as 'The Lizard Kings' unloaded their equipment. I watched from top of the loading dock as three guys unloaded the truck. None of them looked like he play Morrison. Finally, a bearded guy carried an amplifier off the truck. When he put it down, he looked up and saw me.

"What're you supposed to be dressed up as?" He asked.

"The winner of the battle of the bands competition." I said.

"Not if I have something to say about it."

"You're their Morrison?" I asked.

"Sho' nuff." I didn't know if they were from the south, or if that was his best Morrison impersonation. "You know," he said, "everybody tries to look like the young Jim Morrison. We take the tack of playing their bluesyier material, more the *L.A. Woman, Morrison Hotel* stuff.

"That leaves all the rest of the songs for us." I said, smugly.

"You know what I don't like about most of you guys?" He asked, "most of you guys think you are Morrison. And the whole Dionysian thing, and experiencing everything in life."

"I don't want to sit around remembering my life, I don't want to sit around remembering love, I don't want to sit around remembering my exploits, I want to live them."

"You know what?"

"No, what?" I asked.

"You get Morrison wrong. You got a look, you got a pose, but you don't get the man. You don't see him as a human being. You're thinking of him as an icon and you're not thinking about the audience. You're thinking about yourself. You want people to see you as the icon."

"And what do you want?" I asked.

"We just want to give the audience a *Doors* show. And if you're so into living life to it's fullest, how're you doing that, if you're just mimicking Morrison's life?" I had to admit this guy was good.

"You know," I said, "when I was trying to think of a name for the band I thought of the lizard kings."

"Is that right." He said.

"Yeah, but I rejected it. I thought it sounded too much like a sports team, or something like that."

"But a very cool one."

I walked away, 'so much for sizing up the lack of competition,' I thought to myself.

Swifty Redux

After the show we were celebrating, congratulating ourselves that we had won the competition and more importantly, lived through the tour. Me, and the boys were even talking to each other, smiling, laughing, slapping each other on the backs. Like survivors of some great cataclysm that only those who go through the ordeal can understand. The shared trauma brings you together at the end. We were pushed to the back of the dressing room, amidst a throng that piled out into the hallway. People were shaking beers up and the foam was erupting all around us. It reminded me of the first gig at 'The Place' and I felt the way I did that first night, free. I physically felt the weight lift, but this time I felt free for a different reason. Everyone was telling us we won the competition hands down because, except for one highlight song, they played faithful album versions of the songs. Compared to us, their versions were sanitized. They didn't take any risks in the presentation, relying on the audience's own sense of nostalgia to make the connection instead of trying to connect themselves. I'm sure the Lizard Kings' admirers were telling them they won too.

Amongst the well-wishers, back slapping, and congratulations, I saw a face I hadn't seen at any of our shows, and hadn't expected to see. Making his way through the crowd towards us, Swifty.

"Swifty, what're you doing up so late?" I asked.

"I just came to see what I've been booking."

"How'd you like it?" Johnny asked, grabbing Swifty around the shoulders.

"Just fine, just fine, very impressive. I did want to give you boys this." He said, holding up a bottle of Champagne.

"All right, Swifty! Let's open that sucker!"

We toasted a couple of times to the tour being over. Then Swifty looked serious and said, "but I do have an ulterior motive for being here." Everyone got real quiet and attention focused on Swifty.

"Nothing's happened? Has it?"

"Well, yes. Something has happened." He said. We all looked concerned.

"What is it?"

"I know you boys have had a tough tour, but I just wanted to run another booking past you, to see if you are up to one more show."

"Well, uhh, no." We all started to hedge.

"That's what I thought too, but it's a prestigious booking. That's why I decided to ask you if you had one more show in you. Also, this venue rarely solicits bands, so . . ."

"Who is it?" I asked, intrigued.

"*The Whisky a-go-go* in L.A. The owners have heard what you boys have been doing and want to book you."

"*The Whisky!*" We all shouted in unison and we were celebrating again. *The Whisky* was the launching pad for *The Doors*. I almost jumped.

"Yeah, we'll play!" I said.

"What do you guys think?" Johnny asked the band, "you think we can hold it together and play *The Whisky*?" The boys recognized *The Whisky* as a high profile place to play because of the proximity to record companies and executives. A lot of Rock 'n' Roll careers are still launched at *The Whisky*. They all shook their heads in agreement.

"Are the owners the same guys who owned it when *The Doors* played there?" I asked.

"I didn't ask. That's nostalgia not business." Swifty said. "And it would be best for you boys to remember that too."

We all hung around after Swifty had told us of booking *The Whisky*, talking over our good fortune and our road stories that Swifty was interested in hearing, but I had an ulterior motive of my own for waiting. I had been trying to get hold of Swifty for a couple of days to talk over some plans for my future with him. Now it was seemingly taking forever for the boys to talk themselves out.

"I'm hungry, let's get something to eat." Johnny finally suggested. As they were going out the door, Johnny noticed I was remaining there with Swifty and asked, "you coming?"

"No, I have some personal business I need to discuss with Swifty." He shot me a look of distrust and closed the door behind him. When he was gone I said, "Swifty, I read in the paper that a movie studio is auditioning people for a *Doors* movie." I pulled out a copy of *Variety* I had been carrying around and handed it to him, turned and folded to the appropriate page, of course. He read it slowly.

"You read *Variety*?" He finally asked.

"Sure, I started to read it just to get a feel for things in L.A. L.A. has always been my final destination after this was over. Anyway, when I saw this notice I sat bolt upright in bed. I mean what're the odds that a *Doors* movie is casting just when I'm ready to move on to bigger things? I feel like destiny's child."

"Looks like it's right up your alley, all right," Swifty said, still looking the article over before putting it down. "I know some people in L.A. I think I can probably get you a part as an extra or maybe even a speaking part."

"I want the part of Morrison."

His jaw dropped, "you're kidding, right?"

"No."

"Can you act?" He said, staring at me, and I remembered the litany of questions Jim had run past me when I told him about the idea for the band. "That's the first thing they're going to ask me."

"Sure, just about every night of the past year. C'mon what do you have to lose?"

"Me, nothing." He said, shaking his head.

"Those of us who're going to die have nothing to fear."

He picked the paper back up and read through the article again. "Well, it says the role of Morrison is still uncast. I'll see what I can do."

"Thanks, I appreciate that. Oh, and Swifty, do me a favor?"

"Sure."

"Don't tell the boys."

"Why not?"

"No reason, I just don't think they would understand. And if it doesn't work out, it'll save some embarrassment."

Battle of Bands Review

Draw Declared In Band Battle

Last night at Rugby's there was a battle of the bands. Two different *Doors* cover bands, with two different approaches to the same material presented an unorthodox, almost surreal doppelganger that highlighted the opposites of *The Doors'* career. Since there were two stages available in the nightclub area, the bands took advantage of the opportunity to present direct comparisons to their respective acts. The bands traded off playing *Doors* songs in a veritable Rock 'n' Roll tennis match. 'The Unknown Soldiers' approach *The Doors* from Jim Morrison's stated Dionysian perspective, with lots of screams, falling, and theatrics. While 'The Lizard Kings' were a little more sedate in their approach with album faithful renditions of the material that didn't delve into the theatrics too much except for a couple of 'centerpiece' songs like 'Strange Days' and 'L.A. Woman'. Both acts were presented with such professionalism and enthusiasm that there was no clear winner, except the audience, who noisily voiced their enthusiasm for their favorite songs.

Stark Conclusions

The network had been advertising the wrap up of Hollywood Today's! conclusion of the Jimmy Stark story, trying to drum up ratings and hopefully a self-fulfilling prophecy of hyped up interest. The spotlight lit on Merri on her mark, she looked her usual confectionery self.

"In this, our last report on Jimmy Stark we wanted to speak with Jimmy's parents, but we couldn't find his father and his mother has refused repeated requests for an interview. But we did manage to find an old friend of Jimmy's who knew both Jimmy and his father." They cut to a videotape of a man in a barroom. He looked like he was in his late forties, dressed in a workingman's plaid shirt, dusty blue jeans, and black work boots. He was leaning against the bar, a half drunk beer behind him. Merri started the interview.

"I'm here with Robert Mills, a close friend of Jimmy Stark's."

"Yeah, I met Jimmy a few years after Family Muse, he was eighteen or nineteen. Did I mention I used to be a cop. I have this idea for a TV show." He seemed a little drunk.

"Sorry, I'm just a reporter."

"Can I talk about it?"

"We're trying to find Jimmy Stark." Merri said, trying not to look flustered.

"Let me ask you," he said. Then he stopped like he was trying to remember what he was going to say, "what are you looking for Jimmy for?"

"We want to update his fans on how he is and maybe interview him."

The guy leaned forward on his stool moving closer to Merri, whispering furtively,

"looking for secrets?"

"No, just any information you have about Jimmy and his father."

"I used to drink here with Jimmy and his father." He said, reaching back to the bar for his beer.

"How did they get along?"

"I think I knew Jimmy better than his father did. The old man didn't seem too interested in Jimmy, except when he needed money."

"Did Jimmy give it to him?"

"Yeah, usually, but it was usually a day or two after that, that Jimmy would make the papers or get fired from whatever show he was on, or worse, both. Of course, they both didn't understand each other."

"How so?" Merri asked.

"Well, there was the night Bill came in, that's Jimmy's father, he sits down and says 'I'm nothing,' and I said, 'what do you mean?' And he says, 'I wanted to have a different life. I wanted to be something. To give my family what I didn't have. And look what happened, Jimmy.'"

"So I said to him, 'Bill, Jimmy didn't do it to hurt you.'"

"Then he said, 'maybe my wife did.'" Then Robert looked at Merri, "do I get paid for this interview?"

"Sorry, we don't pay for interviews."

"Oh." He looked thoughtful for a moment, then asked, "can I buy you a drink?" The interview ended there.

Merri was back in the studio at her podium. She tried to martial a smile, but it looked forced and uncomfortable. "As we said earlier in this report we wanted to interview Jimmy's mother, Mabel Stark, but she turned down our requests. However, we were able to track down an old interview with her." They cut to the tape, which looked grainier than the previous reports. By the clothes she wore and her hairstyle, it looked like the interview was done in the 70's. It looked dated, like everything from the 50's looked in the 70's, that's the gift of videotape, to show us how fast we can age. Then Jimmy's mother was talking.

"I think it really is all my fault. I pushed Jimmy to become famous, to be something and someone. And before you ask me if I was trying to live out my fantasies through Jimmy, let me tell you." She looked directly into the camera, or at the interviewer standing next to the camera, whichever it was, it was an appeal to be understood either self-consciously or not. "It was more about letting Jimmy being able to live out his fantasies." I wondered what the question was that this was in response to. "I saw a biography of Orson Welles and how his parents raised him as a child genius. And I thought, how splendid."

Then it was back to Merri in the studio to bring all the contradictory images and actions of Jimmy's life together. To sum it up in twenty-five seconds, then cut to the commercial, and then on to their next story.

"It was our intention to bring you an update of Jimmy Stark and his whereabouts for this report, but our investigation hasn't yielded Jimmy Stark in the flesh. Nor has it answered any of the questions of his life. Like, why did Jimmy Stark who had such a promising career in front of him throw it away with such ruthless abandon? What was he looking for? What is any of us looking for? In that light, maybe its impossible to understand Jimmy Stark's life, or any other one person's life through the eyes of others."

The Beat Trail

I lay in bed staring at the ceiling I couldn't sleep, I was still keyed up. I was thinking of all the things I needed to do, fast. It was my time, my future was here. I could stand on the same stage as Jim Morrison! If time and space met, maybe I could feel his ghost blow by me. I tried to sleep, I tossed and turned in bed. I couldn't sleep. I got up and dressed, packed my bag and left it by the door. I knocked on Tom's room door. After a moment he opened the door. I could see he had been lying on the bed watching TV.

"Tom, do you still have the receipts from last night's gig?" I asked.

"Yeah, why, man?" He made no move to let me in the room.

"I need them."

"Uh, I don't know if I can do that. Did you ask Swifty if it's OK?"

"I'm going to L.A. I'm going to be like the advance man, I'll get the accommodations for you and the band, and set some things up."

"I don't know, man." He didn't sound convinced but by the look on his face I knew he was convinced.

"Look, man, your uncle is going to represent me, just think of the money like an advance. A loan against future earnings." And one final push. "C'mon, man, I was the one looking out for you, making sure you got your own room. Who's encouraged you in pursuing your art without making fun of you." He still looked unmoved, "it's a loan, guaranteed, it's a lock. I'm going to have so much going on in L.A., I just have to get there early and get it all worked out."

"All right." He said, relenting. He went over to the bed, reached under it, and pulled out a locked attache case, it was the most out of character looking thing I'd ever seen him with. "There it is, a thousand dollars."

"Just tell Swifty I have the money, and I'll see you guys in L.A."

Caitlin Redux

As soon as businesses opened in the morning, I went to the nearest car rental agency and rented a car. I started driving to Caitlin, fueled by the adrenaline of playing *The Whisky*! Everything was coming together for me. Now there was only one thing left to complete, the personal as well as the professional transformation.

Eight hours later, I was standing outside her house, looking at the warm light emanating from within it. Suddenly, I didn't know what I was going to say. I hadn't really thought about it. My energy had been devoted to getting there. I had only a half formed, vague idea of what I was going to say. I rang the bell. Now, staring at Caitlin's front door, what had seemed like a good idea ten hours before, suddenly didn't seem like such a good idea. 'Of course it is,' I told myself, 'just blurt it out. Your intentions are true you know what you want. Just tell her.' Finally, the door opened.

"Michael, what're you doing here?" She asked.

"I just drove all day to see you."

"Come in." She looked perplexed, looking behind me for the rest of the band as I walked in.

"Will you marry me?" I blurted out, my adrenaline pumping again.

She stepped away from me, "um, I, I don't know what to say."

"You asked me once why I started a band. I know now it was a search for love, it was a search for you."

"That sounds like one of your well exercised lines."

"No! So? The first night we met you said one of my jokes was closer to the truth than I was willing to admit. Yes, I have told other girls I love them, but what I realized is, it's the truth with you. I was just floating it out there before, hoping the other person would make it the truth, hoping I wouldn't be rejected. I don't know, maybe I was just trying to communicate it to myself."

"So, now you have religion?" She asked, skeptically.

"I didn't realize that until just recently, I love you."

She stood there thinking a minute. "What happened on the road? Did you guys get fired? A bad review? A girl you madly loved, dump you? Something in your life is going wrong that sent you into a panic. And for some reason, you think I'm what you need to attain whatever you're looking for."

"No! Just the opposite!" I said, "everything is going great! We're going to L.A., we're going to play *The Whisky*! Then who knows what can happen from there, the sky's the limit!"

"Why me?"

"You're everything I'm looking for in a woman." She looked even more skeptical than before.

"A father with connections in Los Angeles."

"Remember when you asked me what can I do for you? It stopped me dead. No one has ever asked me that before, it meant something."

"Michael, that's so sweet," she said. I thought I saw a smile curling at the corners of her mouth, then the look dissolved, "but don't you see, you're still seeing it as what I can do for you? You still don't see me, or even us in there. Just you. You only want to be with me because of what I represent to you. Maybe that's flattering, but you're living in a fantasy world."

"What's wrong with trying to live out your fantasies?" I asked. "If some people didn't live in a fantasy world, the world wouldn't change. Jim Morrison imagined himself a star."

"Jim Morrison," she said, shaking her head. "Talk about living in a fantasy world, nice and safe that he's not alive. A dead Jim Morrison is a Jim Morrison you can handle. What about you? What does Michael Gray feel?"

"I don't know what you're trying to get at."

"That's because you're blocking it. Don't be afraid to let your defenses down, let yourself feel it. Then you won't need to be afraid of it anymore."

"I don't know what you want."

"You! Just you, Michael Gray." I thought I knew what she wanted, but I couldn't go through that door. I couldn't reach out across those seas of self, afraid to be vulnerable, I was afraid, afraid to let it hurt me "I can't." I said, finally.

"I thought for a brief shinning moment there may be some hope for you. I could almost see it in your eyes."

"What?"

"That you could forget yourself and reach out to me, but there's too much Jim Morrison there. I was part of my father's image. I don't want to be part of anyone else's fantasy anymore. I want to be part of someone's reality, you're just another collector Michael. Go to L.A., enjoy your success and forget about me."

"Listen, I know you're probably worried about stability, but I won't have to live hope to hope, see," I took the almost thousand dollars out of my pocket and put it on the table, "see, I can support you. We'll be able to be comfortable."

She picked up the receipts from the last show, "where did you get all this money Michael?"

"It's an advance." I stood there a moment. "It's mine, I earned it." I said, petulantly.

"Michael," she said calmly, letting the money slip through her fingers "I don't want to be part of the confusion of your chaos." She was mad now. "Morrison said love was the answer, who do you love? I think it's time you left."

"I need you!" I cried.

"Oh Michael, don't be so melodramatic. No one 'needs' anyone else."

"If you don't want to be with me, fine, I don't need you. I'll find someone who wants to be with me. You know," I said, as I turned for the door, "I know I made my bed a long time ago, but I thought you of all people would understand. I thought that bed would be more comfortable with you in it." Silence. She hadn't moved, no emotion flashed across her face. "Umm, can I ask you one last favor?"

"Sure." She said, brusquely.

"Uh, well, do you think you could introduce me to your father?"

"Is that what you wanted all this time?" She laughed, "that's pretty pathetic, Michael. Sure," she said resolutely. "If that's what it takes to get you off my back. You're lucky, I don't think he's touring. I'll give him a call and you can look him up when you get to town. I don't know how you think he can help you. I can't promise anything, but at least he'll probably be able to give you some advice."

At The Crossroads

A truck stop in the middle of nowhere America, somewhere Utah, it was five in the morning, I was tired but I was crossing the country at a rate even the truckers would find amazing. I didn't even know where the nearest town was, it was just the place where two highways intersected, a crossroads, x marks the spot. Morrison who was raised in the South, mentioned the crossroads quite a bit in both poetry and his lyrics. It was that time between night and day, the opposite of twilight, whatever that may be, day would soon consume the night, it was a time of all possibilities, it was waiting for the sun, a new day would begin, and a new world would await.

It was a greasy spoon of a restaurant and it seemed an all too literal of a description. The waitress came up to the counter and clattered a coffee cup down in front of me, and reached over grabbed a pot from the machine and filled the cup.

"What can I get you?" I looked up at her, she was 17, tall and lithe, her smock uniform pressed against her body following its every curve.

"What's your name?" I asked.

"Grace." She was absolutely beautiful and looked out of place here among the other waitresses, a flower growing through the concrete, a star waiting to be discovered. I smiled at her, she smiled at me. I wondered if I should ask here to come to L.A. with me, I could tell her she didn't belong here, I'd be her hero. The shifts were changing and waitresses were walking around gathering their belongings, depositing their belongings, talking amongst themselves, talking to their new customers or collecting their last tips of the night from their tables. Another waitress passed behind her who was once probably as beautiful as Grace, but that time was long gone, only the remnants of that life remained, the coiffed up hair, the make-up that took on gargoyle proportions, but they didn't see each other, Grace probably wouldn't be able to see herself in the other until it was too late. I knew if I came through here again in ten years I'd still find her here, and the years of fending off truckers, the body bending work of waitressing, and the backseat romance of gropings by boys would age her twenty years in that time, the other waitress passing would look at Grace and nostalgically see herself and know this was all true.

Grace was probably the prettiest girl in this town, like Pam was, but who was I kidding? I couldn't help Grace, I couldn't help Pam, I couldn't help Caitlin, I definitely couldn't help Wanda, they all wanted something different from me, something I couldn't give to them. I couldn't help any of the people I'd met this passed year. Before I could help any of them I had to help myself.

"Just the coffee. Thanks." I wondered where fortune would take her in life. I had to get to L.A. I had one great truth left to create, I had a new world to create.

BOOK II

LOST ANGELES

"The west is the best, get here and we'll do the rest."

Jim Morrison, The End, The Doors.

The City

I blew into L.A. streaking down the freeway, the song *L.A. Woman* blasting out of the car speakers, the wind in my hair, the music in the wind. The first thing you notice about L.A. is that it's overflowing with people, tourists, the homeless, the starstruck, it was like an old fashioned boom town, a few ghosts wandered it's streets but it was still booming, if L.A. lived off the people that were successful, the city would be awfully empty. I wanted to see all the sights of my Hollywood dreams, and I wanted to start at the beginning, I went to the 10,000 block of Sunset Boulevard to see one of those old houses built by those crazy old movie people of the 20's. I was looking for a specific address, but all I could see were flowers fenced in, dared to grow. Either I had forgotten the address, or it didn't exist. Venice Beach was my next stop, all roads lead to the ocean. I arrived in L.A. a couple of days before the band, while they drove the rickety van full of equipment. I had called Swifty and told him I was making the arrangements for the band. And I would, at my convenience. Besides, the appointment that Swifty had made for me with an agent and Caitlin arranging for me to meet her father, I had arranged a few appointments of my own.

The first reason for my early arrival in L.A. was purely utilitarian, learn the lay of the land. I had never been in L.A. before. I wanted to live in the L.A. Morrison had, experience it as he had. I decided to open myself to whatever experience came my way. Let fate and fortune be my guides. My guidebook to the fates and fortune was my well-worn copy of *No One Here Gets Out Alive*. The only acceptable guidebook I found.

Almost the second I stepped out onto Venice Beach, I felt the presence of *The Doors*. I heard, coming from a kiosk, a guy playing *Light My Fire* on an acoustic guitar. I wondered how cool it must be for Robby Krieger to come out here and hear a song he wrote twenty something years before, still being played. The echoes of *The Doors* still reverberate to this day. I thought it was a good omen. In keeping with my philosophy of seeing L.A. the way Morrison had, I trudged through the sand down the beach to smoke a joint. I sat down digging my feet into the warm sand. There were people all around me, but everyone had staked out their territory and no one was paying any attention to what anyone else was doing. I dug the joint and lighter out of my pants pocket, lit it, and inhaled the dusky smoke.

"Welcome to the edge of the continent." I said to myself, "you can't go any farther without falling off." I kept the joint cupped in my hand. Every once in awhile I looked around furtively to make sure no cops were coming up behind me. I watched a woman walking along the shoreline close to the water, whenever a wave would wash up she walked just a little higher up the beach to avoid the water, unconsciously mimicking the sandpipers. I saw a guy walking across the beach he stood out from everyone else, he was wearing sandy khaki's and a striped shirt that looked like it'd been on a few days, and he was walking as fast as he could across the beach, he must have seen me too, he came right up to me

"Hey, dude, can you give me a hit?"

"I thought I was being cautious." I said, as I handed him the joint.

"Nah, I spotted you from down there." He said, pointing to the water.

"Where you going man?"

"Mexico, want to come along?"

"Mexico?"

"Yeah, I took some speed last night and I decided to walk to Mexico, I just figured I'd follow the shoreline all the way down."

"What're you going to do when you get there?"

"I don't know dude, have a beer. People down there will just give you quarters and you don't need as much to live as up here, and you can sleep on the beach and it's pure white sand, not dirty sand like this."

"Good luck."

"Thanks." He said handing the joint back to me, and he was off again heading down the beach. I don't know where he started, or how much speed he'd taken but I wondered where would he wake up when he crashed? At the end of this dirty beach? Or on the crystal beach of the Mexico of his dreams?

I took another hit off the joint. Ray tells the story of how he met Jim on the beach. One afternoon he was sitting on the beach meditating when he sees Jim Morrison walking down the beach, Ray calls him over and asks what he's been doing, Jim says writing some songs, Ray asks him to sing one, Jim sings *Moonlight Drive*, and Ray says those are the best Rock 'n' Roll lyrics he's ever heard and they should start a band and make a million dollars, and Jim says that's exactly what he had in mind. It's become almost a scripted response to interviewer's questions, but he tells the story as if it were a Rock 'n' Roll inevitability, predestined. But Morrison didn't come to L.A. to be a rock star. He came for the same reason everybody else comes to L.A., he wanted to be in the movies, he wanted to make them. At UCLA his films were met with derision. His films were 'poetic and nonlinear.' He was undisciplined and had the sixties taste for the experimental. Leaving film school with no prospects for a film career in sight. The movie industry at the time was run by old men, the businessmen who had started the studios fifty years before, modeling their studios after Henry Ford's assembly line, art was an after thought or an accident. They saw no profit in Godardesque films. Morrison didn't have the skills for success in the movie business. But in the music world he was a remarkable vehicle for his times, for those very same reasons. Rock 'n' Roll as a business hadn't yet solidified. No one knew what would be successful. The bands that played the strip reflected this collage of styles from *The Byrds* to *Frank Zappa*, *Buffalo Springfield* to *The Doors*. The men who ran the record companies, if they wanted to break into Rock 'n' Roll, had to rely on the advice of their younger producers. There were 'no experts.' It was an experimental industry for everyone concerned. But those days in music and movies were long over. I had no such delusions about art and industry. I was going to get the part of Morrison in that movie. I knew what people wanted to see and I was gonna give it to them! I finished the joint and sat watching the waves. The gulls swooped and dived at the bounty of the sea's harvest. Time seemed to bunch up out here. You can watch the sunrise on tomorrow, while it sets on today. Then I saw bubbles shimmering in the waves that seemed to be a dragon riding in the roiling surf. "Wow." I knew the boardwalk would be more fun now.

The boardwalk was a Renaissance faire. A kaleidoscope of swirling colors, people and shops. There were T-shirt stores, bookstores, restaurants, tarot readers, sand sculptors, roller blading guitar players, political activists, incense makers, astrologists, numerologists looking for god in the numbers, and the homeless dressed either for a meteorological apocalypse or the tropics, the deformed and reformed. Not bad for an area that Robbby Krieger once described in an interview as 'no one used to come down here except the bums.' A dreadlocked hippie came out of the crowd up to me,

"Dude, you wanna buy some 'shrooms."

"No thanks." I said, as I watched him melt back into the crowd. I wondered if the Chamber of Commerce paid him to be local color, or if he was an undercover cop. I wondered if they realize how much they owe to Jim Morrison and the legend of *The Doors*. Of course, they couldn't very well put a bare chested sculpture with a plaque on it that read, 'Jim Morrison dropped a lot of acid here.' Could they? I walked down the boardwalk trying to take it all in. Then rising above some low buildings I saw it. On the side of a blue building, a bare chested leather clad mural of Morrison. I stood in the middle of the boardwalk studying it. I was like a rock in a river, everything flowing around me. After leaving UCLA and not knowing what he wanted to do, Morrison spent the summer living on a friend's rooftop where he wrote poems that became the basis of the first two *Doors* albums, I know of no greater act of alchemy than of turning words into gold. You can still feel that vibe of creation in the air there were a lot of dread-locked poets walking around the beach with notebooks stuffed with poems, everyone in L.A. was here for the same reason, they wanted to create something, they wanted to change the world, they wanted to create a new world! The air was practically humming, I felt like the guy walking to Mexico, I could feel the vibrations surging through my body with the excitement of that creation, and when I was done here which beach would I awake to find myself on?

I walked around to the alley behind the building, the mural wasn't on the building, it was in the paint. It looked like tiny waves of stucco had washed across the face of the building and out of the froth and foam Morrison's mural was left. It was a pontillistic Morrison. The expression on the mural, pupils dilated, a glazed over look on the face, Jim looked stoned. I wondered if this was someone's way of signaling that this was Morrison's rooftop perch where he had visions of rock concerts in his head. It looked like it could be the building. There was a fire escape up the back and a rail over the lip of the top of the building. It matched the descriptions I had read and how I imagined it would be. It is generally assumed Jim met Ray accidentally that day on the beach, both Ray and Jim told the story that way. They knew a good tale when they heard it. And maybe Ray never realized, it wasn't an accident. Jim knew Ray was in a band, and Jim had been in one of Ray's movies, so he knew where Ray lived. All Jim had to do was hang out until Ray showed up. It's Rock 'n' Roll's version of the myth of Lana Turner being 'discovered' in Schwabs Pharmacy. It's romantic, but only half the truth. Jim didn't 'bump' into Ray. Jim was looking for Ray.

I wondered what Morrison would be like if he was one of the bare chested, dreadlocked kids on the beach today, carrying around a notebook stuffed with poems. Would anybody pay him any notice? I tried to picture what he would look like if he were an up and coming rock star. I had a vision of a Morrison for a new century, the leather would still be there, of course, strategically ripped or tattered. There would be a nipple ring, some other piercings, definitely tattoos. Maybe, 'Jesus, save us babe' across one breast or above his groin. The band would probably still be called *The Doors*. That would still be a freaky name for a band, but what type of music would they be playing? Punk? Rap?

In an interview in the later part of his career Morrison was asked if he would do anything differently. He said, "I think I would have gone for the quiet, undemonstrative artist, plodding away in his own garden." Would the new century Morrison have made another choice, poet? Or had he lived, would it be like Robby feared, Morrison was destined for Vegas like Elvis? A parody of his former self in leather pants and an oversize belt buckle. Playing to an aging but adoring audience trying to recapture their youth.

As I walked back to my car, I saw a flyer stapled to a telephone pole. John Densmore was going to be playing with the poet Robert Bly. I wondered if all the remaining *Doors* were going to tour with their own personal poet.

After I left the beach, I drove around Los Angeles listening to *L.A. Woman*, the album was conceived as L.A. in microcosm, so it made a natural soundtrack for seeing the city, it's a great way to see the city. I noticed that the different areas of L.A., Venice, Santa Monica, Westwood, at one time had been separate entities. Cities in their own right, the suburbs of Los Angeles, but over the years with the influx of people, it had melded into one huge metro area. Yet, not quite homogenous, Koreatown speaks for itself, Westwood had a middle-eastern community, but all had lost individual identity to greater Los Angeles, a city from mountain to ocean, a victim of those seeking fame and fortune. Jim Morrison was right, the concept of the city is based on a circle, at least this one was. The streets ran East and West, North and South. It was easy, you couldn't get lost. It was the machinations of the city itself that got you lost in those circles. Depending on your perspective, it was either Dante's circles of Hell, or the Renaissance belief in the different levels of Heaven.

By the time the song *L.A. Woman* came to the line, "if they say I never loved you, know they are a liar." It seemed to me that it was a purposeful restatement of *Light My Fire*, "you know it would be untrue/you know I would be a liar/if I was to say to you/girl, we couldn't get much higher". At the beginning of Morrison's career, even though his vision was dark, it was optimistic. The lyrics to *The Crystal*

Ship illustrate this the best, "deliver me from reasons why/you'd rather cry/I'd rather fly." However, by *L.A. Woman* the optimism was gone, "a cold girl'll kill you/in a darkened room." Even though Morrison didn't write *Light My Fire* it was the song most closely associated with him, there seemed to be a circularity of theme, the restatement, a purposeful summing up, Morrison's circle of the city.

I drove downtown, into the city proper. I walked the streets of L.A. getting to know the streets I would soon make mine. Sort of the inverse tour Morrison took in his last days in L.A. where he seemed to be trying to memorize the city. I visited Morrison's haunts. I walked up into the neighborhoods, Beverly Hills, then over to Norton Avenue where Morrison once lived, and struggled with his common law wife/girlfriend Pam. The neighborhoods were like any other quiet suburban neighborhood, insulated from the urban noises and sounds right outside the square of the neighborhood. They were cool and green, like putting on a pair of sunglasses.

Walking down Santa Monica boulevard to the Alta Cienega Motel I saw two homeless homosexuals, one pulling at the pants zipper of the other, I ducked through the entrance of the Alta Cienega before I witnessed some street level sex act. I came out under an archway into the enclosed court yard parking lot, the motel was two story's and it took me a moment to find the small tar shack office that was against the far wall of the building. I walked into the office, it was cramped inside and behind the counter sitting watching TV was the owner, an aging Chinese man. He showed me one of the rooms, they were small, with a bed, a TV, and the ceiling was only wooden slats.

"Are all the rooms like this?" I asked a bit disappointed.

"Yes."

"What about Morrison's room?"

"Morrison's room?"

"Yeah, room 32. Were you the owner in the 60's?"

"No." He sighed, "c'mon." I followed him around the balcony of the upper floor, he opened the door to number 32. I could tell this was the deluxe room of the motel it was a little larger than the others and had a plastered ceiling. It was the room Morrison preferred, it was still just four walls, a cheap TV, a bed, but it was the dramas, comedy, sadness that was invested in the plaster, years of graffiti covered the walls, notes to Morrison, poems by faithful fans inspired to art. I could understand why fans fought to inhabit the same space Morrison had. Perhaps a chance to tap into some revenant energy, or maybe a chance to pick up some inspiration in the form of some loose DNA that still might be floating around. This was Morrison's refuge when he and Pam weren't getting along, and it was the center of his universe at the height of his fame. Everything he needed was all within stumbling distance of the motel, the recording studio, *The Doors'* offices, Themis, Pam's boutique, their Norton street apartment, and Barney's Beanery.

"I'll take it." I said. I don't know what I did to arouse the owners suspicions but from then on whenever I would come in or go out he would be standing at the office door glowering at me.

Day of the Living Dead

I woke up early the next morning, too early. But I couldn't get back to sleep, I was too excited, I was going to meet Caitlin's father, Jerry Osprey! One of the things I wanted to do in L.A. was to find a writer. In the same issue of *Variety* that I saw the notice of the impending *Doors* movie, I found an ad for a freelance writer in the classifieds section. While I waited for the day to begin, I flipped through the TV channels reliving my childhood. Watching reruns of *The Brady Bunch*, *The Beverly Hillbillies*, and *Gilligan's Island*. Morrison mentioned TV frequently in his poems, convinced we were becoming voyeurs to our own lives instead of participants. Finally, I couldn't take it anymore. Dawn's light was creeping over the horizon so I decided to walk off some of my energy.

The early morning streets were quiet and a haze hung in the air. Walking down the street I saw a prostitute. As she passed by she asked, "you wanna date?" she was dressed in a dirty short white dress. Through the thin fabric I could see she wasn't wearing a bra. Like Kerouac, Morrison liked to frequent the skidrow side of town but he was a tourist on the seamier side of life, he could walk out any time he wanted. I on the other hand could find myself caught here, enmeshed in the day to day tribulations of survival, caught in the lives of those around me.

I walked fast and soon found myself on Hollywood Boulevard. I was surprised to see the streets alive with people, all at discrete angles to each other. Drag queen Madonnas, boys standing around practicing looking stunning, hoping for the day someone will ask them to pose; and runaway kids with dirty hair and dirtier *Pennywise* T-shirts, the homeless in the corners and crevices of the dirty streets. Occasionally, one or two would crawl over the concrete, reminding me of *The Night of the Living Dead*. Morrison was right to emphasize tragedy in his songs. L.A. is a tragic place. From mansions to people sleeping in the streets, all within a couple of blocks of each other. I felt a hand grab me.

"Help a guy out?" The voice beseeched.

"Sorry, I can't."

"Check your pockets."

"Fuck off." I said, pulling free of his grip. I walked a little farther down the street when I heard another voice cry out of the wilderness.

"Somebody give me some money to get drunk!" I looked down at the guy sitting on the sidewalk, his face was dirty and unshaven, his clothes ripped way past being fashionable, a cigarette resting between two fingers, more filter than anything else. But I recognized him. Through all the dirt he still looked like himself. He was America's little boy, everybody's brother or friend, he was a child star of my childhood, even though, like most child stars, he hadn't quite grown into his face. He stabbed out the remains of the cigarette on the sidewalk. The Walk of the Stars, where every tourist in the world comes to gawk. I looked at the name on the star in front of him, it was his, Jimmy Stark. "It's like visiting your own grave." He said, "which is what a lot of L.A. is like anyway. Scrape away the dirt and underneath you'll find the stars."

"Then it is you? You are him?"

"Yeah, I'm me." He said, a bit wearily. "You a tourist?"

"Not really."

"You have any money?" He asked.

"Some."

"How would you like to see the real L.A.? What the tourists are really looking for, but get ripped off on every time."

"It sounds intriguing, but . . . ."

"Don't you wanna hear the rest of my pitch first?" He said, impatiently. "I've been everything and nothing in this town, from star to street. I can show you things and tell you stories no tour guide could possibly know."

"How much?" I asked.

"A hundred bucks a day, and a place where I can wash up and a couple of meals." I considered it. "No, can't sorry."

Then he said loudly, "You know most people who walk down this street avert their eyes and try not to see, but I want to see, what about you?"

"See what?"

"The truth, the city you're really here to see. Maybe the city you're afraid to see." He said motioning back towards the homeless guy I had rebuffed earlier.

"I don't know the streets well enough to drive around, yet." I said.

"I can drive you around to your appointments, and point things out. We got a deal?" He asked, extending his hand. It seemed like it could be fun. Jimmy Stark was known for his wild nights in Hollywood, maybe he could find a party or something later.

"C'mon, I'm starting an entourage." I joked.

"All right, the price is the same though."

"All right," I said, "let's go back to my motel."

I came back to the motel room with two breakfasts of huevos rancheros wrapped in tinfoil. Jimmy had washed up and changed into clean clothes, mine.

"I hope you don't mind?" He said, seeing me notice the clothes, "but which is better, a clean former child star, or a reeking transient?"

"I see your point." I said. We lay on the bed eating the breakfasts and watching TV, 'Family Muse' came on. He couldn't take his eyes off the TV.

"I think we need to amend the Constitution," he said, "to include the right of everyone to be on TV." Then the image of Sandra Wright, his TV mom, came on the screen.

"I had a crush on her when I was a kid." I said.

"Me too," Jimmy said. "The difference is, I did her."

"What?"

"It was a few years after the show ended, you have to remember when the show was on she was only in her mid-thirties, and she's still beautiful. It's the only way to do your mom without any Freudian repercussions."

"It is?" I asked.

"Well, maybe a few." He laughed.

When we were finished eating I asked him, "what happened?"

"What do you mean, what happened?"

"How'd you get to living on the street?"

"Well," he said, giving himself a second to think, "I lived in a bigger make believe world than most kids when I was on TV. And when the show was over and I was thrust back into the real world, I didn't know anything else, so I sought the comforting unreality drugs provide. Basically, I traded on what little talent I had, I traded on my cuteness, I traded on my looks, and I traded on my celebrity. I traded on everything until there wasn't anything else left to trade on. I just always thought there'd be more."

"So you left show business?"

"You know how before you die you're supposed to see your life flashing by?"

"Yeah."

"Well, it is my life flashing by on that screen." He said, gesturing at the TV, where the child Jimmy still cavorted, running, and playing. "I couldn't watch those ghosts anymore."

"Yeah, I guess I can see that." I said, feeling sorry for him.

"Come on, don't feel bad," he said, swaying towards me playfully. "I've lived the life I wanted to. I've had a lot of experiences writers would kill for. I've had girlfriends rock stars would be jealous of. I've lived in houses and places the rich only dream of, and oh yeah, I had a lot of fun." I looked at the clock.

"C'mon we gotta get going."

"Where we going?" Jimmy asked.

"To see Jerry Osprey."

"You know him?"

"Not yet."

"I always liked his music," Jimmy said, "although I always thought the name Jerry and The Osprey's sounded like it should be a surf music band."

Jerry And The Osprey's

Jimmy was driving us back into the hills to Jerry's Laurel Canyon address that Caitlin had given me. He was taking the turns and curves pretty fast, but there was a certain confidence in his reckless abandon. He wasn't scared, so neither was I. The top was down on the car and flowers scented the air. I was getting off on being chauffeured around by someone famous, no matter how far removed. I flipped through the pages of *No One Here* and told Jimmy, "we have to go on Rothdell Drive."

"No we don't, not to get to the address you gave me."

"Just go that way." I said. As we rounded Rothdell, Jimmy turned up the street and I discovered the house Jim and Pam had lived in, that Morrison had memorialized in song. On the front lawn was a totem pole that had Morrison's, Hendrix's and Joplin's likenesses. The house was a wooden frame but looked like no one had lived in it in a while or hadn't taken care of it, I could see the wood on the porch was splintered and weather beaten, I felt the urge to go pry off a piece of the wood, I guess it would be proof that I was there like having a relic of the one true cross, but I resisted the urge it all was beginning to feel like a pilgrimage to a past, not the discovery of the future I was looking for. "I see you live on love street." I mumbled.

"What?"

"Nothing, just part of a song." Jimmy eased the car down the road and around a corner, and there was a store that had a large white façade that said 'Canyon Country Store,' it had a wooden front porch that looked like any general store off Main street, or out of Mayberry and that without much imagining I could see it hadn't changed that much since 1968. "The store where the creatures meet."

After my sightseeing detour of Morrison's life, it was time to get back to the reality of my unfolding life. Jimmy found the address. Soon, we were standing on the front porch of a wooden beam house. I rang the doorbell. It took a moment or two of Jimmy and me looking around, smiling politely at each other before the door was opened by a beautiful blonde girl holding a baby in one arm.

"Yes?" She asked.

"I'm here to see Jerry Osprey."

"Are you Michael?"

"Yeah."

"Come in." She said, holding the door open for us. We walked into a bright naturally lit, open space with a lot of wood and natural materials, a stairway ran up the side of the room to the second floor, and the girl walked over to an intercom on the foyer wall, pressed a button and said, "Jerry someone to see you." Then turned back to me, "he'll be right down, Caitlin called and told us all about you," she said, "oh, I'm Dana, Jerry's wife." She held out her free hand to shake, I shook it, "and this is Sam." She said bouncing the baby.

"Samantha or Samuel?" Jimmy asked.

"Samantha." A man's voice answered, coming from the stairs. I turned to see a barefooted man in jeans, his long gray hair pulled back into a pony tail, coming down the stairs, "thank you, honey." He said, kissing Dana. She looked like she was younger than Caitlin. I wondered how that all worked out. He tosseled the baby's wispy blond hair.

"Oh, this is . . ."

"Jimmy Stark." Jerry said.

"How'd you know?" I asked.

"Don't you know, everybody in L.A. knows each other." He said, with a wink. "It's worse than mentioning a high school and people ask if you knew Joe Blow or Cathy Smith. C'mon let's go into the living room." We followed Jerry into the next room. Dana went the other way. Jerry noticed us watching her leave.

"Pretty good, huh? One of the perks of being a living legend, she's my third wife. We have children and hold such high hopes for them to create a new world, but we start to let them down right away, conditioning them in the same old ways and nothing new is accomplished, so I'm trying to make up for my past mistakes, staying home with the kid, and being a good father. I try to make it up to Caitlin, too." The house was open and airy. It had lots of windows, the sun shining in. Outside the patio doors was a rather large yard for L.A. The grass was green and some pretty pink flowers were growing on the fence that surrounded the yard.

We all stood staring out at the yard. Jerry broke the silence, "oh man, I've lived here forever. Look at those houses out there. A real neighborhood now, but I don't think I know any of the people in those houses. Back in the sixties, when there weren't so many houses and they were further apart, I <u>did</u> know almost everyone who lived up here. I remember Jackson Browne lived around here, David Crosby, Peter Tork for god's sakes. It was an artists community, we were all young. And if we weren't in the music business proper, we were musicians playing for the joy of being alive. Making music that no one else had heard before. I remember one of us would write a song and walk over to Crosby's or whoever's house, play the song, smoke a joint, and then someone else would come over, then someone else would show up. Some really famous parties started just by going over to someone's house with a song." Then he ended his reverie and looked at us, "but you boys didn't come up here to hear me babble about the past."

"No, it's great to hear those stories." I said.

"Have a seat guys. So, you're friends with Caitlin?"

"I met her on a tour of my *Doors* cover band."

"Oh, how history does like to repeat itself."

"I don't think that'll be a problem." I said.

"That's too bad. Caitlin turned out all right in spite of me, or maybe despite me. A *Doors* cover band, huh? How come no one wants to do a cover band of me?"

"That would be cool." Jimmy said.

"Nah, I still need to make a living touring. *The Doors* don't, certainly not Morrison." Jerry said, shaking his head in amazement. "The fucking *Doors*, Morrison was a dick!" He said, then thought about it, "but then so was I. It was a little past my hits and the start of the living legend crap, and he was on his way up. I probably took myself a little too seriously. I'll tell you, if you want to feel already dead, being called a living legend will do it. You gotta give it to Morrison he probably played the cards right, leave them wanting more, if he had lived he'd probably be in my shoes, a living legend, but who bought my last album? Much less know there is one. But you know, every once in awhile one of the old songs makes it into a movie and sparks some interest in the old musicarino. And a few months later I trot out to my mailbox and pickup a nice juicy royalty check. Not bad for a few hours of writing I did almost thirty years ago, and I suppose when I die what I've done lately will be worth something."

"Caitlin said you toured with *The Doors*," I said. "Did you ever talk with him?" Before he could answer, "did you ever have a beer with him? What was he like?"

"Hold on. Morrison was a just a guy who happened to be in the same business as I was, who I happened to meet a few times. He was a little younger than me and seemed a little fucked up. I don't understand how Manzarek and the others who knew Morrison can keep answering the same questions over and over again. But it does explain why they haven't hit the mass popular audience since Morrison died, because, everything they do is tinged by Morrison, the legend, nothing they do can ever live up to the legend. I don't think even *The Stones* had to deal with that when Brian died." He looked at me, then smiled, it was a peaceful calm, calming look, like a priest. "But that doesn't help you much. What can I do for you?" I heard in that Caitlin's plaintive voice asking the same question.

"I was hoping you would have some contacts and that maybe you could introduce me to some of your friends in the industry?"

"Whatdya do?"

"*The Doors* cover band thing."

"You sing?"

"Yeah, but I'm not really a singer. I can't write songs or music. I'm up for a part in a movie"

"What movie?"

"They're going to make a movie about Jim Morrison."

"Oh, you're an actor?"

"Not really, I've been doing Morrison for a year now. I've read just about everything there is about him. I know how'd he react in any situation."

"What about a part in the next movie? Or the part after that?"

"My story?" I ventured, "or, maybe I'll write a book on *The Doors*. I'll be the foremost authority on them. Then when anything *Doors* related happens, they'll call me asking for my thoughts and ideas on the subject. And everybody will be hanging off my every word."

"Wow. I can really see what Caitlin meant." I wondered what he meant by that. "Then you'll end up in the same boat as *The Doors*. No matter what else you do in life, they'll always ask you about Morrison. Don't you want to create something for yourself? Of yourself?" I didn't know if it was a rhetorical question or not. "Look, you seem a true believer in the myth of Morrison. You have to remember the legend always did more drugs, slept with more women, jumped higher, and ran faster than the man. I've heard stories about me and I wish I had been there." He looked at me, shaking his head. "And to tell you the truth Michael, any contacts I had are twenty-five years old or older. I go out on tour once or twice a year now and those aren't the big promoters any more.

And every once in a while, it's one of those nostalgia festival rock shows where the receipts are split between five or six bands. As for recording, none of the record companies want to record me, not even the small independent one's. I don't think I can be of much help to you." Jerry looked at me thoughtfully and said, "what do you see when you look at me?" I didn't know how to answer. "I'll tell you what you see, an unreconstructed hippie. And now that I'm looking down the leg end of legend as it were, the only thing I know is I managed to keep my idealism intact. In the sixties we sung of freedom, flowers, and love." He said, a faraway look in his eyes, "and those damn songs of peace, love, flowers and hippies are what's left of my idealistic youth. We were almost like real troubadours. I had my heroin period, acid, coke, pot, booze. And this is what I'm down to." He said, lighting a cigarette, "and I'm trying to quit. Sometimes I wondered if all that idealism was just platitudes, words to be mouthed. So I decided to live by my lyrics. The point is I came out the other side, idealism restored. I've been around this town long enough to know that actors can tell the false reality of the situation because as soon as he walks onto a set he's in the fantasy but he can still see the reality behind the fantasy, he can see the cameras, the crew, when a rock star walks out onto the stage all he sees is the seas of adoring fans and the adulation they're giving you, it's the seduction. Isn't that what you saw on stage?"

"I don't get what you're trying to say." I said.

"I gave myself the chance that Morrison didn't have, or maybe didn't allow himself. Jimmy knows. You better be careful if you're just pursuing fame for the sake of fame. You'll be severely disappointed. Rock 'n' Roll really isn't about sex, drugs, and Rock 'n' Roll. Maybe it's not even about the music." He stopped and thought a moment, "no, I guess it has to be about the music, doesn't it? It's about changing the world. Look how its changed the world. Rock 'n' Roll should be in a continuous state of revolution. Morrison got that one right. Look, I never wanted to be famous. I was just this little cat who wanted to play the guitar better than anyone else. Everything else was an accident, no one even thought we could make a living at it for a life time, it was something to do for a while when you're young, have some fun, make an artistic statement, and maybe make a little money before getting real jobs and becoming a productive member of society. Hell, when I started the only person that made a lot of money in Rock 'n' Roll was Elvis."

We walked out of the house and I lost it, "screw him! Washed up old hippie, he's the past. I don't need Jerry Osprey. Onto the future."
"Where's that, man?"
"Hollywood, my good man, Hollywood."

Writers on the Storm

We pulled up in front of a u-shaped apartment building that opened into a courtyard, the address the writer gave me. Jimmy and I walked up to the apartment. It looked like I was expected, the inside door was opened and I could hear the TV show *The Price Is Right* coming from inside. I knocked on the screen door, loudly. A woman came to the door, she was in a bathrobe and looked to be in her mid to late 40's. Her hair was disheveled, she didn't have any make-up on, and she was swaying a little.
"Michael?" She asked.
"Yes, I'm here to see Tory Pearson."
"I'm Tory. Who's this?" She asked looking Jimmy over.
"Jimmy Stark, the star of Family Muse. Remember that show?" This didn't seem to impress her. "He's kind of my entourage," I said.
"Come on in," she said as she flipped the latch on the screen door. The apartment wasn't that big. There was a desk in the middle of the room with a typewriter on it surrounded by a mess of papers. A cigarette smoldered in an ashtray, next to it, a half filled glass of whiskey. A crack ran through one wall behind a picture that was askew it gave me a queasy feeling, like we were perpetually in an earthquake. Sitting in a chair opposite the desk was a barrel chested man intently watching the TV, he was also dressed in a bathrobe, but his was open, belted at the waist with a leather belt. His hair was

gray and black, Bryl Creamed back, there was a bluish tint to it. His beard was stubbly gray. There was something Hemingwayesque about him. "This is Joe." She said introducing the man. Jimmy sauntered in behind me.

"Hey Joe!" Jimmy said.

"Oh, shit." Joe said, seeing Jimmy, then took a slug from a glass sitting on a TV tray in front of him.

"You know each other?" Tory asked.

"Yeah, he played the lead in Tender Fury." Joe said, brusquely.

"It is, after all, a small company town." Jimmy said sarcastically.

"And drove me up the wall," Joe said off handedly.

"Yeah, but I was nominated for an academy award."

"Fucking actors," Joe rumbled, "can't even start to be, without a writer writing it."

"You're in the movie business, Joe?" I asked.

"Joe wrote the novel Tender Fury." Tory said.

"I loved that book!" I enthused, "it's a classic!"

"The movie screwed up my book."

"How'd they do that?" I asked.

"They tacked on a happy ending and got it wrong!"

"Hollywood's heavily into wish fulfillment," Jimmy said.

"You should know," Joe said, belligerently. "Hollywood loves the happy ending, but in Hollywood you can't have a happy ending. From the starlet who ends up a hooker, to the happily married star who suddenly gets a divorce."

"They're just supplying what everybody is looking for," Jimmy said. "And what they can't find."

"The problem is they're supplying an answer they don't take in their own lives, they love the bucolic small town middle America virtues; the exact opposite of the choices they made. The city is built on this fault." Joe said and swallowed some whiskey from his glass. "All I have is the truth, and the truth is you're not going to get the happy ending, not if life has anything to do with it."

"Are you out here writing a screenplay?" I asked, trying to change the subject.

"No, I write books that others make into movies. I'm a writer in the old fashioned sense of the term, L'escritor." He said, with a flourish, writing in the air with a finger.

"Are you working on anything new?"

"Read, breed, or retreat, I've chosen retreat." He said, finishing his whiskey. He turned his attentions back to the TV, with some relief on my part. I turned to the business I'd come for.

"Tory, have you written anything I would know?"

"I wrote the book Breaker and the screenplay for the movie. Do you know it?"

"No. Is it fiction?"

"Nonfiction, it happened to me and my husband, he was a cop. I was kidnapped and a lot of people died. The episode really screwed up our lives, it made all the papers."

"I must've missed it, what happened?" I asked.

"It's hard to explain if you weren't there. I mean, he wasn't my husband when it all started but I fell in love with him, and when it was all over, I discovered he'd betrayed me. But where else could I go? Maybe I let the circumstances control me, but who else could understand? After all the horror, I chose love. It was a life or death situation, good and evil, black and white. When you're pushed together like that how can you not help falling in love? Love conquers all, right?"

"It sounds pretty intense." I said.

"It was, but it was really only a few minutes out of our lives. Moments that were a little too real, if you know what I mean," she said, taking a swig from the glass of whiskey. I shook my head knowingly. "But you know there are really only a few moments in our lives where life and death is decided. Moments which can either make us heroes or reveal us to be what we are, human, afraid."

"That sounds about right," I said.

"That's from the book," she said, finishing the whiskey.

"I remember the movie now. You don't look like the girl who played you."

"She was beautiful wasn't she? Even after she was supposed to be kidnapped and tortured. The irony is when we met her she wasn't beautiful. I guess in L.A. you just need the potential to be beautiful. The potential to be something other than yourself."

"All stories are true sooner or later, boy." Joe said, obstreperously interjecting from his chair. "Unless it's science fiction or some crap like that."

"Then reel life takes over, if you know what I mean," Tory said. I must not have looked like I knew what she meant. "Like reel, as in a movie." I shook my head yes. "And you go to all the glamorous parties, the premieres and you don't even notice the clock is ticking on your fifteen minutes of fame. The question is, what do you do when the movie's over? What are you supposed to do you do in that sixteenth minute?"

"Uh, yeah." I said. I didn't know what to say and was trying to think of ways to change the subject again. "How long have you guys been married Joe?"

"Joe's not my husband," Tory said. "My husband is probably out trolling the bars hoping one of the girls who played Jimmy's sister on Family Muse comes in. So, Michael," she continued, "what are you looking for a writer for?"

"I need someone to write my story," I said.

"And what's that?" She asked.

"MY story, the true story of my life. I want it to be the story of an everyman who comes from nowhere and makes it big. I want it to be a real Horatio Alger story!"

"People don't want to hear the truth, they want a story they can believe is the truth," Joe bellowed.

"Shusssh," Tory hissed at Joe, before turning back to me. "I just have one question, who are you?"

"What?"

"Who are you? And why would anyone want to read YOUR story?" She forcefully expelled a cloud of cigarette smoke in my direction and propped her arm up in the air, agitatedly flicking the cigarette between her fingers.

"I'm in a band, I sing."

"Which band?"

"I don't know if you've heard . . ."

"Hold it right there," she said, "if you don't know if we've heard of your band, how do you expect anyone else to have heard of it?" She sounded irate, then the expression on her face relented a little, "OK, let's try this. Do you have a literary agent?"

"No."

"Do you have an advance from a publisher for your story?"

"No."

"Do you have any interest from a publisher?"

"No."

"Well, how do you propose to pay for my services?"

"Half interest in the book upon its publication." She looked over at Joe, deeply concerned, who was finishing off another glass of whiskey.

"Let me get this right, you want me to write your book on spec? That means speculation."

"You know," Joe started to say in his oversize tones, "you look neither blank enough to write a story upon, nor interesting enough to write about?"

"What if you don't hold up your end of the bargain?" Tory asked.

"I've never backed out of a deal in my life."

"I have books published. My work has a market value," she said. "Let me give you some friendly advice, when you're ready to have a biography or an autobiography written, writers will be coming to you. Until then, go see a movie, read a book."

"Hey kid!" Joe bellowed out the door, as Jimmy and I walked to the car, "all stories should end in death, the death of the hero. Give us a call when you're dead!"

Barney's

I whipped the rental car, tires squealing, into the parking lot of the Alta Cienega. The Chinese owner of the motel came to the door of his office. He'd been watching my comings and goings ever since I checked in. I don't know if he thought I was a troublemaker, or if the aura of chaos that surrounded Morrison clung a little too closely. The appearance of Jimmy that morning didn't seem to ease his concerns. I nodded at him as we walked passed the office and out onto Santa Monica Boulevard. We crossed the street and went to *Barney's Beanery*.

Barney's Beanery was a shoebox shaped building and looked a little out of place of the surrounding buildings, but was from a different time. It had started life as a roadside cafe on Route 66 beside a poinsettia farm. It seemed like it could be any roadside cafe that existed off of route 66, except that movie stars embraced Barney's early, chauffeurs would line the street picking up their employer's hamburgers. There was a bar as you walked in, all the tables were booths, a pool table in one room, and newly squeezed in the back by the restrooms, pinball machines and video games. The decor covered the walls with the quirky miscellany found in art classrooms or corporate restaurants masquerading as quirky local hot spots.

"A Bushmill's and ginger ale." I barked out to the bartender, "make it a double. What dya' want?" I asked Jimmy.

"A beer." I slammed the first Bushmill's in a gulp.

"I've never been so fucking humiliated in my life, and it's only, what time is it?"

"About two," Jimmy said.

"Jesus! What a morning!" A tall blond came in and sat next to us at the bar. I noticed she put a taped up rolodex down on the bar as she sat down. I nudged Jimmy a little to draw his attention to her.

"Hi." I said.

"Hi," she said as the bartender came up to her, "whiskey sour."

"Pretty heavy drink this early?" I asked.

"I like the cherries," she said, smiling wickedly.

"What's your name?"

"Gina."

"Nice to meet you Gina, I'm Michael and this is Jimmy Stark. He's my entourage." I said, liking the idea more and more each time I said it.

"*The* Jimmy Stark?"

"That's me," he said, "I'm just showing him some of the sights. How're you?"

"Well let's see, I got fired last week and today my daughter tells me her boyfriend is in jail."

"You must be so proud." I said, smugly.

"That's why the whiskey sour." She took the cherry out of her drink and sucked on it.

"Can I ask, what's that?" I said, nodding at the rolodex.

"The fruits of my labor." She looked at me like that should've been a good enough answer.

"Oh, well, you don't look old enough to have a daughter that old." I said.

"Oh, that's so sweet," she said. "Do you mean it, or is it a line?"

I smiled, "it's my second day in L.A. and . . ."

"So, what're you doing in town sailor?" She asked.

"Career stuff." I said, downing the other Bushmill's and motioning the bartender for another.

"Dude, everybody's in L.A. for career stuff'"

"So what do you, I mean, did you do?" I asked.

"Former personal assistant for a record producer."

"Oh, yeah?" I asked. My interest piqued, "my band is playing at *The Whisky* this weekend."

"That sounds really cool. So what're you doing sitting in Barney's drinking?"

"Oh, the usual stuff, a bad meeting I'm trying to shake off. But on the good side, I met Jimmy here." I said, slapping Jimmy on the back.

"We met a couple of writers," Jimmy said to Gina, laughing. "You should have seen them, they were pretty drunk and got pretty loud, pretty fast when they found out we didn't have a check for them."

"Sounds like a pretty good movie to me."

"I was trying for a book deal actually."

"I'm sorry."

"That's all right," I said, finishing my drink. "I still have the band."

"Well, be careful what you ask for here, you just may get it."

"Good," I said, smugly. "I'm tired of being a big fish in a small pond. I want to make it big."

"Again, that's everybody in L.A.," she said, "and this isn't a pond, it's the fucking ocean, with all the same kinds of creatures, including some sea monsters." She chugged down the rest of her drink and said, "c'mon lover, let's go." she got up from her stool and waited patiently for me to make my decision.

"Where to?" I asked.

"I have a friend who works at a movie studio I have to meet. Wanna' come?"

"Sure, why not!"

A couple of minutes later we were in her convertible flying down the boulevards, popping over hills and bottoming out the car.

"Take it easy!" I yelled, "these are mountains!"

"Nah, these are the hills. The mountains are up there," she said pointing to the mountains that ran right up to the city. Gone was the happy go lucky maneuvering of Jimmy. It seemed like the car would spin out of control at any second. Something else was driving her she tackled the traffic like she was trying to conquer it, instead of going with it. It was the difference between an artist and a forger. The car swerved and a red Geo flew passed us. I didn't think she was paying attention to driving.

"Geo driving freaks!" She swore, after the car, then looked at me, "relax, I've been driving around L.A. since I was a teenager. I once drag raced Tom Cruise."

"Who won?" I asked.

"I don't know, we were both kinda showing off our toys," she said.

"Free Tibet," Jimmy said.

"What?" I asked. He thrust a finger between us at the car in front of us.

"Free Tibet," he said pointing to the bumper sticker on the car. "Only in L.A., freedom is easy when you can afford a Mercedes convertible."

"What studio are we going to?" I asked Gina.

"Right here, Paramount." She pulled off Melrose to what looked like a side entrance. Gina honked her horn, the gate opened, and she pulled the car in. The guard checked her name against his guest list, handed us a map, drew a line to the building we wanted, and directed us to the parking lot. As we got out of the car Gina took the rolodex out from under her car seat and brought it with her.

We followed the line drawn on the map by the guard, walking among the neatly manicured concrete and hedges, passing buildings labeled The Clara Bow Building, Zuker, DeMille, even a Roddenbury Building. This was the factory town of old Hollywood, built on the premise that everyone in the world would put a nickel down to see flickering images of light on the wall, movies on an assembly line basis. And finally, our destination the Lubitsch Building.

"Whose office is this?" I asked her.

"A producer, but we're not here to see him. My friend is his personal assistant." She said, opening the screen door and walking in.

Inside, there were two women seated at desks. The one farthest away was on the phone.

"Gina!" The woman at the closest desk screamed as she jumped up from her chair, came around, and gave Gina a hug and a kiss.

"Sarah," Gina said, disengaging from the woman, "this is a friend of mine, Michael Gray."

"Jimmy is that you!" Sarah exclaimed as Jimmy came in the door.

"Oh, hi good to see you again," he said, obviously not remembering her.

"I was a PA on Tender Fury," she said.

"I see you've moved up in the business." He said, effortlessly moving to conversational tones.

"I'll be a producer yet. Michael nice to meet you," she said, holding out her hand. "Gina, let's go to the office in back. Jimmy and Michael make yourself at home, look around. Oh, Bridget," she said to the woman on the phone, "I have Steve Guttenberg on hold for you. He's missing a limo." The woman at the second desk picked up the line. "We're having a premiere in New York tonight," Sarah said to me confidentially. Then she and Gina walked off to an office in the back and closed the door.

Jimmy and I sat listening to Bridget talk to Steve Guttenberg. "Steve, the limo will be there in fifteen minutes. I got off the other line with the limo company right before I got on with you." She held the phone away from her ear and rolled her eyes, smiling, she looked excited, like she had found her dream job. There wasn't much to look at except the pictures of movie stars on the walls. Some of the stars had their arms around the shoulder of a shorter, preternaturally tanned man who had brilliantly white teeth, I assumed he was the producer who's office we were in. I listened to Bridget allaying Steve Guttenberg's concerns. When she got off the phone I tried to talk her up.

"Have you worked here long?"

"A couple of years, I came in for an interview and the phones were ringing off the hook and I started answering them and have worked here since." The phone rang again, she took the call, and I went back to studying the pictures. Finally, the waiting had seemed to become a game, at that moment in flitted the most flamboyant gay guy, he was dressed in a lavender body suit with an orange taffeta skirt, he did literally flit from one desk to another like a nervous moth, before landing on the edge of Bridget's desk just as she hung up the phone.

"Who are these cute boys?" He asked, archly. It was a little too surrealistic even for L.A. Finally, the door to the back office opened, and Sarah and Gina came out. I didn't know what business they had transacted, but I did notice Gina no longer had the rolodex she had been clutching when we came in. By the way they were acting about it, I thought that whatever they were up to was at the very least unethical. She hadn't told us anything about it and it wasn't my business anyway, but there was an air of mystery and intrigue surrounding it.

"You ready to go tiger?" Gina asked.

"As soon as you are I guess," I said.

"Uh, can I ask a favor?" Jimmy asked, "can you give me a lift to my agent's office?"

"You have an agent?" I asked, surprised.

"Of course I do! This is Hollywood. I thought since I'm all cleaned up and we're so close by you wouldn't mind. It's only up at Hollywood and Vine."

"It's not that far. Let's go," Gina said.

"Before you go," Sarah said, "there's a party at the Chateau Marmont tonight. Would you like tickets?"

On The Trail of the Woodvine

After another jarring ten minute ride through L.A.'s traffic. Gina pulled up into a parking lot right on the corner of Hollywood and Vine, next to a smoothie stand.

"You mind if I come up with you?" I asked Jimmy.

"You looking for an agent too?"

"Yeah, I'm interviewing one the day after the show at *The Whisky*."

"Like the writer?" He asked, smiling broadly, teasing me. "Sure, c'mon." Gina decided to wait in the car.

We walked into Jimmy's agent's office. There was a receptionist sitting in front of two open offices, in each office was a man sitting at a desk. In one office was a boy and his mother. The boy was dressed like Michael Jackson in his Billie Jean period, a fedora, glittering red shirt and one sequined white glove. Something about the office seemed familiar. I looked at the man in the other office and recognized him. He must have been wearing a lot of make-up on his interview on Hollywood Today! And the room had the same wood paneling I'd seen on TV, it was Jimmy's agent, and this is the office he was interviewed in. I could almost figure out the camera angle and where everybody had stood. Jimmy went up to the receptionist.

"Mind if I see Max?" Max looked up upon hearing his name.

"Jimmy! I wasn't expecting you." Jimmy walked into the office, shook the man's hand and closed the door. I smiled nervously at the receptionist.

"Are you with Jimmy?" She asked.

"Yeah."

"Have a seat." I looked around the office. There were the ubiquitous pictures of stars on the walls. I took a seat close enough to the open door of the remaining agent's office to see and hear everything going on in the office. His desk was cluttered with what looked like pictures of actors headshots. He was reading information off the back of the headshot of the boy.

"What's his name?" The agent asked the boy's mother.

"Preston."

"Princeton! Hi! How ya' doin?" The boy grinned revealing a toothless smile. He did a shy little turn, proud of being the center of attention. "OK."

"How'd you name him? After the college?" The agent not seeming to care that he had misheard the boys name.

"The lord gave it to me."

"Oh?" The agent said, arching an eyebrow.

"I didn't have a name for him," the mother said, "even up to the time they brought him to me. And when they asked me what I wanted to name him, I closed my eyes and said, 'Lord, whatever name you could give me for this child, I would be grateful.' And just then the name came to me."

"Oh." The agent said. They were speaking different languages and neither seemed to be aware of it. Jimmy came out of the other office.

"Everybody looks like somebody." I said, motioning towards the little boy.

"Far out," Jimmy said, "I used to be that kid! My mother dragging me around to auditions, dressed up as all different kinds of things. The thing is, in Hollywood you don't have to look like somebody else, it's the guy who looks like himself that gets the gig. Man! I wish that was me again. I'd do anything to be famous again! Hey kid," Jimmy said, leaning into the office, "good luck." And we left. "Who knows," Jimmy said, "one day that kid might be famous and in an interview tell the story about the day I discovered him."

"What happened in your meeting?" I asked, as we walked back to the car.

"He didn't tell me much that I haven't heard before. He said I should get into A.A., if anything just to make contacts."

"Contacts?"

"Yeah, you can meet anybody there, producers, directors, writers, actors, everybody! I've heard of people going to meetings who aren't even alcoholics." He leaned close and whispered, "if you ask me, I think he's just trying to get me to go to A.A." It was getting late in the day and I remembered I hadn't eaten since breakfast.

"Are you hungry?"

"Thought you'd never ask," Jimmy said. "I know just the place."

Street Scenes

Jimmy gave directions to the restaurant from the back seat as Gina drove. The night air was heady scented with ozone and flowers, the wind was blowing through my hair. I wasn't paying attention to directions, I was just letting the neon signs shimmer my eyes as we cruised the streets of L.A. in the car next to me I saw a woman whose hairdo made her look like an Inca. L.A. is where you can see all the possibilities, and the different combinations of possibilities.

We parked the car about two blocks from the restaurant. Space is always at a premium in L.A., lawns a rarity. When people do have them they're fenced off, and fussed over. And businesses exercise proprietary rights over washrooms. So, when you park in L.A., leave the car where you parked it and walk to wherever you're going. We were walking from the parking lot to the restaurant when we came upon a movie being filmed. Klieg lights, cameras, canvas reflectors, thirteen or so technicians all sequestered behind crime scene tape with walkie-talkied production assistants fending off the crowd and answering questions. We stopped and watched a couple of run throughs. The scene they were filming was, a car pulls up to a phone booth, the actor jumps out of the car, dials a number and delivers his lines then drives away. After each take, three or four people would surround the actor, apply make-up, primp his hair, give him water, or just talk to him. I didn't recognize him.

"Pretty good odds, huh!" Jimmy said. He was watching the action longingly. His eyes had glazed over, I would have sworn he was either on drugs or in love.

Then a guy, who had to be the director, went up to the actor who was talking with the cameraman, the crew parted from around the actor for him. He and the actor chatted quietly, then the director had the actor practice his lines, trying a different delivery each time.

"Pick up the phone, asshole." Sounding tough.

"Pick up the phone, asshole." Defeated.

"Pick up the phone, asshole!" Mad.

"And George, can you motivate at this mark?" The director said, standing at the point at which he wanted the actor to act. "OK, we're ready!" He yelled. "Clear the set!" The technicians scattered from around the actor.

"Rolling!" The director yelled.

"Rolling!" Echoed an assistant director.

"Action!"

"Pick up the phone, asshole!" The actor said, delivering his line with the chosen perfect intonation, the first inflection. While the director gave silent hand signals to the cameraman, the actor got in a car and drove six feet and screeched to a halt.

"Cut! That's perfect," the director yelled, "everyone back to one, we're going to do it again."

"I can see what you mean now about the unreality of this place," I said to Jimmy.

"L.A. has become a giant set for itself." He said, as we continued to walk to the restaurant.

Dominick's

Dominick's was a dimly lit restaurant with a warm ambiance. Well dressed people sat in the booths drinking martinis. On the walls, were the same pictures I'd been seeing all day, the pictures of actors and actresses that you see everywhere, even at the smallest hot dog stand. As we walked in the maitre'd started shouting in thickly Greek accented English.

"No, no, Mr. Jimmy, you can't come in here, you can't come in here without money." Jimmy was laughing, saying, "Dominick, Dominick," trying to settle him down. "It's OK, it's OK, we have money." Jimmy turned to me and said, "you better show him some money, man." I pulled out my wallet and showed him my money.

"Well, that's different. Why didn't you say so . . . Come this way."

On the way to the table I asked Jimmy, "what was that about?"

"I used to work here," Jimmy confided. "I was the maitre'd, they only hired me because I was famous. They thought the novelty of it would bring in customers."

"What happened?"

"That was back in my wild days. People would buy me drinks and I would get totally ripped. One night I tore the place apart."

"Why?"

"The customers would buy me drinks, right? Well, this one particular night I was in the bar, right over there," Jimmy pointed to the adjoining room. "I was signing autographs and I was in there a long time, right? Then, out of the crowd this guy says 'Jimmy, Jimmy, can you sign this for me?' And he holds up a freakin' lunch box! You know, one with my picture on it, and to this day, I don't know if that guy had been carrying that lunch box around with him everywhere he went, or if he ran home to get it. Anyway, I went apeshit! I said, 'you can't sign a fucking lunch box!' I grabbed it from him and stomped the shit out of it, all the while yelling, 'I'm not a fucking product! I'm not a thing! I'm not anybody's fucking little brother!' I was walking on the tables and almost literally climbing the walls. People were cheering me on! It made all the papers."

"You freaked out over a lunch box?" I asked.

"It wasn't that. They used me, all those products, they used me. Do you know what it's like to be used?"

As we got ourselves settled in a booth a waitress handed us the menus. Aside from having worked here, I suddenly understood why Jimmy liked the place, as I read the menu, the most inexpensive thing on it was a turkey sausage gumbo. I ordered it.

"Dig that!" Jimmy exclaimed as a beautiful young girl passed with her date, an old guy wearing a loud shirt, which ballooned up over the top of his control top pants. He was tan, wore a gold necklace and bracelet. His hair was so coiffed, it unintentionally resembled a bad toupee. He looked pregnant with money and producers' cards.

"That's the one thing I hate," I said. "An old guy with a girl our age."

"L.A. is proof of the evolutionary principle that no matter how fat, old or ugly you are, you can have the prettiest wife and/or girlfriend money can buy."

"That's because every guy thinks it's his sexual manifest destiny to have an ice blond on his arm," Gina said.

"Rock 'n' Roll is the same," I said. "Put a guitar in a guy's hands, put him on-stage, and no matter what he looks like he'll get a beautiful girlfriend."

"Where's yours?" Jimmy said, laughing.

"Very funny," I said. "I'm going to the washroom."

There was a bank of phones by the washrooms. The door to the men's room was locked, so I decided to wait. On one of the phones was a guy hustling a movie deal.

"I sent the screenplay over today with four different endings." He listened as the person on the other end talked. "Version A is a romantic comedy ending, version B a dramatic ending. I don't care about the ending. You can have all the endings you want, all the way down to Z where bugs rule the planet. Look, this isn't *Doctor Zhivago*. Yeah, I'll hold." He looked up and noticed me listening. "Hey kid," he said, "mention a book here, it scares the hell out of them. They'll think you're a genius." I nodded at him. And it occurred to me there are any number of alternate endings available in L.A., and all the possible outcomes that can be created by any one person.

Chateau Marmont

After dinner, and with no after dinner floor show from Jimmy. It was off to The Chateau Marmont to meet Sarah. The Chateau Marmont is a hotel built in the 1920's, with a history as old as Hollywood. It has the art noveau design favored by designers of the age, but it doesn't have the flimsy construction materials of today, everything is oak, stone or marble, and the history is as solid as the construction, from stories of Douglas Fairbanks swinging on a chandelier across the room, to Jim Morrison hanging off the balconies, or John Belushi OD'ing in a bungalow a few years before.

The hotel was hosting an open house for art dealers, it was crowded in a bar area people gathered around Kim Basinger, I squeezed through the crowd, and ran around the hotel pretending to be interested in the paintings, looking for food and alcohol. The turkey gumbo hadn't gotten me very far, I found more alcohol than food. I went to the balcony of a room overlooking the courtyard where I saw Gina and Sarah, sitting at a table in the back of the courtyard, there were a couple of wine bottles between them. I spit ice cubes from my drink down toward them. They looked up and waved, "come on down!"

"Ah, the rolodex conspirators." I said, as I sat down.

"Shussssh!" They both hissed at me, "keep your voice down."

"Any wine left?" I examined each wine bottle for traces of alcohol then asked, "so, Gina, what's with the rolodex?"

"Simple, I told you I got fired, so I took the rolodex, which I built up myself, mostly anyway, and gave it to Sarah." She looked at me, "I told you there are all kinds of sea monsters here."

"So, what're you going to do with it?" I asked Sarah.

"We're brokering it, maybe we'll start our own production company, or see how much capital we generate with it."

"I like that, so it's called *generating capital* now?" A lanky guy in black jeans, black shirt, and cowboy boots came up to our table. He had a script in one hand.

"Hi Sarah!" He said, "I've been looking all over for you."

"Stan!" She jumped up and gave him a hug. "Stan this is a business partner of mine Gina, and Michael Gray. Stan is an actor, he was in *Wayne's World*."

"I don't remember you in the movie," I said.

"I was the guy in the back seat throwing up."

"Oh! Great performance, I think." I said, looking perplexed.

He laughed, "that's OK, I know what you mean. Sarah," he said, "thanks for giving me a ticket. Here's the script you wanted to see."

"You wrote it?"

"Yeah and I'm playing it at the Mirror Playhouse next weekend. I'll leave a couple of tickets under your name at the box office."

"Thanks," Sarah said. "Stan is one of the most intellectual actors around."

"Thanks," Stan said sincerely. "And if you want a script read, Sarah's the one to get it to. She knows everybody."

"Is that right?" I asked. Sarah smirked smugly at me.

"I gotta get going," Stan said. "I just wanted to get the script to you and thank you for the tickets. See you next week." And he disappeared back into the hotel. We all sat for a moment, Gina and Sarah sipping at their wine.

"So, did you enjoy your day Mr. Mojo Risin'?" Gina asked me. "Did you get to see enough of the sea life?"

"What makes you think I'm that into Morrison?"

"Who're you kidding?" She said. "All dudded up in those leathers."

"Because I wear leather pants and a black shirt makes me Jim Morrison?"

"No, it's the way you wear them, careful to match his style. And I've watched you, a conscious effort to move like him."

"Yeah, I saw enough of it." I said, thinking a moment. "Is that why you brought me around on your 'errands' today, so you could show me the underbelly of show business?"

"Just trying to keep someone's idealism intact."

"I'm not all that innocent, you don't know what I did to get here," I reached across the table and grabbed her hand, stroking it a little, "I'll tell you what," I said to her softly, "I'll get rid of Jimmy, and why don't you come to the motel with me?" She pulled her hand away from mine.

"Back to the pond little fishy." Sarah laughed at this, I looked up to see Jimmy smiling at me, holding a glass of wine as he watched the whole scene unfold.

"You know I've been watching you two all day, flailing around like a fish drowning in oxygen. Gina, do you really think that rolodex is going to make you the next big producer? And Michael, you're even more desperate than she is, your show at *The Whisky* is your rolodex."

"How?"

"You think it's going to solve all your problems, do you think there's going to be a moment of clarity where everything is explained, or you're going to fall in love during the montage? We've all become convinced we should be able to solve all our problems over the course of an hour TV show, or after two hundred pages of a book. With everything we have, we still feel a void in ourselves. And we look outside ourselves, we look for 'things' to fill that emptiness. You guys are chasing ghosts. I'm a fraud and a fake but at least I know it. The rolodex and fame won't change your lives, they'll only change the circumstances of your life."

"Why shouldn't we?" I asked, "it's the mythology we were all raised on, in the movies, on TV, isn't it supposed to be some reality of our lives on those screens? Why shouldn't our expectations live up to that?"

"Because it's all make believe. You've watched all that stuff and believe, but you've never considered failure."

"I believe in the transformative power of art?"

"Everybody is on their way to being something," Gina said.

"It doesn't exist. Did it transform me?" Jimmy asked.

"Yeah, you were a kid who everyone remembers. Your name will live on."

"Is that what you want? Immortality? Kill a few people you'll be infamous, as all the victims run for the TV cameras. Sometimes I try to imagine what my life would be like if my mother hadn't taken me to Max. What would my life be like today? I would've had a childhood with playgrounds and friends. The reason I quit show business is," he swallowed the last of his wine, "is the reason I took the part in Tender Fury, it had a death scene. And I wanted to know what it's like to die. But there was no illumination, no insight. I was just playing like any kid on a playground that goes 'bang, you're dead.' You fall over, twitch a little, hold your breath awhile, and when the bell rings and you go back in to class. It was empty, I was mimicking life, and I wanted to live a life." We were all quiet for a minute. "Look at them," Jimmy said, pointing to the wall behind us. There were cockroaches crawling up the whitewashed wall. "While we scurry around searching for whatever it is we're searching for, they're just sitting there, waiting to inherit the earth. I think it's time for me to be going." He put the wine glass on the table.

"Where you going?" I asked.

"I'm not too far from where you picked me up, I'm going back to the streets."

"Do you want to come to *The Whisky* Friday night, it'll be good publicity for the both of us. Of course, it's good for me to have a celebrity friend there, and it'll be good for you to be seen, maybe a producer will be there or something."

"I think you're looking for something I can't give you," he said. "I've exhausted every invitation I've had in this town. There wouldn't be any advantage for you to have me there." He sighed.

"Do you want the money I owe you?" I asked.

"You know the only time in my life I've felt like I'm running scared is when I've had money. I've found that when you don't have money, you don't get what you don't need. It's easy to let go of things, its mostly letting go of your fears. Besides," he said a little louder, "you paid for the tour. Hell, you got everything except an earthquake!" Jimmy turned to leave.

"You want to go back to the street?"

"You see me as a tragedy, a failure living on the street but for once I'm living my life, that's living in the moment, out there are all the issues of life and death, what's important, what's not. No one bothers me, the street is democracy in action, everyone is pretty equal out there. I made my peace with the streets a long time ago.

They give me freedom and besides, I don't think the streets can change without me there to witness them."

"Hold on," Gina said, "we'll come with you." Gina and Sarah left with Jimmy out into the night behind the clanging of the gate. I'd lost my entourage, it was time to go.

The day had come full circle, I found myself much like I had that morning trudging along between Sunset and Santa Monica. The difference now was I was drunk and tired. Each step seemed to come with a price. I was passing a coffee shop. Sitting by the window was the hooker I'd seen that morning, still in the same off white dress, maybe a little dingier. She was eating a white frosted angel food cake, the one luxury of her labors I supposed. I shifted my position and saw my reflection in the window. I remembered what Joe had said about seeing the face of a former starlet in the face of a hooker. The reflection shifted again and I wondered if I saw my future in her face, then it shifted again, like reaction shots in a movie. I thought of Gina's sea monsters, was there a monster in that reflection?

The Body Shop

I woke up hung over. I had hoped staying in the room Morrison preferred would invoke his spirit, or perhaps a revisit by dream, but no dream or vision was forthcoming. I guess that was asking for too much. But maybe I was closer to Morrison than I realized. How many times had he awakened in this room hung over? I lay in bed staring at the ceiling thinking. Towards the end L.A. had become a city of night for Morrison. He had dissipated a lot of energy in frenetic action, in activities that seemed to have no meaning, at least to a bystander. I couldn't shake the same feeling. I got up and went to the bathroom. I came back into the room and I saw the remnants of yesterday's breakfast and other evidence of Jimmy's having been there. It was too empty and too sad. I decided to get something to drink to ease my hangover. I didn't wear my 'Morrison uniform' I threw on a pair of old jeans, a pair of gym shoes, and an old sweatshirt.

I walked into one of the many newsstands that are around L.A. I was absently looking through magazines. When I looked up from whatever magazine I was looking at, I saw a beautiful girl round the corner. I put down the magazine and followed her. She had picked up a magazine and was looking through it. She looked like a model. Trying to look cool, I picked up a magazine and leafed through it, all the while watching her. She was my queen of the magazines. I put on Morrison's persona and walked up to her. She glanced up and smiled a little as I approached.

"Excuse me," I said. "Are you a model?"

"Yeah."

"I thought so. Do you live in L.A.?"

She looked up from her magazine and looked me up and down and said, "sorry, I'm not interested." She put down the magazine and walked out. I felt like a stalker.

Walking down Sunset I happened upon a white stucco building that had in large letters next to the door, *The Body Shop*, a strip club, one of the still existent clubs from the sixties that Morrison frequented. I understood why Morrison preferred the nondescript motels and strip clubs. It was the anonymity, the strippers are jaded and don't care who you are, which must have appealed to a man who felt he was being pursued by fans, the press, and bandmates. Often he would take interviewers to the strip clubs to throw them off. The walk up there helped clear my head, but as soon as I walked into the club I was overpowered by the synergistic effects of thousands of nights of cheap perfumes mixed together. I started feeling nauseous again.

Inside, it was all brass and glass, someone's idea of taste and phony class. There were three sweaty looking businessmen at a table at the end of a catwalk stage, hooting and hollering whenever a dancer came near them. I sat at a table, when a waitress came over I ordered a beer. Sitting at the bar were four or five dancers dressed in varying amounts of undress, nursing drinks, waiting for more customers to come in, or their turn to dance. I watched the businessmen two tables away, in their suits, ties loosened. They licked their lips and tried to grope the dancers every time they came near them, ending with the dancer retreating from that end of the stage as fast as they could. The dancers were young and fairly pretty, and the old guys were fairly fat and lecherous. At their table was a dancer dressed in an *I Dream of Jeannie* seven veils costume. I concentrated on my lukewarm beer the waitress brought and watched the dancers. They really weren't dancing, following the music, or moving in time to it, it was more like rhythmic writhing, that was the same no matter what song was on. After you're in a strip club a while the novelty of semi-clad women wears off and all you want to see is a dressed woman, it even seems kind of sexy.

"Hi." I heard a female voice say as I felt a hand run across the back of my shoulders. I looked up it was the girl who had been sitting with the sweaty businessmen. I looked over, they were gone. "Mind if I sit down?" She asked.

"No."

"My name is Sheryl." She said, holding her hand out delicately. I shook it.

"Michael," I said, "do you know if Jim Morrison hung out here?"

"I dunno. But you look a little like him."

"Thanks. I've heard that once or twice before," I said a little self-consciously. "What happened to the old dudes?"

"Oh, they were perverts." A waitress came over.

"Too bad."

"Would you like to buy the lady a drink?" The waitress asked.

"Sure."

"I'll have a Champagne cocktail," She said.

"I'll have another beer," I said. The waitress went back to the bar. "You like being a dancer?"

"Yeah, I'm trying to save money so I can build a house in Silver Lake." The waitress brought our drinks and I paid for them.

"That sounds cool. How long before you get your house?"

"I figure by the time I'm thirty."

"How old are you now?"

"Nineteen."

"You can make that much dancing?"

"Well," she whispered, "I do some side work outside of dancing, if you know what I mean." It took me a second to realize her second profession was the world's oldest profession.

"All of them too?" I asked, motioning to the other dancers sitting at the bar.

"A couple of them," she said. They didn't look like the proverbial hookers with the hearts of gold, they looked as if their hearts were as thin as paper. "My shift is up after this last dance, if you want, you know, do something more, we can. Think it over, I have to get ready, don't go away." She got up and went backstage to wait for the dancer on-stage to finish her routine. Sheryl came out the music throbbing, her body moving. She stood in front of me on-stage, swaying in time to the music. She danced, bending and shimming, swaying her pastied breasts in my face, while running her hands through my hair. When the dance was over she came back to the table. She was playing with one of her pasties, then handed it to me.

"Here, put it back on," She instructed, her nipple staring me in the eye. "Lick it and stick it back on." I licked the pasty and placed it over her nipple and pushed it on. She sat back down.

"Do you want another drink?" I asked, finishing mine.

"My shift is over, I don't have to stay, do you want to come with me for a little more private party?"

"How much?" I asked.

"Hundred an hour." In the changing light I looked at the other dancers at the bar, they were a couple steps removed from the hooker I saw begging for tricks on the street, they weren't that desperate, but they looked the way I felt, it felt like a sleazy score, and it really had nothing to do with them or even the sex, Sheryl and I weren't that different, she had a dream and a plan too. It was me, I hadn't had time for anything except sex, and now that's all that was left, I was empty and it would be an empty act, and that seemed to matter now.

"No."

Sheryl looked at me, "do you want a private dance?"

"No."

"Well, I've spent a lot of time over here. You see the bartender over there?"

"Yeah."

"He times us. I have to give the house a cut of my time."

"Here," I said, handing her forty dollars. I finished my beer and left.

Who Do You Love?

I was alone, I felt empty and lonely. I realized I'd felt this way ever since arriving in L.A. and had been doing everything to fill that void, the stripper in New Orleans, the stripper in L.A., no real connections made on the road. Sex could be gotten anywhere, and when sex is that available you can't hold onto the experience. Maybe that's what Alex had been trying to tell me in New Orleans, the emptiness of sex without love. Who do you love? Caitlin had asked me. I thought about my past with women, Deidre I know I didn't love, I didn't even think I liked her. Caitlin, I thought about calling her again, to be scathingly honest with myself, I loved the idea of her, the fantasy of what a great couple we'd make, her a Rock 'n' Roll legacy, me, a budding star. She'd made her feelings pretty clear anyway. Pam? Did I love her? Did I *love* her? I asked myself again, trying to get a real answer, she loves me. *The Doors'* version of Bo Diddley's *Who Do You Love?* Kept running through my head, it was a languid stroll through the 'forty-four miles of barbed wire,' that is love.

Maybe I shouldn't have come to L.A. Morrison had L.A., Hemingway and Fitzgerald had Paris, Thoreau had Walden Pond. Morrison had followed his literary heroes to Paris, but when he got there he found he was out of step, out of time. Pilgrimages are a problem, whether to a virgins womb or the abandoned cafés of Paris, every path has a way, he'd followed his path, they theirs. What they found there didn't exist for him. Maybe that's the truth Morrison had found in Paris, and what Morrison found in L.A didn't exist for me. In L.A. the truth that love and sex aren't free is all around you, they come with emotions that if we're riding the snake, those feelings are the dragons tail that comes whipping around. Maybe the truth I found is, to avoid being alone is; all you have to do is ask.

Calling Pam

I put about three dollars in change in the pay phone and dialed her number. It rang I tried to drown out the traffic going by on Santa Monica Boulevard.

"Hello?" She said.

"Hi, I'm sorry I haven't called sooner."

"Oh, hi," she cooed softly. "Where are you?"

"I'm in L.A. me and the band, we're going to play *The Whisky* this weekend."

"That's great!" She said.

"Can you come out here to see us?" I asked.

"Us?"

"Yeah, I mean me."

"You left here in such a hurry the last time I saw you."

"You told me you had a boyfriend. What was I supposed to do?"

"It still hurt, especially after what we shared."

"You were hurt?" I said, "you're the one with the boyfriend."

"I thought we had more than that together."

I thought for a moment. "I miss you. Things haven't been going as well as I had hoped and I'm just trying to get things together."

"Isn't it a little late?"

"No, the gig is still three days away, it came up suddenly, I didn't have time to do anything except make the arrangements and get out here. I've been running around finding a motel for the band and sending out invitations to the show to movie producers, and every newspaper in L.A. And the morning after I have a meeting with an agent, I really want you to come." There was silence on the other end. I could feel her wavering ambivalence. I felt her moving away from me. I didn't want to lose her, "let me tell you the truth, I don't really feel like I belong here. I feel like I'm a fraud."

"You belong there, I believe in your talent."

"Then come," I said, plaintively. "I need someone who believes in me, and someone I believe believes in me, if that makes any sense."

"But why do you want to be with me?"

"I see the parts of me in you that I miss. I wish I could be quiet again, that I didn't have to howl to get noticed. I'm an oddity no matter where I go. In my family, at the college, in my own band! Even the bars where I feel the closest to comfortable, I talk about life and death, and the construction workers look at me suspiciously. I talk about existential dilemmas and the yuppies walk away shaking their heads."

"Um, OK," I knew she had made a decision. "What about my boyfriend?"

"Just come, I miss you." I said, "or stay in that one horse town, and when you marry Billy Carlson, the farting mechanic you've known since third grade, send me an invitation." I paused, hoping to hear her laugh. "Look, I have money. I can send plane fare, you can be here tomorrow, and we can rent a house on Norton just like Jim and Pam. Or up in the hills, anything you want." Another silence, "look, you came to me, now I've come to you."

Irony In The Garden

In the couple of days I had left before the gig at *The Whisky* I didn't have that much to do. I finished the little chores I had left, I'd gone out that morning and reserved rooms for the boys at the first motel I ran across. To kill the time in between I spent it the same as Morrison had, drinking. Walking back to the motel room from Barney's, I was thinking how I wouldn't have to deal with the boys after tomorrow night. Pam was supposed to arrive sometime today. She hadn't told me what time to expect her, but I gave her the hotel name, room number and address. As I walked up the steps to the room I noticed the door to the room was open. I thought maybe Pam had talked the owner into opening the room for her. "Pam?" I said as I walked in.

"I'm not interrupting am I?" She asked. She was lying on the bed naked.

"Hi honey, no, I don't think you are." We spent the next couple of hours making love.

I was lying awake afterward staring at the ceiling. Pam woke up.
"Did you sleep?" She asked.
"No." She looked at me.
"Why do you still look that way?"
"What way?"
"You, don't look . . . comfortable," she said. "You're with the girl you love and tomorrow will be your introduction to the world."
"I've done things I'm not proud of to get here. I met this woman who told me L.A. is like the ocean, full of sea monsters . . ."
"Everybody has to do that to get where they are. That's the price of fame."
"I think I'm losing myself. I feel like an actor playing a role."
"Maybe that's all we're meant for, we're all actors bound to playing ourselves."
"The irony is I am playing a role! And it's not myself! Every night I get out on-stage and play Jim Morrison, but I'm not! And everybody knows it, but every one comes up to me calling me 'Jim' or 'Morrison' and they expect me to be some aspect of him, and depending on what they expect, they'll either love me or tell me to 'fuck off.' I can't win."
"I'm sorry, baby." She cooed.
"Look at me, I'm just a Rock 'n' Roller dressing the same as I did in high school, dressing up like Jim Morrison, acting like some kind of kid giving the finger to the teacher, refusing to grow up. I can't tell anymore where I begin and Morrison ends. I've adopted so much of this into me, I can't stop it!" I said, tensely. "I saw myself in the faces of those I read about, Hemingway the hero, Kerouac the loner, Morrison the poet. I've always thought of myself as being a great adventurer through life. You know, going on archaeological digs, climbing the Himalayas, being the next Spielberg or Hemingway."
"You will be," she implored.

"I guess, I just thought I'd wake up and *be* something, transformed, like turning into the wolfman, just being. I guess, I just never knew how to get there."

"You're almost there, baby." She said, curling around my body.

"But I don't know if I'll ever be comfortable, satisfied with what I have . . ." I stopped to think a minute, "Morrison once said that he never wrote a song where you feel completely at home, comfortable."

"So?"

"Maybe if he did, I'd be able to feel it." And then I realized, with horror, it was the truth.

"Relax baby," she said, clinging to my chest. "You're just nervous, you're almost home."

"At least you have a home. I don't think I've had a home since I was a kid. I want to be normal, I want to be comfortable, to have a home. I want someone to be there, I want to eat when I'm hungry, sleep during the night, I feel like some kind of vampire."

"You'll have those things."

"I read that before *The Doors* hit it big, Morrison met with some film school friends at the UCLA Botanical Gardens. I've always kind of pictured it, the night air is cool, the grass wet, they're sitting off a stone path on a bench surrounded by the green hedges. He's lithe, dressed in black jeans, and a T-shirt, his hair curling around the collar, sand in the wrinkles of his jeans, or at the back of his neck. Maybe he's still living at the beach, or with Ray and Dorothy, or even bouncing from girlfriend's to girlfriend's apartment. It doesn't really matter, the point is his friends are trying to talk him out of being in the band.

'There's too much competition, the band will never make it.' One said.

'Your film career is going great,' said another.

'You don't want to be in a band with those guys Jim, they're not going anywhere.' shit like that. And Morrison seeing the irony in that, that's what others had told Ray, Robby and John about him. I've always seen it as a Garden of Gethsamane scene. You know, his moment of doubt before fame."

"That's all it is, baby, a moment, a little fear of the unknown. All you have to do tomorrow is do the gig at *The Whisky*. And the next morning, step through that agent's door into your new world. The life you . . . we deserve. Remember, you are the band! You are him! Morrison was the spark for *The Doors* and you're the spark for that band. They need you!" That evening I showed her around the world Morrison stepped into.

The Whisky

"This is where it all started for Morrison." I said, to Pam. *The Whisky A-Go-Go*, a blue stucco building on the corner of Sunset and San Vincente, the marquee "pops" out at you in hot pink neon. The marquee read, The Unknown Soldiers. I rapped on the glass of the front door until I got the attention of one of the bouncers. I explained who I was, the band had been here earlier this afternoon to set up, and that I was waiting for them to come back from dinner so we could do the sound check before the doors opened. He let us in. I had met Mario briefly earlier, he was one of the original owners of *The Whisky*. It was largely a ceremonial introduction, like meeting the Pope and then you're whisked away to deal with the people who do the real work. He was a burly ex Chicago cop, and he looked it, or maybe a Mafia Don. There didn't seem to be much difference in methodology to me.

The interior was cool, dark, and small! It was only about fifty feet deep. There's a bar directly across the room from the door, the ceiling was low, and the stage jutted out into the room. I walked out onto the concrete floor, the room opened up. There were stairs running up to a second floor. I ran my hand across the stage like it was a sacred shrine. All the equipment was on the stage, it was going to be a tight fit up there. How did Morrison do any of the jumping, twirling, falling, everything I had read about? Of course Morrison was fueled by a combination of ambition, acid, and youthful energy. I'd seen pictures of *The Whisky* from the sixties there had been booths and Go-Go dancers in cages. There had been tapestries on the wall and it had been light. Now it was stripped down and dark, able to cram in as many paying customers as you could. Behind the stage hung black curtains used to close off what must have been the rest of the club. They had changed it since the sixties, but it's the history of the place that counts. *The Doors* jamming with *Them*, Janis sitting in a booth with a bottle of Southern Comfort in front of her, Hendrix dropping by and jamming. It was the ghosts that still dance in this space, the sounds that still reverberate in the walls that is important.

Pam and I were having a beer that I had talked the bartender into giving us. We watched as the *Whisky* employees scurried passed, like stagehands across a darkened proscenium. Finally, the band came in. Following in tow were 'the girlfriends,' a phalanx of glittering guards.

"Hiya boys!" I said, my feet up on an empty stool, shades on, as they marched in. "Ready for our last gig?"

"Hey asshole, could you have found us a shittier motel?"

"I thought you'd fit in there."

"Some drunk band was running around all night playing hacky sack. They broke one of our windows."

"Sounds like you fit in," I said.

"What have you been doing here all this time?"

"Exploring," I said. "Getting the lay of the land, resting, taking it easy."

"Exploring?" Johnny asked sharply.

"Yeah, probably getting laid and exploring the bars and strip joints," Brian said.

"You could've at least checked out *The Whisky* before hand and let us know the lay of the land.'"

"Why? It wasn't that important. According to Swifty we didn't have to be here until today to sign the contract, show us where to setup, sound check, blah, blah, blah, it's all just a formality."

"Why should anything be different." Johnny said, a smile on his face. "By the way where's our money?"

"Good question," Brian said, sounding fairly pissed off. "Why don't you tell us."

"After tomorrow you won't have to worry, I'll have more than enough."

"I don't care about the money per se," Johnny said, "it's the symbolism of the act that makes it a betrayal, man. Not the money, but the willingness to rip us off."

"Man, I'm the personification of sixties ideals," I said.

"What ideals? Corruption, betrayal, avarice? Sounds like all the same old ideals, dude." Ian said.

"After tonight's gig," Johnny said, "we're done. And just so it's in words you can understand, this is the end."

"The end!" I yelled. "This is only the beginning! We're all going to be famous."

"How are WE going to be famous?" Johnny asked.

"Uhh . . . ."

"Swifty told us about your audition."

"Oh." I wondered how the innocent always manage to catch the guilty off guard so they sound innocent.

"You went behind our backs to audition for a movie," Johnny said.

"I knew you couldn't be part of it, so I didn't . . ."

"And how did you know we couldn't have been a part of it? You didn't care, you acted in your own selfish self interest."

"Why did Swifty tell you?"

"Don't worry," Johnny said, "Swifty didn't betray you. Funny thing, we had already decided we'd had enough of you and this *Doors* shit, so we asked him to represent Ghost Dance, after this final show."

"And he told us," Brian said picking up the story, "we were too good a band for someone as small as him. He said he'd make some calls since we were already going to be in L.A."

"And he offhandedly said he'd do that for us since he was already doing it for you."

"And Swifty really knows the music business. Unlike you, who knows only what he's read in books. Every theory you've put forth has been wrong. We didn't want to tell you because everything was going well, so we carried you and glossed things over hoping an owner or promoter would straighten you out."

"Do you think my rantings have been just that? That they have no purpose? They we're meant to educate you, to alter your perceptions of the world. I don't really think any of you learned a thing, still the small town wannabe's that you'll always be."

"And who the fuck do you think you are to decide we need to be educated?" Mitchell said. I wasn't going to tell them because no one was asking questions. It was all accusation, no one listening to the other.

"Do you really think they're going to hire a guy no one has heard of to play Jim Morrison?" Johnny asked, smugly.

"Fuck you." I said. "OK, so I did it, it's part of the deal. It's not a party until you break something and it's not work until you bleed. Don't be hypocrites. You took the rewards that came with this band, the beautiful girlfriends, the new equipment, the tour."

"Were those things supposed to distract us? Buy us off? To make us forget our own dreams? We made a bad deal, we're trying to fix it."

"A bad deal!" I said incredulously. "You played bigger audiences than you ever could have because of me. You even made it to L.A. because of me! You think I like this deal? I'm tired of living in dormitory conditions, sleeping on other people's couches, picking up pennies when people should be shoving dollars into my hands."

"Do you think WE liked it in that cramped, reeking van? Or putting up with your bullshit? It was the joy of the music that got us through." Suddenly, we were surrounded by gawking *Whisky* employees and at the back of the room, coming from the office was Mario and Swifty.

"What?!" I said, incredulously.

"That's your problem, that's what you're missing, and that's why this isn't bringing you what you thought it would. It's the joy, the joy of creation, the joy of accomplishment."

"You've got to be kidding. I get to L.A., one of the most jaded and Machiavellian cities in the world, and all anybody can talk about is the joy of creation? This was all my . . ." I paused, trying to gain some composure then said, "I did it for you too." The circle of surrounding employees opened as Mario and Swifty walked up.

"Is this your idea of a sound check?" He asked, taking the cigar out of his mouth. We all ignored him.

"No, you used us." Johnny continued, "you mimicked the talents of a genuine rock legend. Everything comes through that, none of this is yours. We're the ones supplying the talent. What have you created here? Nothing except a testament to your ego and you want to be recognized for it? You've created nothing yet you want the honors, rewards and status that comes with creation?"

"It's the spoils of Rock 'n' Roll. I didn't make the rules."

"You can't proclaim yourself an idol!"

"You want to know why I can do this? I'll tell you why! I am him! I am Jim Morrison. I am Hemingway. I'm every hero you've ever heard of, standing right before you, I made you a band! I'm the hero of this story! I've worked for the right."

"No, Morrison did." Brian said.

"Either you did the things you did to replace that joy," Johnny mused, "or to make up for it with a false sense of victory. And that's why you're hiding in the same places as Morrison did, alcohol and drugs. In your Morrison mania you didn't see that Morrison got lost on the road."

"Boys," Swifty interjected, "this isn't the place to air family problems. Michael, what you fail to see is Rock 'n' Roll isn't the healthiest of environments. Morrison wasn't perfect. He was on stage literally screaming for help, but he took advantage of what he had, his talent and his looks, which by the way are advantages you all have, and most people have, if they would just turn to themselves instead of looking to idols. I've seen so many bands that had potential but they were blinded by what their *heroes* were doing they couldn't find their own voice or even search for it."

"You know why this is all falling apart?" I asked the band. "It's all because none of you has any belief in this."

"Belief?"

"The kind of simple belief that Ray Manzarek had when he heard Morrison's songs on the beach that July day, the belief I had in you as the band that could do this."

"But not enough belief to let us follow our own course." Brian said.

"If it wasn't for our belief in this band we wouldn't have held it together for so long." Johnny said.

"See, that's belief in your own little band and not belief in the larger concept of what I'm trying to do."

"Which is?"

"This is about changing the world, it's lead to gold, alchemy!"

"Lead to gold?!" Johnny said, "and what do you think art is going to change you into?" I felt the anger building in me, but I could sense the betrayal, mine, the betrayal of myself that was so close, but I couldn't reveal myself to them, to be naked in front of everyone if I gave myself away what do I have left? I paced the space I had in this circle, fuming and made my decision, "we're not performing." I turned to the band. "It's my idea, my band and we're not performing."

"Your band!" Johnny exploded. "It's always been OUR band." He said motioning to include the four of them. "You keep saying 'the band' as if it were a tool, a thing for you to use. It's an entity to us. It is us. What you have failed to realize in all of this is you needed us more than we need you. WE DON'T NEED YOU!"

"Morrison died for your sins man," Brian said.

"All right boys. All right," Mario interjected. "What all of you fucks have failed to realize is," he said, holding the cigar between two fingers, the chewed wet end of the cigar stuck in my face, "is that a lot of people including me have worked for you, have done what they have promised to do for you. You think you can just not perform without any consequences? You think you hold all the cards here? You don't. I've been in this business more years than all of you've been alive put together, and seen a lot of bands. You owe them and me. If not a performance, money. If there's no performance we will sue you." He started to walk away, then said to me, "listen kid, jumping around on stage, and wearing leather pants don't make you Jim Morrison."

I spent the night by the bar, my back pressed against the wall by the sheer volume of people crowded into the bar. "We" were the only band scheduled to play that night. I sat through two sets of Ghost Dance getting drunker and drunker. The boys made up for not being able to play their songs. Only half of the first set were *Doors* songs, the other half and the second set were all originals. At least an album's worth of songs. Johnny was using his anger, I could swear he was stealing moves I'd done on-stage, but there was something different about it too, he was giving himself to the audience. The audience liked them. Cheering them on with growing enthusiasm with each passing song until I couldn't take it anymore . . .

L.A. Times Review

"Tribute" Band Perishes

Last night at *The Whisky A go-go*, a *Doors* tribute band was supposed to play. They did and they didn't. Due to a falling out with the band, lead singer Michael Gray refused to perform prior to the doors opening. But the band, which goes by the name "Ghost Dance," played their own original material. Due to contractual agreements, they also played a set of *Doors* songs. They handled *The Doors* material well, delivering the hits with enthusiasm. But they really delivered the goods on their original songs, giving the audience a performance maybe unrivaled since *The Doors* played *The Whisky*. Admirably debuting their talent and potential. The only blemish of the evening wasn't their fault, an audience member apparently moved by the music jumped on-stage screamed a few things at the audience and was dragged off by security. All in all, Ghost Dance realized the opportunity presented to them and took it. I hope they'll have the opportunity to play *The Whisky* again. If they do, be sure to see them.

"Shit," I said as I read the review, for, perhaps, the millionth time. I crumbled up the paper, it was the sound of seeing your dream become a nightmare, I threw it at the corner of the room.

Mourning After

The next morning I woke up early again. Not due to excitement, but to my anxiety and nerves. I lay in the bed staring at the ceiling and the sloppy whitewash meant to cover it. I left Pam sleeping in the room to run out to the newsstand to get a newspaper. I made it back to the room without reading it. No matter what the reviews said about the band, it held nothing good for me. There was no redemption of a performance, only the uncertainty of what might have been. I read the review.

"Oh, shit." I said out loud.

"What is it, baby?" Pam asked, the sleep still in her voice.

"Sorry, I thought you were still sleeping."

"Not with you running in and out of the room."

"I don't think I should go to that meeting today."

"At the agent's?"

"Yeah."

"Why not?"

"Here, read this." I said, handing her the review.

"So?" She said after reading it. "What does it have to do with the audition?"

"That show was supposed to be like the audition, the basis for me getting in their door."

"I don't think so. Look," she said sitting up in bed, "they're looking for someone who can act like Jim Morrison, which you can do better than anyone else out there. It doesn't matter if you're in some band or not. You sent them a tape, right?"

"Right."

"So they know you can handle that part. What they want is someone who can look like Jim Morrison, act like him. And if they want someone who has proven they can do that, they have to come to you."

"You think so?"

"They'll probably give you a screen test, but that'll just be to make sure you're comfortable in front of a camera. But the band doesn't mean anything. Last night doesn't matter to them. I bet you they didn't even go to the show last night. And you know why?" She paused for dramatic effect, "because it wasn't necessary for them to."

"I guess so," I said, my voice betraying my lack of confidence.

"Look, you can either melt away now, and throw away all the work it took to get you here, or you can let it strengthen you, it's your choice." She was right, this was the alchemical moment! What I'd been striving for, the fire of the annealing process, I could either burn out or burn brilliantly, Pam was right, I didn't need the band and I didn't need to perform last night.

I dressed in my full Morrison regalia again. Pulling on the leathers, I felt like a matador getting ready for a corrida. Then into Morrison's character, it fit like a warm glove.

"How do I look?" I asked.

"You look fine." Pam said, straightening my collar.

I took a taxi over to the Capital Records building on Sunset for the appointment with the agent. As the cab drove down Sunset, I watched as the landmarks of my imagination passed by like a movie. The streets were empty this early, and didn't have the energy or magic they possessed at night. Pam was right, I was him. A facsimile, but still the closest they could come to Jim. The cab pulled up in front of the building, it was built to look like a stack of records. I sized up the building, this is where my destiny was to be decided, everything had led to this moment, I was Morrison. I was the embodiment of his ideals, I was what they were looking for! I felt larger than the building, I could feel myself looming over the city, I felt larger than life, I felt like a rock star.

The Casting Couch

I sat in the large outer office of the agent, staring at the pictures on the wall, the receptionist keeping a polite eye on me as she went about her duties. As I waited my fears and doubts started to creep back in, finally her phone rang.

"You can go in now," she said, putting the phone back down. As I got to the door of the inner office, it opened and Johnny and the rest of the band walked passed me. They didn't say anything. They didn't have to, the hostile looks on their faces said it all. They weren't supposed to be here. I wondered what was going on.

"What're you doing here?" I asked.

"Leaving the past behind." What was that supposed to mean? I walked into the office. It was much more palatial in size to Swifty's Milwaukee office, almost regal in it's demeanor, in color and tone it resembled a Rembrandt painting, the browns of the paneling, the murky black of the leather furniture, Swifty's office in comparison was a pencil sketch compared to this masterpiece. A desk sat in front of a wall sized window with a panoramic view of downtown L.A. Behind the desk sat a man with Swifty to his left. Sitting across the desk from them was another man, his back towards me. As I came in, he got up and turned towards me, it was Johnny's father. He buttoned his jacket, smoothed away some insignificant dust molecule, and smiled wolfishly at me. Swifty got up to greet me, he looked glum as he shook my hand.

"Good morning. Mike we have a lot of things to discuss. Last night was certainly a mess." He said, quietly. "This is my son, Don," Swifty gestured towards the man behind the desk. He rose, hand extended.

"How're you," he said perfunctorily. Then he carried on the conversation, "and over here," he said motioning towards the far end of the office where two men were sitting on a couch, a couple of drinks on the table in front of them, "is Ben Craven, he's from the studio producing the movie, and Jerry Glavin, he's a music producer working as the music supervisor for the movie." They each nodded and shook my hand. Each was the fit, sophisticated executive of my imagination, who played a couple sets of tennis before or after a meeting. "And of course you know Mr. Ryder."

"Of course." I said, tersely.

"Now," Swifty said, taking charge of the meeting, "Michael before you get to Mr. Craven and Mr. Glavin, we have to resolve the issues you have with the band, and the money you owe." I got a bad feeling in the pit of my stomach. "But I think we have a solution for you, if you agree."

"Which is?" I asked.

"I'll let Mr. Ryder explain."

"I paid the remainder of the debt the band owed to Mr. Leonard, including the 'advance' you took upon yourself to *borrow*."

"Great!" I said, "I didn't like the idea of being in debt to anybody."

"I did it for my son and his band, which means," he said, evenly but with a tone of controlled genteel hostility in his voice, "I own the contract. The balance of which is owed to me."

"I see," I said. "what's the kicker here?" I asked, as if that weren't enough. I looked over at Swifty to see how he could have sold me out so easily.

"You sign this promissory note here," he said, picking up a typed page from the desk. "Or you might be subject to legal trouble if Mr. Leonard decides to press charges."

"Would you do that, Swifty? You know I'm good for it."

"It's your choice Michael, I told you this was a business, it's time to live up to your responsibilities. If you duck out on those who have helped you, there are repercussions." I heard the click of a pen and Johnny's father holding it out to me, a smug smile on his face.

"Fine," I said grabbing the pen and signing the note. "For all the good it will do you. You'll get the money back prior to whatever the terms are. Now, if you'll excuse yourself I have the business I came here for, to attend to." I tossed the pen onto the desk.

"That's all I wanted," he said gathering up the note and pen before leaving.

"We're done?" I asked Swifty. He shook his head sadly affirmative as he sat back in his chair.

I went over to the couch where the movie executives were sitting. Swifty's son came over and took the last remaining chair, aligned with theirs'. I faced a triumvirate. I took the final chair in front of the table across from them. Next to their drinks I saw a manila folder spread open across the table, a headshot of me and the tape I sent them.

"Sorry about the old business," I said.

"First of all, we want to thank you for sending us your audition tape of your performance, we're sorry we missed you at *The Whisky* last night." Pam was right! I thought, everything was going to be OK! They hadn't seen the show, and they knew what had happened, and the preamble of band business didn't matter to them! They probably had seen worse, after all the residue of show business is scandal. Jerry Glavin, the music producer was first to speak.

"Although we were impressed with the band that did play. They did a lot of originals, the audience loved them, they're going to be big someday, we're glad you helped get them here. We approached them with a contract."

"You were at the show?" I asked, shocked, realizing they had been at the *Whisky*, they missed me because I didn't perform. "Did they take it?"

"On the advice of their parents they're looking for representation right now, but I'm sure we'll be able to make a deal." I looked over at Swifty and he was shaking his head affirmatively.

"Now, regarding the reason we're here, the movie," Swifty's son said. "Sorry Mike, but we've decided to go with an actor." I looked around the room at the cast of characters before me. The music producer was looking out the window at the view trying to be aloof, Swifty's son professional, the appointed trigger man, but the guy from the studio, Ben Craven, I could tell from his demeanor he was used to being in charge, the power behind everything happening here. He sat back watching and listening to everything with interest, but never betraying any emotion. Like a camera, recording everything, cold, omnipresent, but keeping a professional distance making sure the will of the studio was carried out, his will.

"Why?" I asked, directing my comments to Stark. "I know everything about Morrison, ask me something. There's nothing I don't know about the guy. I can bring so much to the role."

"It's not a matter of knowledge," Swifty's son replied. "It has nothing to do with that. We need an actor. To tell you the truth, it's easier to teach an actor to sing, than a singer to act."

"But I can act, I do it every night on-stage. I know those songs better than Morrison. I've been singing them longer than he did."

"We've decided to go with a proven actor." There was an uncomfortable silence. "The decision has already been made. But, because we appreciate what you do, and don't want you leave empty handed, we are prepared to offer you a small speaking part in the movie."

"How much?"

"Scale." Swifty's son said, coolly.

"No," I said. Swifty's son looked at his at his father, then to Ben Craven.

"Mike, do you know how many people would kill to be in your position?"

"Mike," Swifty said from the desk, "a small speaking part gets you some money and into the union, and who knows where you can take that to."

"This has always been an all or nothing deal for me," I said. He looked at me in awe, either for my bravado, or the foolhardiness of my grandeur.

"Well, then . . ." Swifty's son said smiling, "our business is concluded, thank you and good luck." He stood, extended his hand to shake. That was it? No negotiation? I looked around the room for anything, I didn't know what I was looking for. Ben Craven, Swifty's son, and the music producer huddled closely, talking. They acted like they were moving on to other subjects. The moment had no tension, no soundtrack to tell me what to expect. It was a flat. 'No, the decision has been made, thank you,' business as usual. I got up to leave. I took a couple of steps and looked back, they looked up expectantly.

"Who do you think you're going to get to play Morrison for your little movie!" I yelled. They looked at me blandly. "I can even give you a verbatim recitation of the albums, how about *Absolutely Live?* " There was silence, they shook their heads sadly, and went back to their conversation. I left.

I walked out onto Sunset Boulevard. The colors of the city swirled around my head, cars racing up and down the street, souvenir shops, tourists, the dirty streets and just underneath, stars inlaid into the concrete. Suddenly, it was like a fevered dream. Was any of this real? Had I really appeared in front of audiences? I could see it all in my mind, I saw it was me on the stage, I remember how it felt. I remembered everything, every club, every person, every night, but it didn't feel real, it didn't feel like that was me. Was I asleep? Was it all a mad dream? Would I wake up and find everything was OK, I'd find myself happily next to Deidre, and that it was all just a dream? It all combined into a vertiginous tumble.

The 16th Minute

And that's how it ends? Another broken dream on Sunset Boulevard? No. I tried to get acting jobs, aside from a few extra parts, and a briefly seen scene in a cameo as Morrison, nothing. I tried to get another band together, but musicians coming to L.A aren't interested in being in a tribute band. Maybe at the beginning I did have a Hollywood vision of things, where the hero overcomes adversity and triumphs, nothing occurred to me except triumph. I was a dreamer, all I ever had are dreams, dreams staring at the ceiling in a night time bed of what I'd be . . . I lived the first twenty-three years of my life in my imagination. I came close to making those dreams real, and I did create something, all those shows with the band we created something, conjuring out of the air, pulling something out of the ether, there were times I felt as if I were just a vehicle for something greater than me. I felt the fires of creation and it makes you immortal, if only for a few minutes. What we created was maybe a little something of what a real *Doors* show was like.

Caitlin was right, I walked that edge that Morrison did, stared into the abyss. I wanted to learn about that existence to see what lay on the other side, to see what I could learn about myself. I did learn a lot about what was going on in Morrison's head, but what had I learned about what was going on in my head, Michael Gray's? What had I been trying to accomplish? I was looking for transcendence. I thought I'd be transformed into something greater than myself. Why Morrison? Why *The Doors*? That had always been a question since the beginning, the only conclusion I can come to is that, the legends that survive are the ones we see our own reflection in.

Johnny was right too. The only reason to be on that stage was joy. The joy I first felt on being onstage, at living out a dream, but I couldn't maintain . At first I savored each experience of being on-stage as a meal. Then I hungered for more until I was gorging myself, but never being filled. Maybe that's what Morrison was trying to do? Experience the joy he found in the music and experience it in other parts of his life, like the drug addict who needs more and more to recapture the first golden high that addicted him. The lights were in my eyes and I didn't see the devastation until I came down off that stage. Every once in a while I miss the music, I'll go out for a walk in the rain, and as the raindrops flutter across the puddles it looks like music.

I guess I thought I was after something concrete but all the real answers in life aren't; they're yours to find. A mirror reveals nothing that you don't bring to it, Morrison had been my mirror. Johnny and the band had that joy. I chose love, I married Pam we stayed in L.A. and now, one night a week I sit in front of the stage mirror preparing for a performance on the last stage I have. Every Saturday I throw on the leather pants and do a show for my audience of one, the only audience I want. She is the bit of unreality I need in the world to get through life. I've come to realize I did find my new world, in Pam and the love she offered. My new world of thought and feeling was being able to acknowledge that love to myself. Pam and I live in apartments that we change as our fortunes change, but the thought still haunts me that maybe if Morrison had found a home in the world I would have been able to also. But I was close, real close. So, I decided to write the book myself, and why not? I don't know how to write a book, I can't type and my grammar is poor, but I had been the lead singer in the premiere *Doors* cover band, and I hadn't known anything about music either when I started the band. But I did it, and it was successful. People came. And I do hope for a Rock 'n' Roll resurrection, some day they'll all be interested in my story and I'll be the authority then. When others want to write books they'll have to come to me. Now, all I have is to reflect upon those years and write my memoirs. I'll come back night after night if I have to, reliving my past glories until I get them right, that's my life. I blew out the candle that had burned down a couple of hours more, crumbled up the paper, and threw it at the garbage can. The night of "writing" ended. The page still blank.

Acknowledgments

When I first wrote this book I wanted to use a name of a band that didn't exist so there would be no mistaking the band in my book for an existing band. When I came up with the name The Unknown Soldiers no tribute band was using the name (I even Googled it), since then a band has picked up the name. I just want to reiterate that band and the band in my book are in no way related. The incidents revolving around the band are things that I saw hanging around with various garage bands, or they're extrapolations of things I witnessed, in other words fiction.

As with any book it took many people to help bring it to fruition. I'd like to thank The Doors whose inspiration and existence made the tableau of this novel possible. My sister Connie for providing shelter, and editing services, and for her putting up with my complaining about her taking out all of my prepositions. And my mother for the proofreading and all the stories she read to me.

Ms. Rickey Mallory for another exceptional cover (www.rrmillary. com). Mr. Dave Benzinger, guitar player extraordinare, for his technical help about things musical (www.davetheguitarplayer.com). It should be noted that any mistakes about the music or playing of instruments are mine. Alex Patton for publishing excerpts of this work and his continued support (www.newdoorstalk.proboards43.com). Jim Hunt for sharing his insights into the poetry of Jim Morrison and the meanings in the song 5-1.

And I'd like to thank the people who read the rough drafts and offered critiques and encouragement Michael White, whom Jim

Morrison would've hung out with. And to those who provided unknowing inspiration and literary succour. Mr. Lewis Shiner whose novels **Glimpses** and **Say Goodbye** every fan of Rock 'n' Roll should read (www.Lewis shiner.com). And as always Charles and Barbara Post for the years of friendship and encouragement.

CPSIA information can be obtained
at www.ICGtesting.com
Printed in the USA
FFOW02n0817020915
16479FF

9 781413 495409